THE ISLAND OF DOCTOR MOREAU
A POSSIBILTY
and Other Stories

The Island of Doctor Moreau

A POSSIBILTY

and Other Stories

———◆———

H. G. WELLS

with an Introduction and Notes by
EMILY ALDER
Edinburgh Napier University

WORDSWORTH CLASSICS

This volume is dedicated by the publisher to
ANTONY and **ROSEMARY GRAY**,
who typeset and proofread our books
from 1994 to 2017, with affection
and gratitude.

The H. G. Wells titles were the last
project Antony worked on.

Readers who are interested in other titles from
Wordsworth Editions are invited to visit our website at
www.wordsworth-editions.com

First published in 2017 by Wordsworth Editions Limited
8B East Street, Ware, Hertfordshire SG12 9HJ

ISBN 978 1 84022 740 6

Typeset in Great Britain by Antony Gray
Printed and bound by Clays Ltd, Elcograf S.p.A.

Contents

The Island of Doctor Moreau: A Possibility
page 9

Aepyornis Island
page 115

The Sea Raiders
page 127

The Empire of the Ants
page 139

GENERAL INTRODUCTION

Wordsworth Classics are inexpensive editions designed to appeal to the general reader and students. We commissioned teachers and specialists to write wide-ranging, jargon-free Introductions and to provide Notes that would assist the understanding of our readers rather than interpret the stories for them. In the same spirit, because the pleasures of reading are inseparable from the surprises, secrets and revelations that all narratives contain, we strongly advise you to enjoy this book before turning to the Introduction.

KEITH CARABINE
General Adviser
Rutherford College,
University of Kent at Canterbury

BIOGRAPHY OF THE AUTHOR

Herbert George Wells, known as 'Bertie' or 'H. G.', was born on 21 September 1866 at Atlas House, on the High Street of what was then the Kentish market town of Bromley. His father Joseph, a former gardener, kept a shop and played professional cricket; after his father broke his leg when Wells was ten, Wells's mother Sarah returned to domestic service at the country house Uppark, near Midhurst, in Sussex.

Wells's elder brothers had both been apprenticed to drapers, a trade that Sarah Wells considered to be highly respectable. Wells was apprenticed to drapers in Windsor and Southsea but was much keener to continue to be educated, and he persuaded his mother to let him become a pupil-teacher at Midhurst Grammar School. Wells's exam results at Midhurst were so strong that he won a scholarship, aimed at increasing the number of science teachers in Britain, at the Normal School (now Imperial College London), under 'Darwin's bulldog', the biologist T. H. Huxley. Wells drew extensively on his experiences as a student for his 1900 novel *Love and Mr Lewisham*. Ill-fed, poor and increasingly discontented by both the quality of the teaching he received and the social organisation of the world, Wells became more and more interested in politics and in imaginative literature, especially Plato, Blake and Carlyle. He also began writing, providing articles and a time-travel story, 'The Chronic Argonauts', for the college magazine, the *Science Schools Journal*.

Wells failed his final exams and found work as a teacher in Wales. After being fouled in a rugby game, he suffered severe kidney damage, and for much of the 1890s Wells feared he would die prematurely. Returning to London and completing his degree, he worked as a correspondence tutor and in 1893 wrote his first books, *Honours Physiography* and *A Textbook of Biology*. His writing branched out into literary journalism and popular scientific writing, and in 1895 alone Wells published four further books: *Select Conversations with an Uncle*, *The Wonderful Visit*, *The Stolen Bacillus and Other Incidents* and his masterpiece, *The Time Machine*. This first 'scientific romance' was swiftly followed by *The Island of Doctor Moreau* (1896), *The Invisible Man* (1897) and *The War of the Worlds* (1898). None has ever been out of print since; Wells was swiftly hailed as a man of genius by his contemporaries. Both sociable and irascible, Wells became friends, and fell out with, other writers such as George Gissing, Joseph Conrad, Stephen Crane, George Bernard Shaw, Arnold Bennett, Ford Madox Ford and Henry James, whom Wells would later cruelly lampoon in his 1915 novel *Boon*, the climax of a long disagreement between the two writers about the purpose and nature of the novel.

Wells never wanted to be limited to writing scientific romances, and during this period he also wrote realistic prose fiction set in a recognisable real world, whose disorganisation and unfairness these novels sought to diagnose: *The Wheels of Chance* (1896), *Kipps* (1905), *Tono-Bungay*, *Ann Veronica* (both 1909) and *The History of Mr Polly* (1910). Wells's early-twentieth-century science fiction, such as *The Food of the Gods* (1905) and *In the Days of the Comet* (1906), increasingly showed a vision of the world as Wells would want to order it. His political and utopian writing from *Anticipations of the Reactions of Mechanical and Scientific Progress upon Human Life and Thought* (1901) to *A Modern Utopia* (1905) also demonstrated Wells's commitment to creating a utopian government, a World State that would ensure that mankind would never go to war.

Following the First World War, Wells's passion for this project intensified, and he embarked on an ambitious collaborative scheme to write the first history of the world, hoping that if future generations were better educated, then rivalries between nations would be unnecessary, and world government would follow. *The Outline of History* (1919) was Wells's best-selling book in his own lifetime, selling millions of copies internationally, and was followed by the school version *A Short History of the World* (1922) and by equivalents for science, *The Science of Life* (1930), and social science, *The Work, Wealth and Happiness of Mankind* (1931). At its height, Wells's fame was as much as a thinker and public intellectual as a novelist. He met or corresponded with the greatest figures of the first half of the twentieth century: Winston Churchill, Lenin and Stalin, Theodore and Franklin Roosevelt, Albert Einstein and Sigmund Freud. His later novels from *The New Machiavelli* (1911) onward tend to be more overtly engaged with Wells's 'Open Conspiracy' to convert his readership to his own political point of view, often at a cost to these books' literary merit and subsequent afterlife.

Wells had married his cousin Isabel in 1891, but the couple proved incompatible and he left her for his pupil Amy Catherine Robbins, whom he rechristened 'Jane'. In spite of Wells's many infidelities, which Jane seemed prepared to tolerate, the couple were happily married until Jane's death from cancer in 1928; and they had two sons, Gip and Frank. An affair with the writer Amber Reeves produced a daughter, Anna Jane, and Wells's long affair with novelist Rebecca West led to the birth of a further son, Anthony West. Wells also enjoyed liaisons with, amongst others, Dorothy Richardson, Elizabeth von Arnim, Margaret Sanger and, following Jane's death, Odette Keun and Moura Budberg.

Wells's writing was prophetic in both senses of the term: as exhorting humankind to mend its ways, and in foreseeing the future. His writing imagined before they existed the aeroplane, the tank, space travel, the atomic bomb and the internet. In later life, the emphasis of his political writing turned more towards the rights of the individual, and his 1940 book *The Rights of Man: Or, What Are We Fighting For?* is a key text in the history of human rights.

Wells often despaired of his warnings being sufficiently heeded, declaring that his epitaph should be: 'God *damn* you, you fools – I told you so.' None the less, the influence of his hundred and fifty books and pamphlets of science fiction, novels, politics, utopia, history, biography and autobiography has been enormous throughout the twentieth century and beyond.

SIMON J. JAMES
Professor of English Literature at Durham University
and author of *Maps of Utopia: H. G. Wells,
Modernity and the End of Culture*

INTRODUCTION

H. G. Wells was fascinated by questions about relationships between humans and animals, and returned to them continually in his fiction and science writing in unusual and inventive ways. *The Time Machine* (1895) and *The War of the Worlds* (1898) draw on future times or other planets to imagine the fate of the human race and encounters between species. The four stories collected here confine their scenarios to the terrestrial present day – but the distant location of three of these stories, on remote islands or in unexplored lands, allows Wells superb opportunities to stretch the limits of what is realistic or believable. These stories could – almost – really have taken place in such unknown corners of the globe. Even more chilling is the reverse strategy, as when 'The Sea Raiders' (1896) brings fearsome sea creatures right into the cosy English homeland – maybe not so differently from Martian invaders after all.

If these four tales are not science fiction in the futuristic, extra-terrestrial sense, they are, in Wells's own term, *scientific romances*. Suspenseful, funny, horrifying and outrageous by turns, they are adventure stories with plausible-enough frameworks of scientific practices or theories. Wells later said he wrote them by substituting 'an ingenious use of scientific patter' for magical or supernatural plot devices.[1] But perhaps Wells is being too modest here. Trained and well read in biology and anatomy, he drew on the latest theories of animal evolution, physiology and surgery. He had also a sharp eye for human foibles and eccentricities, and his stories often bear a keen satirical edge.

THE ISLAND OF DOCTOR MOREAU

The Island of Doctor Moreau (1896) shocked many of its early readers with its representations of vivisection and its equally cutting satire of religion, imperialism and civilisation – but it also fascinated readers, and continues to do so. Wells is a perceptive storyteller, and what remains striking about *The Island of Doctor Moreau* is the degree to which we as readers are persuaded to accept this far-fetched tale. In a

---

1 H. G. Wells, Preface to *the Scientific Romances of H. G. Wells*, p. viii. For full details of all works cited, please see the Select Bibliography at the end of this Introduction.

classic narrative model, a carefully-constructed surrounding frame-work acts powerfully to make the main story seem convincing and authentic. Before the main narrator, Edward Prendick, takes up the story, we read an 'Introduction' written some years later by his nephew, Charles. Charles's tone is factual and objective, which suggests to the sceptical reader that his words can be trusted. Rather than have Charles urge us to believe what will follow, Wells casts him in the role of a man reluctantly obliged, out of a sense of duty to his relative's wishes, to admit the facts surrounding his uncle's otherwise patently unlikely account.

Certain public facts are all stated – including the date of the loss of the *Lady Vain* on 1 February 1887 (presented as a well-publicised incident akin to the real-world disaster of the wrecked *Medusa* in 1816), the date of Prendick's rescue eleven months and four days later, the existence of a possible island (Noble's Isle), and the existence of a schooner called the *Ipecacuanha*. At the same time, room for doubt is maintained – between the latitude and longitude of the *Lady Vain*'s wreck and the coordinates of Prendick's rescue there is a sense of a blank space. This space may or may not be occupied by Noble's Isle (which is by no means conclusively proved to be Moreau's island) and by Prendick's 'strange account of himself'. Indeed, Prendick's story does not so much explain the mystery as do the opposite – it sounds so outlandish that, his nephew writes, he is 'supposed demented', scarcely a witness to be relied upon. This short 'Introduction' may present corroborating information in a factual manner that at first glance seems unimpeachable, but on closer inspection it is full of holes.

How, then, are readers to weigh up what follows? One answer is in the structure of the rest of the narrative. It has twenty-two chapters, corresponding structurally although not temporally to the eleven months he spends on the island (plus the final four days accounted for by his time in the boat). This is an orderly, sane piece of narrative organisation, far from 'demented' in either structure or style. Rather, Prendick's written expression is mostly clear, detailed and frank – with the crucial exceptions of his delirium in Chapter 1 before his rescue by the *Ipecacuanha*, and the trauma of his final months on the island in Chapter 21. In other words, his otherwise lucid story is topped and tailed by portions in which we *doubt* his ability to record the experience accurately. Out of this combination of methods – narrative structure, real-world facts, matter-of-fact writing style and a compelling ambiguity – Wells forges a sophisticated authenticating strategy that prepares readers for the story ahead.

Such careful preparation is necessary because *The Island of Doctor Moreau* is not a story that pulls any punches. It is usually remembered as a horrific story about animals being surgically transformed into people – a process originating as a London scandal recalled by Prendick as the 'Moreau Horrors'. All this is dwelt upon later, though; Prendick's account of the action doesn't begin on the eponymous island, nor with animals, nor even in London. It begins at sea. Chapter 1 finds Prendick 'In the Dinghy of the *Lady Vain*', drifting in the Pacific with two companions. Lack of provisions soon makes them desperate and brings them up against the so-called 'custom of the sea' – the drawing of lots to decide which man will be killed and consumed to save the lives of the others. Prendick agrees reluctantly, but is spared from taking part in cannibalism by a quarrel that tips the other two men overboard. He is rescued, nearly dead, by the *Ipecacuanha* and Moreau's assistant Montgomery, engaged in transporting a puma and other animals to Moreau's island. Combined with the ambiguous introduction, Prendick's aimless drifting and confused delirium further helps to secure the secrecy of the location of Moreau's island. All we really know is that it is in a plausible but unverifiable area of the Pacific west of Peru. Prendick's stressful narrow escape from cannibalism also launches one of the novel's central themes: that the veneer of civilised behaviour by which Victorians – and by extension, all of us – lived might be worryingly thin.

In Chapter 2, Prendick awakes to meet his rescuer Montgomery, a former medical student and fellow Londoner. What Montgomery is doing on this boat and why Prendick keeps hearing savage growling noises from above are, for the moment, perplexing mysteries. Nor are they solved when Prendick is well enough to leave the cabin. His first outing, in Chapter 3, 'The Strange Face', brings him face-to-face with 'a misshapen man' who 'turned with animal swiftness' and whose 'black face . . . shocked me profoundly'. This is Montgomery's servant, M'Ling, and neither Prendick nor reader knows at this point that he is one of Moreau's Beast People, someone created out of at least one animal. The first few Beast People Prendick meets he thinks are native Pacific islanders, and his description here of M'Ling, indeed, resonates with Victorian anthropology, which saw many colonial peoples as primitive and animal-like, further down the evolutionary scale from white Europeans. The irony is that this comparison has already been undermined – in the dinghy it was white men who turned, or intended to turn, to the stereotypically 'savage' practice of cannibalism. As readers, even as early as Chapter 3 we are by now alert to *The Island of*

Doctor Moreau's destabilisation of numerous commonplace binaries –
such as human/ animal, civilised/ savage, European/ native, or coloniser/
colonised – in readiness for the story that unfolds on the island. The
social structure of Moreau's island, for example, imposes rules of human
behaviour on the Beast People in a parody of the kind of imperial
relations in which the British Empire imposed its own culture and
control on colonies.

The Beast People embody contemporary ideas about race and imperial
relations, as well as about humans' animal identity. M'Ling, who is one
of the most successful of Moreau's creations, is a particularly intriguing
figure. Anxious as Prendick, Montgomery and the *Ipecacuanha*'s crew are
to distance themselves from him – Montgomery won't have him in the
cabin, and the crew won't have him on deck – there is nevertheless
something tantalisingly familiar about him. Convinced he has never seen
anyone like this before, Prendick 'experienced at the same time an odd
feeling that in some way I *had* already encountered exactly the features
and gestures that now amazed me'. Unaware, of course, of Moreau's
achievements, Prendick is unable to interpret this uncanny moment.
The green shining of M'ling's eyes strikes Prendick as 'stark inhumanity'.
He thinks he is looking upon a human equal, and there is a mismatch
between his expectations and what he sees. Does he unknowingly
recognise in M'Ling the familiar animals from which the servant has
been forged, or do M'Ling's startling features remind him of the beast
inside other humans he has met – or in himself?

Moreau himself first appears in Chapter 5, to unload his animals
from the *Ipecacuanha* – and to refuse to unload Prendick. The vicious
drunkard Captain Davies sets Prendick adrift in the dinghy again, until
Moreau, at Montgomery's behest, finally allows him to land. In
Chapters 6 and 7, although Prendick is now on Moreau's island and
able to observe the islanders, the new animals and the laboratory set-up
of Moreau's dwelling, his questions only increase in size and scope.
Who are the 'deformed' islanders, what are the animals for, what are
Montgomery and the white-haired leader up to? Learning Moreau's
name, Prendick is reminded of the 'Moreau Horrors', in which 'a
prominent and masterful physiologist' had been driven out of London
in a scandal over cruel surgical practices after 'a wretched dog, flayed
and otherwise mutilated, escaped from Moreau's house'. This is another
public event, outside Prendick's narrative but within the storyworld,
to which Prendick's account can appeal for validation. The title of
Chapter 7, 'The Locked Door', is also significant, suggesting the secrets
and answers from which Prendick is currently barred, and it ends on

cliff-hanging questions that invite us to share his puzzlement: 'What could it mean? A locked enclosure on a lonely island, a notorious vivisector, and these crippled and distorted men?'

Wells's contemporary readers would already be filling in some blanks here with topical knowledge. With Moreau's notoriety, Wells invokes a long-running public controversy in late-Victorian Britain over vivisection – the dissection of living animals for scientific purposes. Animal welfare generally grew more prominent in the public consciousness during the course of the nineteenth century (the RSPCA was founded in 1824, the Vegetarian Society in 1847, and the RSPB in 1889), and anti-vivisectionists vigorously protested the practice from the 1870s onward. *The Island of Doctor Moreau* foregrounds the painful and gory process of vivisection, in its descriptions of the puma especially, which cries 'as if all the pain in the world had found a voice' and whose face Prendick later glimpses in Chapter 17 as 'hellish, brown, seamed with red branching scars, red drops starting out upon it, and the lidless eyes ablaze'. The novel is clearly implicated in vivisection debates, but is it against the practice, or for it?

Interestingly, contemporary reviewers drew mixed conclusions. *The Times* saw it as a sensational representation of diabolical experiments, while the *Spectator* took it for an anti-vivisection attack.[2] Moreau's arrogance and cold indifference to suffering may lead readers to condemn his treatment of the animals and thus the practice of vivisection. But perhaps surprisingly, as Anne DeWitt explains, what motivated campaigners the most was '*not* primarily the ethics surrounding human treatment of animals, but rather the consequences for the vivisector'.[3] In this way, Moreau's hard heart reflects his flawed motives – personal ambition rather than an altruistic desire to better the condition of the human race. Pain, in his eyes, is 'such a little thing' in the grand scheme of existence.

None the less, Moreau's physiological and surgical achievements are considerable, and Wells himself was not an anti-vivisectionist but thoroughly in support of the advancement of scientific knowledge. Martin Willis suggests that Moreau's eviction from the London scientific scene owes more to the fact that he was bringing into disrepute the kinds of practices that scientists preferred to keep out of the public eye, than to objections to what he was actually

2 These and several other reviews are collected in H. G. Wells, *The Island of Doctor Moreau*, ed. Mason Harris.

3 Anne DeWitt, *Moral Authority, Men of Science, and the Victorian Novel*

doing.[4] Wells is thus criticising attitudes to laboratory science, not laboratory science itself. Much later, in a 1927 essay, Wells argued that

> anti-vivisection is not really a campaign against pain at all. The real campaign is against the thrusting of a scientific probe into mysteries and hidden things which it is felt should either be approached in a state of awe, tenderness, excitement or passion, or else avoided.[5]

So, although vivisection is a prominent theme of the novel, *The Island of Doctor Moreau* also taps into some profound questions about the purpose of science and its implications for how people understand the world.

Those questions included debates about evolution following in the wake of Charles Darwin's *Origin of Species* (1859). Darwin's theory proposed that species had gradually evolved on earth over millions of years, through a process of 'natural selection' whereby those who were fittest to survive in their environment lived to pass on their characteristics to the next generation. Evolutionary theory ran counter to the biblical creation story in which God made all species, including humans, in their current form, which was fixed. Natural selection, instead, implied that evolution was not a fixed state but a continual process. Moreover, adaptation to the environment did not necessarily entail steady progress towards increased complexity, but could run the other way – it could lead humans back down the evolutionary ladder towards simpler animals. Moreau's Beast People in *The Island of Doctor Moreau* are a clever innovation by Wells through which the narrative can explore the implications of humanity's relationship with animals.

By Chapter 9, 'The Thing in the Forest', Prendick has encountered several individuals who strike him as 'human in shape' but with 'the unmistakable mark of the beast'. He infers from their animal-like features that Moreau is turning people into animals, a situation that seems possible because of the new Darwinian perception of an uncomfortably close human-animal relationship. Prendick's conclusion is in line with Victorian anxieties in the 1890s about degeneration – the fear that humanity had ceased to progress and was now physically and morally in decline. These fears were memorably articulated in Max Nordau's book *Degeneration* (1892, translated into English in 1895),

---

4 Martin Willis, *Mesmerists, Monsters, and Machines: Science Fiction and the Cultures of Science in the Nineteenth Century*

5 H. G. Wells, 'Popular Feeling and the Advancement of Science. Anti-vivisection', p. 228

and also fuelled by the living conditions of Britain's populous inner cities in which crime, disease and malnutrition were rife.[6] Seeing the Beast People as animalised humanity is much more conceivable to Prendick than imagining the possibility of humanised animals.

Yet the clues are there. Chapter 10 is titled 'The Crying of the Man', which may be closer to the truth about the puma than Prendick realises at this point. Moments after Prendick has been deposited 'on all fours' by his hammock and experiences a 'sense of animal comfort' from eating food, he hears the puma crying, but '[i]t was no brute this time; it was a human being in torment!' In a swift, dramatic sequence, he tears open the laboratory door, glimpses the scarred puma, is flung out again by Moreau, grabs a makeshift club, and flees into the forest. We enter into Prendick's feelings of fear and confusion as he is gripped with 'a chaos of the most horrible misgivings' and a conviction that the same 'hideous degradation' will shortly be his own fate at Moreau's hands.

Chapter 12, 'The Sayers of the Law', forms a sort of grotesque interlude in the main action. An ape-like being escorts Prendick to the Beast People's dwelling, where he finds himself repeating with them the Law, which covers injunctions laid down by Moreau to keep them under control and prevent them from reverting to animal behaviours:

'Not to go on All-Fours; *that* is the Law. Are we not Men?'
'Not to suck up Drink; *that* is the Law. Are we not Men?'
'Not to eat Fish or Flesh; *that* is the Law. Are we not Men?'

This chant bitingly parodies the Ten Commandments, and also echoes Rudyard Kipling's poem 'The Law of the Jungle' from *The Jungle Book* (1894), which sets out animal behaviours, particularly for the wolf pack. Moreau's laws, however, impose on the Beast People a set of *human* behaviours they cannot understand.

Instead, fear of Moreau is what ensures obedience: '*His* is the House of Pain', the chant concludes, a raw reminder of what each of them once endured. The Beast People repeat the Law blindly. To Prendick it is an 'idiotic formula', a 'mad litany'. The Law mocks the rules of behaviour that govern civilised human societies and draws attention to their arbitrary nature – especially as many of them have already been violated by the novel's human characters. The meaninglessness of supposed distinctions between animals and humans (of any kind) – shape, behaviour and language – is thrown into sharp relief. Moreau

6   For discussions of the late-Victorian city and Gothic literature, see e.g. Linda Dryden, *The Modern Gothic and Literary Doubles: Stevenson, Wilde and Wells*.

understands this on a profound level, explaining to Prendick in Chapter 14 that '[a] pig may be educated'. The mind was no less shapeable than the body. According to Moreau, much of 'moral education' is just 'artificial modification', keeping in check the '[c]ravings, instincts, desires that harm humanity' but which are no less a feature of humans' existence than of animals'.

Bodily similarities between humans and animals are one thing, but claiming morality and language as qualities that animals are capable of was even more shocking to Wells's readers. Prendick suspects Moreau of having induced 'a kind of deification of himself' in the Beast People. Their worshipping chant of his rules and powers, and his appearance as 'a white-faced, white-haired man, with calm eyes' suggests his God-like image. Like Victor Frankenstein, Moreau usurps the role of Creator. In 1933, looking back, Wells described *The Island of Doctor Moreau* as 'an exercise in youthful blasphemy'.[7] By this, Wells is acknowledging his own impudence as a young writer as well as the 'strange wickedness' that Prendick identifies in Moreau's decision to sculpt a *human* form. Prendick at first thinks the Beast People are an artificially-degraded kind of humanity, are '[m]onsters manufactured!' Moreau's ambition, though, is to make not just any kind of human, but a superior, perfected human being – to 'burn out all the animal', to out-do both God and Nature through scientific mastery.

As Moreau explains in Chapter 14, the surgical knowledge of grafting and transplantation already existed, and he is devoted to pursuing 'the plasticity of living forms', changing both 'outward form' and 'the physiology, the chemical rhythm of the creature'. Much of Moreau's explanation, in fact, draws verbatim on a scientific essay Wells published in 1895.[8] In theory, many of the kinds of transformations he induces in the Beast People were potentially possible. The novel raises questions over what, exactly, if anything, separated humans from beasts – from *other* beasts, perhaps we should say – and many of Wells's contemporary readers would be able to link the novel to current debates about mechanisms of evolutionary change in species.

And Moreau is dogged by failure. Despite his successes, 'the stubborn beast-flesh grows day by day back again'. As early as Chapter 9, Prendick witnessed the Leopard-man's disobedience of the Laws, including killing a rabbit and drinking from the stream with his mouth. In Chapter 16, 'How the Beast Folk Taste Blood', the killing of another rabbit

7 Wells, Preface to *The Scientific Romances*, op. cit., p. ix
8 H. G. Wells, 'The Limits of Individual Plasticity'

leads Moreau and Montgomery to fear that the constraints the Beast People have internalised are weakening. Moreau leads the men and the loyal Beast People in a mad hunt to make an example of the Leopard-man and reassert his authority. Prendick, accustomed to the odd appearance of the Beast People, has grown to feel some pity for them. Rather than allow the Leopard-man to be taken back to the torture of the vivisection chamber, Prendick mercifully shoots him: 'seeing the creature there in a perfectly animal attitude, with the light gleaming in its eyes and its imperfectly human face distorted with terror, I realised again the fact of its humanity'. In an adroit twist, the Beast People begin to seem more human in their responses than the humans do.

Moreau's imperial control over the island gradually weakens. Prendick has defied him by shooting the Leopard-man and in the next chapter, ominously titled 'A Catastrophe', the vivisected puma pulls her chains out of the wall and escapes. Trailing bandages like an unravelling mummy, she leads the pursuing Moreau to his death. Further attacks follow on M'Ling and the drunken Montgomery, until Prendick is left alone with the Beast People at the end of Chapter 20. For a short time he is able to assert his human authority, but an insidious 'Reversion of the Beast Folk' (Chapter 21) sets in. Moreau's great failure, of which he was well aware, is that his humanising does not last, and 'the stubborn beast-flesh grows day by day back again'. The Beast People gradually lose the capacity for language, and their bodies revert to 'a generalised animalism' made up of their chief animal form 'tainted with other creatures'. The Beast People slide back down the evolutionary ladder, to less sophisticated and less specialised forms.

Significantly, Prendick, too, regresses. Chapter 22, 'Alone with the Beast Folk', covers 'the longer part of my sojourn upon this Island of Doctor Moreau', but it does so in the fewest pages – as if Prendick's storytelling ability is also in decline, or he is glossing over the trauma of these months. 'I too,' he reflects, 'must have undergone strange changes . . . I am told that even now my eyes have a strange brightness, a swift alertness of movement.' Reversion, it appears, is catching. Or perhaps there *is* no real reversion in Prendick, merely an erosion of the trappings of civilisation. An important reason why *The Island of Doctor Moreau*'s readers found it shocking was because it expressed 'not the possible dangers of the human *future*, but the animal, chaotic, bloody origins and hidden nature of the human *present*'.[9] Humans *are* animals, and Moreau's experiments have revealed the beast in everyone.

9 Frank McConnell, *The Science Fiction of H. G. Wells*, p.89

If that is so, then the title of Chapter 22, 'The Man Alone', is curiously suggestive, poignant and ironic. If Prendick, by his own admission, has grown to resemble an animal in some ways during his time with the Beast People, then on leaving the island he becomes a 'man' again, drifting alone in his boat until he is rescued. But the same chapter also covers his return to London where, if anything, Prendick feels more alone than ever before – almost as if he was still among the Beast People. He feels 'as though the animal was surging up through' the Londoners around him. He is constantly reminded of the Beast People in the 'prowling women' and gibbering preacher of the metropolis. Even readers in the library seem like 'patient creatures waiting for prey' while 'the blank, expressionless faces' of commuters are 'particularly nauseous'. The Gothic horror of Moreau's island is reinscribed on to London and Londoners, hinting at the savagery close beneath the surface of even this most modern of cities.[10] Yet at the same time, isolation consoles Prendick and reconciles him to the 'peace and protection' of the cosmos. He has withdrawn from 'the confusion of cities and multitudes' to the reflection and tranquillity of books and astronomy. He has clearly not composed this account of his experiences while 'demented', but in a state of 'hope and solitude', on a note that encourages us, too, to accept the spirit of his story.

The action of *The Island of Doctor Moreau* may take place on a remote island, but its reach is long enough to trouble the same civilised homeland from which Moreau was ousted. Wells's novel is rich and multi-layered, engaging with many of the most prominent concerns of 1890s Britain – imperialism, religion, science, urban living, morality, social behaviour. It rewards many re-reads. The three short stories that make up the rest of this volume also have something to say, in different ways, about many of the same themes. Relationships between humans and animals, false assumptions of human superiority and different forms of imperial domination are all recurring ideas. Like *The Island of Doctor Moreau*, these stories displace important 1890s cultural concerns into fantastic plots, and use sophisticated narrative strategies to draw readers into their strange and often frightening worlds.

'AEPYORNIS ISLAND'

'Aepyornis Island' was published two years before *The Island of Doctor Moreau* in 1894 and the two stories have some interesting affinities.

10 Dryden, *The Modern Gothic*, op. cit.

'Aepyornis Island' uses the same technique of a framing narrative; it too is a retrospective account by a returned traveller of his unusual experiences on a remote island, authenticated by a few real-world details. This time, instead of the scientifically-educated Prendick, the story is told in the plausible, unlearned voice of a professional collector, called Butcher. There are also some thematic similarities between the two narratives – contemporary Victorian scientific culture, encounters between humans and animals, global travel and imperial relations. The story's premise rests on the discovery of three Aepyornis eggs – the Aepyornis being a species of large flightless bird thought to be extinct in the storyworld (and really extinct in our world). Butcher, the collector, is stranded on a coral atoll with the last remaining egg, which hatches a male Aepyornis chick. At first the bird provides company like a pet, but on reaching adulthood it turns aggressive, forcing Butcher to kill it, shortly before his fortuitous rescue by a passing yacht.

Butcher's job as a professional collector is not an unusual one. Over the nineteenth century, geology, fossil-hunting, specimen collecting, and the keeping of aquaria or menageries were increasingly popular as hobbies and pastimes. From abroad, travellers and explorers would bring back exotic specimens of flora and fauna to fascinate and perplex those at home in Britain and to expand knowledge of natural history, while fossils of long-gone species filled public and private museums. For some, like Charles Jamrach, owner of Jamrach's Animal Emporium in London, animal dealing was a profitable business. Jamrach is one of two animal dealers named by Butcher in the story; the other is fictional – his employer, Dawson. As the world became increasingly well-charted and its flora and fauna increasingly (though, as is still the case, far from exhaustively) catalogued, it is easy to understand why dealers would employ travelling collectors like Butcher to bring back unusual specimens from afar – and easy to understand Butcher's excitement at the discovery of the rare eggs.

The Aepyornis, of course, had the added advantage of being supposedly extinct, making his discovery a major coup scientifically. Butcher's dominant interest, however, is in the money. This makes him not a very sympathetic character, especially in the early stages of the story, but none the less a believable one, since he behaves accordingly, beating one of his Madagascan assistants for breaking a valuable egg, and referring to them as 'beggars' and 'heathens'. As in *The Island of Doctor Moreau*, treating colonial others as if they were savage actually serves to expose the savagery of the white man himself. Being stranded on the atoll with the Aepyornis is a direct consequence of this behaviour to his assistants –

in return for his aggression, they attempt to take the canoe and abandon him. He shoots one and discovers the other dead from a poisonous bite, leaving him adrift in the canoe until he reaches the atoll.

Robert Hampson has called 'Aepyornis Island' a 'comic-scientific variant of Sindbad's Second Voyage (crossed with *Robinson Crusoe*).'[11] The stories of Sindbad belong to the collection known as *The Arabian Nights*, narrated by Scheherazade to save her life, night by night. In his second voyage, Sindbad is left behind on an island and escapes by riding on the foot of a roc, a mythological giant bird. He is then stuck in the inaccessible valley to which the roc has carried him, and must figure out a further plan of escape. He attaches himself to a slab of meat, flung by merchants to stick to the diamonds covering the valley floor, and is carried by an eagle to its nest, which merchants then raid to retrieve the jewels. Butcher invokes 'Sindbad's roc' to emphasise the monstrous size of the Aepyornis, suggesting that the Aepyornis was the grain of truth behind the roc legend, but the narrative structure of Wells's story also mirrors Sindbad's voyage. Both stories are recounted within a framing narrative of storytelling, with a two-part structure of abandonment in one location and stranding in another, ending with rescue. Wells takes the fantasy adventure and gives it a scientific framework, with enough real-world detail around its unlikely premise to modernise it for the Victorian present day.

Butcher also alludes to the most famous of shipwreck narratives, Daniel Defoe's novel *Robinson Crusoe* (1719). Crusoe spends twenty-eight years on a Caribbean island, surviving by building his own housing and growing crops. Naturally, Butcher casts himself as Crusoe, resourcefully improving his situation by building a shelter out of the wreckage of his canoe, for example. Crusoe is also a colonial figure, though, re-enacting the European imperial project in microcosm on his island and assuming authority over his native companion, Man Friday. In 'Aepyornis Island', by naming the young bird 'Friday', Butcher is also assuming the role of imperial master. As in *The Island of Doctor Moreau*, the implications are twofold – first, the story can be seen as an allegory of imperial relations between two very different human cultures, and secondly, it can be seen as a fable about human-animal relations in which human superiority is taken for granted. Human mastery of the natural world, including the control and exploitation of non-human species and environments though the collecting and dealing of specimens, for example, is also a form of imperialism.

11 R. G. Hampson, 'Genie out of the Bottle: Conrad, Wells and Joyce', p. 222

Again like *The Island of Doctor Moreau*, 'Aepyornis Island' questions such assumptions. Butcher believes he is the dominant partner in his initially companionable relationship with the Aepyornis. But when it reaches maturity the tables are turned and the bird easily asserts its physical superiority, 'landing out at me with sledge-hammer kicks, and bringing his pickaxe down on the back of my head'. Butcher flees into the lagoon. His admiration for the 'handsome' Aepyornis immediately and amusingly becomes outrage against this 'great gawky, out-of-date bird!' The Aepyornis's rare, near-extinct status now becomes an insult, but the real joke is on the confounded Butcher, who clings in vain to clichés of human superiority: 'And me a human being – heir of the ages and all that.' In his eyes the Aepyornis is a species whose time has come and gone, no more than a 'blessed fossil', whereas humans are supposed to be the pinnacle of evolution. But such beliefs mean little on Aepyornis Island, and being dethroned as the dominant species is hard to take.

Ultimately, though, it is Butcher's human ingenuity and tools that enable him to defeat the aggressive bird, hurling a line around its legs to trip it up and leave it vulnerable to his knife. But after the Aepyornis's death, he grieves. He cannot bring himself to eat the bird, feeling 'exactly as if he was human'. In his loneliness he acknowledges their companionship and their interdependence, perhaps realising that a more respectful exchange can exist between humans and animals – although in the story's final irony it doesn't stop him selling the bones as soon as he gets back to Britain. 'Aepyornis Island' asks us to think about human-animal interactions and imperial relationships, but like the other stories included in this volume, it doesn't necessarily give us answers.

'THE SEA RAIDERS'

'The Sea Raiders' differs from the other three tales because it recounts exotic animals visiting Britain, rather than being encountered by travellers abroad. In the story, one summer some ferocious people-eating cephalopods visit the south coast of Devon and Cornwall and, for extra gruesomeness, their attacks are not on bold travellers, but on ordinary locals and holidaymakers. Wells is very precise about the setting of the action. Naming the coastal Devon towns of Seaton, Sidmouth and Budleigh Salterton allows his readers to map the sea raiders' progress. Once again Wells's narrative strategies work to provide a convincing sense of authenticity. The story is begun by an unidentified narrator, evidently an expert in marine biology who is thus able to locate the events in the context of current scientific knowledge –

by the late nineteenth century, giant squid (*Architeuthis*) were known to exist and Prince Albert I of Monaco did, as described in the second paragraph, obtain cephalopod specimens from whales' stomachs in 1895. The fourth paragraph settles into the accounts of the specific encounters with *Haploteuthis ferox* that took place that particular May, and the expert voice gives way to the third-person viewpoint of an ordinary retiree on holiday, Mr Fison. Again, the combination of authenticating details and a believable, trustworthy witness add credence to a remarkable tale.

Like 'Aepyornis Island', 'The Sea Raiders' is a blend of science and mythology – as indeed were giant cephalopods. The legend of the kraken derived from reported sightings of massive squid-like creatures, but it was not until the 1870s that specimens were first found to establish the existence of a real animal. Real giant squid are not hostile attackers like *Haploteuthis ferox*, but they are often represented that way in literature.[12] Wells's story follows earlier tales involving cephalopods by writers like Victor Hugo and Jules Verne – both Hugo's *The Toilers of the Sea* (1866) and Verne's *Twenty Thousand Leagues Under the Sea* (1869) involve struggles between the human characters and belligerent cephalopods. Wells's innovations are to bring the invaders to the ordinary, familiar and supposedly safe south coast of England, and to invent a new species of cephalopod rather than attributing aggressive characteristics to an already-known type.

Wells's *Haploteuthis ferox* are no ordinary giant squid – they are intelligent, voracious, and work together like a pack of wolves or orca. They are

> in shape somewhat resembling an octopus, with huge and very long and flexible tentacles, coiled copiously on the ground. The skin had a glistening texture, unpleasant to see, like shiny leather. The downward bend of the tentacle-surrounded mouth, the curious excrescence at the bend, the tentacles, and the large intelligent eyes, gave the creatures a grotesque suggestion of a face.   [p. 125]

In this description, the sea raiders anticipate the octopus-like Martians of *The War of the Worlds*, whose 'rounded bulk[s] ... glistened like wet leather', accompanied by 'Gorgon groups of tentacles' and 'immense eyes' of 'extraordinary intensity'. There is something particularly vile and uncanny about these cephalopod shapes, offering plenty of scope for Gothic horror. To the human narrator the Martian is 'unspeakably

12 See 'Kraken', in *Ashgate Encyclopedia of Literary and Cinematic Monstrosity*

nasty . . . I was overcome with disgust and dread.' Similarly, in 'The Sea Raiders', the creatures are 'ghastly-looking', 'revolting', 'abominable', and watch Mr Fison with 'evil interest'. Perhaps the most horrible thing about the sea raiders is, rather like the Beast People, their 'grotesque' distortion of human features – skin, limbs, face. These creatures disgust, hinting, perhaps, at primeval evolutionary pasts humans would prefer to forget, but they also fascinate. The unknown regions of the ocean deep are a fruitful source of such repellent yet compelling monstrosities. In such an environment, writers could imagine strange, alien-like creatures shaped as differently as possible from familiar animals – especially given their tentacles. This is now a rather familiar monstrous limb-type, but it only started to appear in weird tales and science fiction in the late nineteenth century.[13]

The sea raiders are also uncomfortably fearsome because of their intelligence. They communicate with a feline 'soft purring sound', and target the two boats and their passengers with remarkable efficiency. The narrator refers to the speculations of another expert, Hemsley, that having chanced to taste human flesh out at sea, the creatures had begun to seek it out. Alternatively, the narrator suggests, they were driven by 'hunger migration' in a lean year. Despite these rational explanations, an air of fantasy remains over the animals – they are reportedly phosphorescent and are later glimpsed floating 'like creatures of moonshine through the blackness of the water'. But there is no firm explanation for what has happened, no retribution for their attacks. These aggressors are not punished or destroyed as is more common with fictional monsters of the time, such as Dracula or Edward Hyde, or Wells's own Martians – they simply pass on out of the story, never to be seen again.

'THE EMPIRE OF THE ANTS'

The final story in this volume returns to a far-flung setting, exotic yet sinister. This time it is South America, in what is apparently the northern part of Brazil, although many place-names are invented. In 'The Empire of the Ants', Captain Gerilleau is sent with his gunboat to investigate reports of some dangerous, self-important ants threatening inhabitants on an Amazonian tributary. The irony of the story's title runs deep. The unexpected combination of ants with imperialism invites laughter and leads us to expect a humorous story – which indeed it is,

13 China Miéville, 'M. R. James and the Quantum Vampire'

often in some rather black ways. The title mocks the complacency of European empires through comparison with a mere insect community. But yet, as the story progresses, we watch these mere insects utterly trounce the human characters and run rings around their weapons and technology. The story's coda, section 4, dwells in all seriousness on the ants' efficiency and progress – they really are, the narrator fears, building an empire, with Europe itself predicted to be under threat within fifty years.

Like 'The Sea Raiders', the story has a framing narrator, while the action is mainly told through the eyes of Holroyd, a Lancastrian engineer aboard Captain Gerilleau's gunboat. During the journey they hear of some ominous local reports of giant ants with 'big eyes' that 'get in corners and watch what you do'. The suspense builds as Holroyd watches the forested shores, becoming increasingly uncomfortable with a tangled Brazilian landscape in which '[m]an seemed at best an infrequent precarious intruder'. As their forthcoming encounters with the ants make clear, it is not people but the indigenous insects who are fit for this environment. By the end of the story, all human attempts to counteract their advance have been absolutely futile.

Like Wells's Martians, the ants show the human characters what it is like to face and be overrun by a stronger, smarter, more efficient conqueror. The narrator's closing prediction that just a few decades would lead to the ants' 'discovery' of Europe reverses the typical direction of imperial expansion. The ants also stand for a number of European anxieties about their colonial lands – both people and insects were native inhabitants of the colonies and both sometimes got in the way of the colonial project by not behaving the way the colonialists wanted. Charlotte Sleigh discusses the ways in which colonial peoples were linked in the imperial imagination with insects, especially ants: '[A]nts, innumerable and indistinguishable, were the most other-ish of all the insects and the best animals to embody the alien threat lurking within Europe's colonised, supposedly domesticated nature.'[14]

As non-humans, the ants have primitive, unfathomable motivations and thought, suggesting that human intelligence does not have a monopoly on being able to create sophisticated and well-organised societies, as the insect-like Selenite society in Wells's 1901 novel *The First Men in the Moon* also shows. Humans, it seems, have no inevitable right to the top spot in the natural order and might have to give way to

14 Charlotte Sleigh, 'Empire of the Ants: H. G. Wells and Tropical Entomology', p. 36

another species better equipped to thrive. As Holroyd muses after glimpsing overgrown ruins of buildings abandoned by people 'driven back' from the forest, 'Who were the real masters?' He worries about the ants' potential to evolve. If humans had

> emerged from barbarism to a stage of civilisation that made them feel lords of the future and masters of the earth . . . what was to prevent the ants evolving also? Suppose presently the ants began to store knowledge, just as men had done by means of books and records, use weapons, form great empires, sustain a planned and organised war?   [p. 139]

Holroyd's concerns can be seen as analogous to imperial worries about rebellion from within their colonies, and as satirising the sense of shock complacent European imperialists might experience on realising that their own tactics could be adopted and used against them.

The story is still, however, also about actual ants.[15] Wells names his insects after a species known as *saüba*, a leaf-cutting ant, while their behaviour derives from two other kinds of ants familiar to Victorians: driver ants (*Dorylii*) and legionary ants (*Ecitonii*): army ants. Wells's ants are, of course, further embellished. They are unusually big, about five centimetres long, and they have large eyes. Most of all, they are intelligent – a trait that only humans, of all animals, are supposed to have; the leader ants have particularly large heads and their posture suggests they make unusual use of their two front legs (or arms). Amusingly, some of them wear clothes. In the words of Gerilleau, they are 'a new sort of ant'. There are echoes here of the 'travesty of humanity' that is the Beast People, but these ants are much cleverer and more rational than the Beast People. And their intelligence is entirely their own – a scary insect intelligence that humans cannot really understand.

The ants are threatening and seemingly unstoppable, but at the same time, the story mocks the human characters' clunky attempts to kill the creatures and ironically exposes imperial powerlessness. There is humour in the clumsy behaviour of the humans compared to the brisk movements of the ants, vanishing from sight in moments only to watch knowingly from the shadows as Holroyd, the captain and the others puzzle over what has happened. Captain Gerilleau's indecisive leadership is ridiculed, for example, in the build-up to his final important

15 Sleigh, op. cit.

decision, declared like an ultimatum: '*I shall fire de big gun!*' It is fired twice 'with great sternness and ceremony', but it is an empty gesture, with no effect on the ants. In fact, the firing of the gun only underscores the humans' helplessness in contrast to the martial efficiency of the ants, who move like 'modern infantry advancing under fire'. The assumption of superiority of arms is undercut because the ants are too small to shoot and too fast and deft to burn. Once again, Wells returns to the idea of humanity's dethronement as dominant species, as 'lords of the future and masters of the earth', as 'heir of the ages and all that'. Of all the stories in this volume, it is in this one, as its title suggests, that the usurping species comes closest to succeeding in ousting us from that position.

These four stories are excellent examples of the range of ways that Wells's scientific romances, long or short, respond to profound questions that still tax readers and writers today. Questions of what it means to be human and how humans can, do or should relate to other species (and each other) are explored. Wells's remarkable imagination and storytelling skill shape compelling narratives that engage, entertain, and often urge us to confront some difficult home truths. The fantastical plots may revolve around encounters with exotic, fearsome or uncanny animals in (usually) far-flung locations, but they none the less speak back to social, ethical and scientific contexts and debates of Wells's own time – some of which have since become our own.

EMILY ALDER
Edinburgh Napier University

SELECT BIBLIOGRAPHY

Critical Works and Editions

Ashgate Encyclopedia of Literary and Cinematic Monstrosity, Ashgate, Abingdon, 2014

Bernard Bergonzi, *The Early H. G. Wells: A Study of the Scientific Romances*, Manchester University Press, Manchester, 1961

Anne DeWitt, *Moral Authority, Men of Science, and the Victorian Novel*, Cambridge University Press, Cambridge, 2013

Linda Dryden, *The Modern Gothic and Literary Doubles: Stevenson, Wilde and Wells*, Palgrave Macmillan, Basingstoke, 2003

R. G. Hampson, 'Genie out of the Bottle: Conrad, Wells and Joyce', in *The Arabian Nights in English Literature*, Peter Carracciolo (ed.), St Martin's Press, New York, 1988, pp. 208–13

Mason Harris (ed.), *The Island of Doctor Moreau*, Broadview Press, Plymouth, 2009

Roslynn Haynes, *H. G. Wells: Discoverer of the Future*, Macmillan, Basingstoke, 1980

John Huntington, *The Logic of Fantasy: H. G. Wells and Science Fiction*, Columbia University Press, New York, 1982

Frank McConnell, *The Science Fiction of H. G. Wells*, Oxford University Press, New York, 1981

Steven McLean, *The Early Fiction of H. G. Wells: Fantasies of Science*, Palgrave Macmillan, Basingstoke, 2009

China Miéville, 'M. R. James and the Quantum Vampire', in *Collapse*, IV, 2008, pp. 105–28, *Urbanomic.com*

Patrick Parrinder, *H. G. Wells: The Critical Heritage*, Routledge & Kegan Paul, London, 1972

Robert M. Philmus and David Y. Hughes (eds), *H. G. Wells: Early Writings in Science and Science Fiction*, University of California Press, Los Angeles, 1975

Charlotte Sleigh, 'Empire of the Ants: H.G. Wells and Tropical Entomology', in *Science as Culture*, Vol. 10/1, March, 2001, pp. 33–71

W. Warren Wagar, *H. G. Wells: Traversing Time*, Wesleyan University Press, Middletown, CT, 2004

H. G. Wells, Preface to *The Scientific Romances of H. G. Wells*,
Gollancz, London, 1933, pp. vii–x

H. G. Wells, 'Popular Feeling and the Advancement of Science. Anti-
vivisection', in *The Way the World is Going*, Ernest Benn, London,
1927, pp. 221–30

Martin Willis, *Mesmerists, Monsters, and Machines: Science Fiction and
the Cultures of Science in the Nineteenth Century*, Kent State
University Press, Kent, OH, 2006

Biographies

John Batchelor, *H. G. Wells*, Cambridge University Press, Cambridge,
1985

Vincent Brome, *H. G. Wells: A Biography*, London, New York and
Toronto, Longmans, Green, 1951

Michael Coren, *The Invisible Man: The Life and Liberties of H. G. Wells*,
Random House of Canada, Toronto, 1993

Michael Foot, *H. G.: History of Mr Wells*, Black Swan, London, 1996

Michael Sherborne, *H. G. Wells: Another Kind of Life*, Peter Owen,
London, 2010

David C. Smith, *H. G. Wells: Desperately Mortal. A Biography*, Yale
University Press, New Haven and London, 1986

Anthony West, *H. G. Wells: Aspects of a Life*, Hutchinson, London,
1984

The Island of Doctor Moreau
A Possibilty

Contents

Foreword

On 1 February 1887, the *Lady Vain* was lost by collision with a derelict when about the latitude 1' S and longitude 107' W.

On 5 January 1888 – that is eleven months and four days after – my uncle, Edward Prendick, a private gentleman, who certainly went aboard the *Lady Vain* at Callao,[1] and who had been considered drowned, was picked up in latitude 5' 3" S and longitude 101' W in a small open boat of which the name was illegible, but which is supposed to have belonged to the missing schooner *Ipecacuanha*. He gave such a strange account of himself that he was supposed demented. Subsequently he alleged that his mind was a blank from the moment of his escape from the *Lady Vain*. His case was discussed among psychologists at the time as a curious instance of the lapse of memory consequent upon physical and mental stress. The following narrative was found among his papers by the undersigned, his nephew and heir, but unaccompanied by any definite request for publication.

The only island known to exist in the region in which my uncle was picked up is Noble's Isle,[2] a small volcanic islet and uninhabited. It was visited in 1891 by HMS *Scorpion*.[3] A party of sailors then landed, but found nothing living thereon except certain curious white moths, some hogs and rabbits, and some rather peculiar rats. No specimen was secured of these – in view of which this narrative is without confirmation in its most essential particular. With that understood, there seems no harm in putting this strange story before the public in accordance, as I believe, with my uncle's intentions. There is at least this much in its behalf: my uncle passed out of human knowledge about latitude 5' S and longitude 105' E, and reappeared in the same part of the ocean after a space of eleven months. In some way he must have lived during the interval. And it seems that a schooner called the *Ipecacuanha* with a drunken captain, John Davies, did start from Africa with a puma and certain other animals aboard in January 1887, that the vessel was well known at several ports in the South Pacific, and that it finally disappeared from those seas (with a considerable amount of copra[4] aboard), sailing to its unknown fate from Bayna[5] in December 1887, a date that tallies entirely with my uncle's story.

CHARLES EDWARD PRENDICK

Edward Prendick's Story

CHAPTER 1

In the Dinghy of the Lady Vain

I DO NOT PROPOSE to add anything to what has already been written concerning the loss of the *Lady Vain*. As everyone knows, she collided with a derelict when ten days out from Callao. The longboat, with seven of the crew, was picked up eighteen days after by HM gunboat *Myrtle*, and the story of their terrible privations has become quite as well known as the far more horrible *Medusa* case.[6a] But I have to add to the published story of the *'Vain* another, possibly as horrible and far stranger. It has hitherto been supposed that the four men who were in the dinghy perished, but this is incorrect. I have the best of evidence for this assertion: I was one of the four men.

But in the first place I must state that there never were four men in the dinghy – the number was three. Constans, who was 'seen by the captain to jump into the gig',* luckily for us and unluckily for himself did not reach us. He came down out of the tangle of ropes under the stays of the smashed bowsprit, some small rope caught his heel as he let go, and he hung for a moment head downward, and then fell and struck a block or spar floating in the water. We pulled towards him, but he never came up.

I say lucky for us he did not reach us, and I might almost say luckily for himself; for we had only a small breaker[7] of water and some soddened ship's biscuits with us, so sudden had been the alarm, so unprepared the ship for any disaster. We thought the people on the launch would be better provisioned (though it seems they were not), and we tried to hail them. They could not have heard us, and the next morning when the drizzle cleared – which was not until past midday – we could see nothing of them. We could not stand up to look about us, because of the pitching of the boat. The two other men who had escaped so far with me were a man named Helmar, a passenger like myself, and a seaman whose name I don't know – a short sturdy man, with a stammer.

We drifted famishing, and, after our water had come to an end, tormented by an intolerable thirst, for eight days altogether. After the

* *Daily News*, 17 March 1887[6b]

second day the sea subsided slowly to a glassy calm. It is quite impossible for the ordinary reader to imagine those eight days. He has not, luckily for himself, anything in his memory to imagine with. After the first day we said little to one another, and lay in our places in the boat and stared at the horizon, or watched, with eyes that grew larger and more haggard every day, the misery and weakness gaining upon our companions. The sun became pitiless. The water ended on the fourth day, and we were already thinking strange things and saying them with our eyes; but it was, I think, the sixth before Helmar gave voice to the thing we had all been thinking. I remember our voices were dry and thin, so that we bent towards one another and spared our words. I stood out against it with all my might, was rather for scuttling the boat and perishing together among the sharks that followed us; but when Helmar said that if his proposal was accepted we should have drink, the sailor came round to him.

I would not draw lots, however, and in the night the sailor whispered to Helmar again and again, and I sat in the bows with my clasp-knife in my hand, though I doubt if I had the stuff in me to fight; and in the morning I agreed to Helmar's proposal, and we handed halfpence to find the odd man. The lot fell upon the sailor; but he was the strongest of us and would not abide by it, and attacked Helmar with his hands. They grappled together and almost stood up. I crawled along the boat to them, intending to help Helmar by grasping the sailor's leg; but the sailor stumbled with the swaying of the boat, and the two fell upon the gunwale[8] and rolled overboard together. They sank like stones. I remember laughing at that, and wondering why I laughed. The laugh caught me suddenly like a thing from without.

I lay across one of the thwarts[9] for I know not how long, thinking that if I had the strength I would drink sea-water and madden myself to die quickly. And even as I lay there I saw, with no more interest than if it had been a picture, a sail come up towards me over the skyline. My mind must have been wandering, and yet I remember all that happened, quite distinctly. I remember how my head swayed with the seas, and the horizon with the sail above it danced up and down; but I also remember as distinctly that I had a persuasion that I was dead, and that I thought what a jest it was that they should come too late by such a little to catch me in my body.

For an endless period, as it seemed to me, I lay with my head on the thwart watching the schooner (she was a little ship, schooner-rigged[10] fore and aft) come up out of the sea. She kept tacking to and fro in a widening compass, for she was sailing dead into the wind. It never entered my head to attempt to attract attention, and I do not remember anything distinctly after the sight of her side until I found myself in a little cabin aft. There's a dim half-memory of being lifted up to the gangway, and of a big red countenance covered with freckles and surrounded with red hair staring at me over the bulwarks.[11] I also had a disconnected impression of a dark face, with extraordinary eyes, close to mine; but that I thought was a nightmare, until I met it again. I fancy I recollect some stuff being poured in between my teeth; and that is all.

CHAPTER 2

The Man Who Was Going Nowhere

The cabin in which I found myself was small and rather untidy. A youngish man with flaxen hair, a bristly straw-coloured moustache and a dropping nether lip, was sitting and holding my wrist. For a minute we stared at each other without speaking. He had watery grey eyes, oddly void of expression. Then just overhead came a sound like an iron bedstead being knocked about, and the low angry growling of some large animal. At the same time the man spoke. He repeated his question, 'How do you feel now?'

I think I said I felt all right. I could not recollect how I had got there. He must have seen the question in my face, for my voice was inaccessible to me.

'You were picked up in a boat, starving. The name on the boat was the *Lady Vain*, and there were spots of blood on the gunwale.'

At the same time my eye caught my hand, thin so that it looked like a dirty skin-purse full of loose bones, and all the business of the boat came back to me.

'Have some of this,' said he, and gave me a dose of some scarlet stuff, iced.

It tasted like blood, and made me feel stronger.

'You were in luck,' said he, 'to get picked up by a ship with a medical man aboard.' He spoke with a slobbering articulation, with the ghost of a lisp.

'What ship is this?' I said slowly, hoarse from my long silence.

'It's a little trader from Arica[12] and Callao. I never asked where she came from in the beginning – out of the land of born fools, I guess. I'm a passenger myself, from Arica. The silly ass who owns her – he's captain too, named Davies – he's lost his certificate, or something. You know the kind of man, calls the thing the *Ipecacuanha*, of all silly, infernal names; though when there's much of a sea without any wind, she certainly acts according.'

(Then the noise overhead began again, a snarling growl and the voice of a human being together. Then another voice, telling some 'Heaven-forsaken idiot' to desist.)

'You were nearly dead,' said my interlocutor. 'It was a very near thing, indeed. But I've put some stuff into you now. Notice your arm's sore? Injections. You've been insensible for nearly thirty hours.'

I thought slowly. (I was distracted now by the yelping of a number of dogs.) 'Am I eligible for solid food?' I asked.

'Thanks to me,' he said. 'Even now the mutton is boiling.'

'Yes,' I said with assurance; 'I could eat some mutton.'

'But,' said he with a momentary hesitation, 'you know I'm dying to hear of how you came to be alone in that boat. Damn that howling!' I thought I detected a certain suspicion in his eyes.

He suddenly left the cabin, and I heard him in violent controversy with someone, who seemed to me to talk gibberish in response to him. The matter sounded as though it ended in blows, but in that I thought my ears were mistaken. Then he shouted at the dogs, and returned to the cabin.

'Well?' said he in the doorway. 'You were just beginning to tell me.'

I told him my name, Edward Prendick, and how I had taken to natural history as a relief from the dullness of my comfortable independence.

He seemed interested in this. 'I've done some science myself. I did my biology at University College[13] – getting out the ovary of the earth-worm and the radula of the snail, and all that. Lord! It's ten years ago. But go on! go on! tell me about the boat.'

He was evidently satisfied with the frankness of my story, which I told in concise sentences enough, for I felt horribly weak; and when it was finished he reverted at once to the topic of natural history and his own biological studies. He began to question me closely about Tottenham Court Road and Gower Street.[14] 'Is Caplatzi still flourishing? What a shop that was!' He had evidently been a very ordinary medical student, and drifted incontinently to the topic of the music halls. He told me some anecdotes.

'Left it all,' he said, 'ten years ago. How jolly it all used to be! But I made a young ass of myself, played myself out before I was twenty-one. I dare say it's all different now. But I must look up that ass of a cook, and see what he's done to your mutton.'

The growling overhead was renewed, so suddenly and with so much savage anger that it startled me. 'What's that?' I called after him, but the door had closed. He came back again with the boiled mutton, and I was so excited by the appetising smell of it that I forgot the noise of the beast that had troubled me.

After a day of alternate sleep and feeding I was so far recovered as to be able to get from my bunk to the scuttle,[15] and see the green seas trying to keep pace with us. I judged the schooner was running before the wind. Montgomery – that was the name of the flaxen-haired man – came in again as I stood there, and I asked him for some clothes. He lent me some duck things[16] of his own, for those I had worn in the boat had been thrown overboard. They were rather loose for me, for he was large and long in his limbs. He told me casually that the captain was three-parts drunk in his own cabin. As I assumed the clothes, I began asking him some questions about the destination of the ship. He said the ship was bound to Hawaii, but that it had to land him first.

'Where?' said I.

'It's an island, where I live. So far as I know, it hasn't got a name.'

He stared at me with his nether lip dropping, and looked so wilfully stupid of a sudden that it came into my head that he desired to avoid my questions. I had the discretion to ask no more.

CHAPTER 3

The Strange Face

We left the cabin and found a man at the companion[17] obstructing our way. He was standing on the ladder with his back to us, peering over the combing[18] of the hatchway. He was, I could see, a misshapen man, short, broad and clumsy, with a crooked back, a hairy neck and a head sunk between his shoulders. He was dressed in dark-blue serge, and had peculiarly thick, coarse, black hair. I heard the unseen dogs growl furiously, and forthwith he ducked back, coming into contact with the hand I put out to fend him off from myself. He turned with animal swiftness.

In some indefinable way the black face thus flashed upon me shocked me profoundly. It was a singularly deformed one. The facial part projected, forming something dimly suggestive of a muzzle, and the huge half-open mouth showed as big white teeth as I had ever seen in a human mouth. His eyes were blood-shot at the edges, with scarcely a rim of white round the hazel pupils. There was a curious glow of excitement in his face.

'Confound you!' said Montgomery. 'Why the devil don't you get out of the way?'

The black-faced man started aside without a word. I went on up the companion, staring at him instinctively as I did so. Montgomery stayed at the foot for a moment. 'You have no business here, you know,' he said in a deliberate tone. 'Your place is forward.'[19]

The black-faced man cowered. 'They – won't have me forward.' He spoke slowly, with a queer, hoarse quality in his voice.

'Won't have you forward!' said Montgomery, in a menacing voice. 'But I tell you to go!' He was on the brink of saying something further, then looked up at me suddenly and followed me up the ladder.

I had paused halfway through the hatchway, looking back, still astonished beyond measure at the grotesque ugliness of this black-faced creature. I had never beheld such a repulsive and extraordinary face before, and yet – if the contradiction is credible – I experienced at the same time an odd feeling that in some way I had already encountered exactly the features and gestures that now amazed me. Afterwards it occurred to me that probably I had seen him as I was lifted aboard; and yet that scarcely satisfied my suspicion of a previous acquaintance. Yet how one could have set eyes on so singular a face and yet have forgotten the precise occasion, passed my imagination.

Montgomery's movement to follow me released my attention, and I turned and looked about me at the flush deck[20] of the little schooner. I was already half prepared by the sounds I had heard for what I saw. Certainly I never beheld a deck so dirty. It was littered with scraps of carrot, shreds of green stuff and indescribable filth. Fastened by chains to the mainmast were a number of grisly staghounds, who now began leaping and barking at me, and by the mizzen a huge puma was cramped in a little iron cage far too small even to give it turning room. Farther under the starboard bulwark were some big hutches containing a number of rabbits, and a solitary llama was squeezed in a mere box of a cage forward. The dogs were muzzled by leather straps. The only human being on deck was a gaunt and silent sailor at the wheel.

The patched and dirty spankers[21] were tense before the wind, and up aloft the little ship seemed carrying every sail she had. The sky was clear, the sun midway down the western sky; long waves, capped by the breeze with froth, were running with us. We went past the steersman to the taffrail, and saw the water come foaming under the stern and the bubbles go dancing and vanishing in her wake. I turned and surveyed the unsavoury length of the ship.

'Is this an ocean menagerie?' said I.

'Looks like it,' said Montgomery.

'What are these beasts for? Merchandise, curios? Does the captain think he is going to sell them somewhere in the South Seas?'

'It looks like it, doesn't it?' said Montgomery, and turned towards the wake again.

Suddenly we heard a yelp and a volley of furious blasphemy from the companion hatchway, and the deformed man with the black face came up hurriedly. He was immediately followed by a heavy red-haired man in a white cap. At the sight of the former the staghounds, who had all tired of barking at me by this time, became furiously excited, howling and leaping against their chains. The black hesitated before them, and this gave the red-haired man time to come up with him and deliver a tremendous blow between the shoulder-blades. The poor devil went down like a felled ox, and rolled in the dirt among the furiously excited dogs. It was lucky for him that they were muzzled. The red-haired man gave a yawp of exultation and stood staggering, and as it seemed to me in serious danger of either going backwards down the companion hatchway or forwards upon his victim.

So soon as the second man had appeared, Montgomery had started forward. 'Steady on there!' he cried, in a tone of remonstrance. A couple of sailors appeared on the forecastle.[22] The black-faced man, howling in a singular voice rolled about under the feet of the dogs. No one attempted to help him. The brutes did their best to worry him, butting their muzzles at him. There was a quick dance of their lithe grey-figured bodies over the clumsy, prostrate figure. The sailors forward shouted, as though it was admirable sport. Montgomery gave an angry exclamation, and went striding down the deck, and I followed him. The black-faced man scrambled up and staggered forward, going and leaning over the bulwark by the main shrouds,[23] where he remained, panting and glaring over his shoulder at the dogs. The red-haired man laughed a satisfied laugh.

'Look here, captain,' said Montgomery, with his lisp a little accentuated, gripping the elbow of the red-haired man, 'this won't do!'

I stood behind Montgomery. The captain came half round, and regarded him with the dull and solemn eyes of a drunken man. 'Wha' won't do?' he said, and added, after looking sleepily into Montgomery's face for a minute, 'Blasted sawbones!'[24]

With a sudden movement he shook his arm free, and after two ineffectual attempts stuck his freckled fists into his side pockets.

'That man's a passenger,' said Montgomery. 'I'd advise you to keep your hands off him.'

'Go to hell!' said the captain, loudly. He suddenly turned and staggered towards the side. 'Do what I like on my own ship,' he said.

I think Montgomery might have left him then, seeing the brute was drunk; but he only turned a shade paler, and followed the captain to the bulwarks.

'Look you here, captain,' he said; 'that man of mine is not to be ill-treated. He has been hazed ever since he came aboard.'

For a minute, alcoholic fumes kept the captain speechless. 'Blasted sawbones!' was all he considered necessary.

I could see that Montgomery had one of those slow, pertinacious tempers that will warm day after day to a white heat, and never again cool to forgiveness; and I saw too that this quarrel had been some time growing. 'The man's drunk,' said I, perhaps officiously; 'you'll do no good.'

Montgomery gave an ugly twist to his dropping lip. 'He's always drunk. Do you think that excuses his assaulting his passengers?'

'My ship,' began the captain, waving his hand unsteadily towards the cages, 'was a clean ship. Look at it now!' It was certainly anything but clean. 'Crew,' continued the captain, 'clean, respectable crew.'

'You agreed to take the beasts.'

'I wish I'd never set eyes on your infernal island. What the devil d'you want beasts for on an island like that? Then, that man of yours – understood he was a man. He's a lunatic; and he hadn't no business aft. Do you think the whole damned ship belongs to you?'

'Your sailors began to haze the poor devil as soon as he came aboard.'

'That's just what he is – he's a devil! an ugly devil! My men can't stand him. *I* can't stand him. None of us can't stand him. Nor *you* either!'

Montgomery turned away. '*You* leave that man alone, anyhow,' he said, nodding his head as he spoke.

But the captain meant to quarrel now. He raised his voice. 'If he comes this end of the ship again I'll cut his insides out, I tell you. Cut out his blasted insides! Who are *you*, to tell *me* what *I'm* to do? I tell you I'm captain of this ship – captain and owner. I'm the law here, I tell you – the law and the prophets. I bargained to take a man and his attendant to and from Arica, and bring back some animals. I never bargained to carry a mad devil and a silly sawbones, a – '

Well, never mind what he called Montgomery. I saw the latter take a step forward, and interposed. 'He's drunk,' said I. The captain began some abuse even fouler than the last. 'Shut up!' I said, turning on him sharply, for I had seen danger in Montgomery's white face. With that I brought the downpour on myself.

However, I was glad to avert what was uncommonly near a scuffle, even at the price of the captain's drunken ill-will. I do not think I have ever heard quite so much vile language come in a continuous stream from any man's lips before, though I have frequented eccentric company enough. I found some of it hard to endure, though I am a mild-tempered man; but, certainly, when I told the captain to 'shut up' I had forgotten that I was merely a bit of human flotsam, cut off from my resources and with my fare unpaid; a mere casual dependant on the bounty, or speculative enterprise, of the ship. He reminded me of it with considerable vigour; but at any rate I prevented a fight.

CHAPTER 4

At the Schooner Rail

That night land was sighted after sundown, and the schooner hove to. Montgomery intimated that was his destination. It was too far to see any details; it seemed to me then simply a low-lying patch of dim blue in the uncertain blue-grey sea. An almost vertical streak of smoke went up from it into the sky. The captain was not on deck when it was sighted. After he had vented his wrath on me he had staggered below, and I understand he went to sleep on the floor of his own cabin. The mate practically assumed the command. He was the gaunt, taciturn individual we had seen at the wheel. Apparently he was in an evil temper with Montgomery. He took not the slightest notice of either of us. We dined with him in a sulky silence, after a few ineffectual efforts on my part to talk. It struck me too that the men regarded my companion and his animals in a singularly unfriendly manner. I found Montgomery very reticent about his purpose with these creatures, and about his destination; and though I was sensible of a growing curiosity as to both, I did not press him.

We remained talking on the quarter deck until the sky was thick with stars. Except for an occasional sound in the yellow-lit forecastle and a movement of the animals now and then, the night was very still. The puma lay crouched together, watching us with shining eyes, a black heap in the corner of its cage. Montgomery produced some cigars. He talked to me of London in a tone of half-painful reminiscence, asking all kinds of questions about changes that had taken place. He spoke like a man who had loved his life there, and had been suddenly and irrevocably cut off from it. I gossiped as well as I could of this and that. All the time the strangeness of him was shaping itself in my mind; and as I talked I peered at his odd, pallid face in the dim light of the binnacle[25] lantern behind me. Then I looked out at the darkling sea, where in the dimness his little island was hidden.

This man, it seemed to me, had come out of Immensity merely to save my life. Tomorrow he would drop over the side, and vanish again out of my existence. Even had it been under commonplace circumstances, it would have made me a trifle thoughtful; but in the first place was the singularity of an educated man living on this unknown little island, and coupled with that the extraordinary nature of his luggage. I found myself repeating the captain's question, What did he want with the beasts? Why, too, had he pretended they were not his when I had remarked about them at first? Then, again, in his personal attendant there was a bizarre quality which had impressed me profoundly. These circumstances threw a haze of mystery round the man. They laid hold of my imagination, and hampered my tongue.

Towards midnight our talk of London died away, and we stood side by side leaning over the bulwarks and staring dreamily over the silent, starlit sea, each pursuing his own thoughts. It was the atmosphere for sentiment, and I began upon my gratitude.

'If I may say it,' said I, after a time, 'you have saved my life.'

'Chance,' he answered. 'Just chance.'

'I prefer to make my thanks to the accessible agent.'

'Thank no one. You had the need, and I had the knowledge; and I injected and fed you much as I might have collected a specimen. I was bored and wanted something to do. If I'd been jaded that day, or hadn't liked your face, well – it's a curious question where you would have been now!'

This damped my mood a little. 'At any rate – ' I began.

'It's chance, I tell you,' he interrupted, 'as everything is in a man's life. Only the asses won't see it! Why am I here now, an outcast from civilisation, instead of being a happy man enjoying all the pleasures of London? Simply because eleven years ago – I lost my head for ten minutes on a foggy night.'

He stopped.

'Yes?' said I.

'That's all.'

We relapsed into silence. Presently he laughed. 'There's something in this starlight that loosens one's tongue. I'm an ass, and yet somehow I would like to tell you.'

'Whatever you tell me, you may rely upon my keeping to myself – if that's it.'

He was on the point of beginning, and then shook his head, doubtfully.

'Don't,' said I. 'It is all the same to me. After all, it is better to keep your secret. There's nothing gained but a little relief if I respect your confidence. If I don't – well?'

He grunted undecidedly. I felt I had him at a disadvantage, had caught him in the mood of indiscretion; and to tell the truth I was not curious to learn what might have driven a young medical student out of London. I have an imagination. I shrugged my shoulders and turned away. Over the taffrail leant a silent black figure, watching the stars. It was Montgomery's strange attendant. It looked over its shoulder quickly with my movement, then looked away again.

It may seem a little thing to you, perhaps, but it came like a sudden blow to me. The only light near us was a lantern at the wheel. The creature's face was turned for one brief instant out of the dimness of the stern towards this illumination, and I saw that the eyes that glanced at me shone with a pale-green light. I did not know then that a reddish luminosity, at least, is not uncommon in human eyes. The thing came to me as stark inhumanity. That black figure with its eyes of fire struck down through all my adult thoughts and feelings, and for a moment the forgotten horrors of childhood came back to my mind. Then the effect passed as it had come. An uncouth black figure of a man, a figure of no particular import, hung over the taffrail against the starlight, and I found Montgomery was speaking to me.

'I'm thinking of turning in, then,' said he, 'if you've had enough of this.'

I answered him incongruously. We went below, and he wished me good-night at the door of my cabin.

That night I had some very unpleasant dreams. The waning moon rose late. Its light struck a ghostly white beam across my cabin, and made an ominous shape on the planking by my bunk. Then the staghounds woke, and began howling and baying; so that I dreamt fitfully, and scarcely slept until the approach of dawn.

CHAPTER 5

The Man Who Had Nowhere to Go

In the early morning (it was the second morning after my recovery, and I believe the fourth after I was picked up), I awoke through an avenue of tumultuous dreams – dreams of guns and howling mobs – and became sensible of a hoarse shouting above me. I rubbed my eyes and lay listening to the noise, doubtful for a little while of my whereabouts. Then came a sudden pattering of bare feet, the sound of heavy objects being thrown about, a violent creaking and the rattling of chains. I heard the swish of the water as the ship was suddenly brought round, and a foamy yellow-green wave flew across the little round window and left it streaming. I jumped into my clothes and went on deck.

As I came up the ladder I saw against the flushed sky – for the sun was just rising – the broad back and red hair of the captain, and over his shoulder the puma spinning from a tackle rigged on to the mizzen spanker-boom.[26]

The poor brute seemed horribly scared, and crouched in the bottom of its little cage.

'Overboard with 'em!' bawled the captain. 'Overboard with 'em! We'll have a clean ship soon of the whole bilin' of 'em.'

He stood in my way, so that I had perforce to tap his shoulder to come on deck. He came round with a start, and staggered back a few paces to stare at me. It needed no expert eye to tell that the man was still drunk.

'Hello!' said he, stupidly; and then with a light coming into his eyes, 'Why, it's Mr – Mr?'

'Prendick,' said I.

'Prendick be damned!' said he. 'Shut-up – that's your name. Mr Shut-up.'

It was no good answering the brute; but I certainly did not expect his next move. He held out his hand to the gangway by which Montgomery stood talking to a massive grey-haired man in dirty-blue flannels, who had apparently just come aboard.

'That way, Mr Blasted Shut-up! that way!' roared the captain.

Montgomery and his companion turned as he spoke.

'What do you mean?' I said.

'That way, Mr Blasted Shut-up, that's what I mean! Overboard, Mr Shut-up – and sharp! We're cleaning the ship out, cleaning the whole blessed ship out; and overboard you go!'

I stared at him dumfounded. Then it occurred to me that it was exactly the thing I wanted. The lost prospect of a journey as sole passenger with this quarrelsome sot was not one to mourn over. I turned towards Montgomery.

'Can't have you,' said Montgomery's companion, concisely.

'You can't have me!' said I, aghast. He had the squarest and most resolute face I ever set eyes upon.

'Look here,' I began, turning to the captain.

'Overboard!' said the captain. 'This ship ain't for beasts and cannibals and worse than beasts, any more. Overboard you go, Mr Shut-up. If they can't have you, you goes overboard. But, anyhow, you go – with your friends. I've done with this blessed island for evermore, amen! I've had enough of it.'

'But, Montgomery,' I appealed.

He distorted his lower lip, and nodded his head hopelessly at the grey-haired man beside him, to indicate his powerlessness to help me.

'I'll see to *you*, presently,' said the captain.

Then began a curious three-cornered altercation. Alternately I appealed to one and another of the three men, first to the grey-haired man to let me land, and then to the drunken captain to keep me aboard. I even bawled entreaties to the sailors. Montgomery said never a word, only shook his head. 'You're going overboard, I tell you,' was the captain's refrain. 'Law be damned! I'm king here.' At last I must confess my voice suddenly broke in the middle of a vigorous threat. I felt a gust of hysterical petulance, and went aft and stared dismally at nothing.

Meanwhile the sailors progressed rapidly with the task of unshipping the packages and caged animals. A large launch, with two standing lugs,²⁷ lay under the lea of the schooner; and into this the strange assortment of goods were swung. I did not then see the hands from the island that were receiving the packages, for the hull of the launch was hidden from me by the side of the schooner. Neither Montgomery nor his companion took the slightest notice of me, but busied themselves in assisting and directing the four or five sailors who were unloading the goods. The captain went forward interfering rather than assisting. I was alternately despairful and desperate. Once or twice as I stood waiting there for things to accomplish themselves, I could not resist an impulse to laugh at my miserable quandary. I felt all the wretcheder for the lack of a breakfast. Hunger and a lack of blood-corpuscles take all the manhood from a man. I perceived pretty clearly that I had not the stamina either to resist what the captain chose to do to expel me, or to force myself upon Montgomery and his companion. So I waited passively upon fate; and the work of transferring Montgomery's possessions to the launch went on as if I did not exist.

Presently that work was finished, and then came a struggle. I was hauled, resisting weakly enough, to the gangway. Even then I noticed the oddness of the brown faces of the men who were with Montgomery in the launch; but the launch was now fully laden, and was shoved off hastily. A broadening gap of green water appeared under me, and I pushed back with all my strength to avoid falling headlong. The hands in the launch shouted derisively, and I heard Montgomery curse at them; and then the captain, the mate, and one of the seamen helping him, ran me aft towards the stern.

The dinghy of the *Lady Vain* had been towing behind; it was half full of water, had no oars, and was quite unvictualled. I refused to go aboard her, and flung myself full length on the deck. In the end, they swung me into her by a rope (for they had no stern ladder), and then they cut me adrift. I drifted slowly from the schooner. In a kind of stupor I watched all hands take to the rigging, and slowly but surely she came round to the wind; the sails fluttered, and then bellied out as the wind came into them. I stared at her weather-beaten side heeling steeply towards me; and then she passed out of my range of view.

I did not turn my head to follow her. At first I could scarcely believe what had happened. I crouched in the bottom of the dinghy, stunned, and staring blankly at the vacant, oily sea. Then I realised that I was in that little hell of mine again, now half swamped; and looking back over the gunwale, I saw the schooner standing away from me, with the red-haired captain mocking at me over the taffrail, and turning towards the island saw the launch growing smaller as she approached the beach.

Abruptly the cruelty of this desertion became clear to me. I had no means of reaching the land unless I should chance to drift there. I was still weak, you must remember, from my exposure in the boat; I was empty and very faint, or I should have had more heart. But as it was I suddenly began to sob and weep, as I had never done since I was a little child. The tears ran down my face. In a passion of despair I struck with my fists at the water in the bottom of the boat, and kicked savagely at the gunwale. I prayed aloud for God to let me die.

CHAPTER 6

The Evil-Looking Boatman

But the islanders, seeing that I was really adrift, took pity on me. I drifted very slowly to the eastward, approaching the island slantingly; and presently I saw, with hysterical relief, the launch come round and return towards me. She was heavily laden, and I could make out as she drew nearer Montgomery's white-haired, broad-shouldered companion sitting cramped up with the dogs and several packing-cases in the stern sheets. This individual stared fixedly at me without moving or speaking. The black-faced cripple was glaring at me as fixedly in the bows near the puma. There were three other men besides – three strange brutish-looking fellows, at whom the staghounds were snarling savagely. Montgomery, who was steering, brought the boat by me, and rising, caught and fastened my painter[28] to the tiller to tow me, for there was no room aboard.

I had recovered from my hysterical phase by this time and answered his hail, as he approached, bravely enough. I told him the dinghy was nearly swamped, and he reached me a piggin.[29] I was jerked back as the rope tightened between the boats. For some time I was busy baling.

It was not until I had got the water under control (for the water in the dinghy had been shipped; the boat was perfectly sound) that I had leisure to look at the people in the launch again.

The white-haired man I found was still regarding me steadfastly, but with an expression, as I now fancied, of some perplexity. When my eyes met his, he looked down at the staghound that sat between his knees. He was a powerfully-built man, as I have said, with a fine forehead and rather heavy features; but his eyes had that odd drooping of the skin above the lids which often comes with advancing years, and the fall of his heavy mouth at the corners gave him an expression of pugnacious resolution. He talked to Montgomery in a tone too low for me to hear.

From him my eyes travelled to his three men; and a strange crew they were. I saw only their faces, yet there was something in their faces – I knew not what – that gave me a queer spasm of disgust. I looked steadily at them, and the impression did not pass, though I failed to see what had occasioned it. They seemed to me then to be brown men; but their limbs were oddly swathed in some thin, dirty, white stuff down even to the fingers and feet: I have never seen men so wrapped up before, and women so only in the East. They wore turbans too, and thereunder peered out their elfin faces at me, faces with protruding lower-jaws and bright eyes. They had lank black hair, almost like horsehair, and seemed as they sat to exceed in stature any race of men I have seen. The white-haired man, who I knew was a good six feet in height, sat a head below any one of the three. I found afterwards that really none were taller than myself; but their bodies were abnormally long, and the thigh-part of the leg short and curiously twisted. At any rate, they were an amazingly ugly gang, and over the heads of them under the forward lug peered the black face of the man whose eyes were luminous in the dark. As I stared at them, they met my gaze; and then first one and then another turned away from my direct stare, and looked at me in an odd, furtive manner. It occurred to me that I was perhaps annoying them, and I turned my attention to the island we were approaching.

It was low, and covered with thick vegetation – chiefly a kind of palm, that was new to me. From one point a thin white thread of vapour rose slantingly to an immense height, and then frayed out like a down feather. We were now within the embrace of a broad bay flanked on either hand by a low promontory. The beach was of dull-grey sand, and sloped steeply up to a ridge, perhaps sixty or seventy feet above the sea-level, and irregularly set with trees and undergrowth. Halfway up was a square enclosure of some greyish stone, which I found sub-sequently was built partly of coral and partly of pumiceous lava. Two thatched roofs peeped from within this enclosure. A man stood awaiting us at the water's edge. I fancied while we were still far off that I saw some other and very grotesque-looking creatures scuttle into the bushes upon the slope; but I saw nothing of these as we drew nearer. This man was of a moderate size, and with a black negroid face. He had a large, almost lipless, mouth, extraordinary lank arms, long thin feet and bow-legs, and stood with his heavy face thrust forward staring at us. He was dressed, like Montgomery and his white-haired com-panion, in jacket and trousers of blue serge. As we came still nearer, this individual began to run to and fro on the beach, making the most grotesque movements.

At a word of command from Montgomery, the four men in the launch sprang up, and with singularly awkward gestures struck the lugs[30] Mont-gomery steered us round and into a narrow little dock excavated in the beach. Then the man on the beach hastened towards us. This dock, as I call it, was really a mere ditch just long enough at this phase of the tide to take the longboat. I heard the bows ground in the sand, staved the dinghy off the rudder of the big boat with my piggin and, freeing the painter, landed. The three muffled men, with the clumsiest movements, scrambled out upon the sand, and forthwith set to landing the cargo, assisted by the man on the beach. I was struck especially by the curious movements of the legs of the three swathed and bandaged boatmen – not stiff they were, but distorted in some odd way, almost as if they were jointed in the wrong place. The dogs were still snarling, and strained at their chains after these men, as the white-haired man landed with them. The three big fellows spoke to one another in odd guttural tones, and the man who had waited for us on the beach began chattering to them excitedly – a foreign language, as I fancied – as they laid hands on some bales piled near the stern. Somewhere I had heard such a voice before, and I could not think where. The white-haired man stood, holding in a tumult of six dogs, and bawling orders over their din. Montgomery, having unshipped the rudder, landed likewise, and all set to work at unloading. I was too faint, what with my long fast and the sun beating down on my bare head, to offer any assistance.

Presently the white-haired man seemed to recollect my presence, and came up to me.

'You look,' said he, 'as though you had scarcely breakfasted.' His little eyes were a brilliant black under his heavy brows. 'I must apologise for that. Now you are our guest, we must make you comfortable, though you are uninvited, you know.' He looked keenly into my face. 'Montgomery says you are an educated man, Mr Prendick; says you know something of science. May I ask what that signifies?'

I told him I had spent some years at the Royal College of Science, and had done some researches in biology under Huxley.[31] He raised his eyebrows slightly at that.

'That alters the case a little, Mr Prendick,' he said, with a trifle more respect in his manner. 'As it happens, we are biologists here. This is a biological station – of a sort.' His eye rested on the men in white who were busily hauling the puma, on rollers, towards the walled yard. 'I and Montgomery, at least,' he added. Then, 'When you will be able to get away, I can't say. We're off the track to anywhere. We see a ship once in a twelve-month or so.'

He left me abruptly, and went up the beach past this group, and I think entered the enclosure. The other two men were with Montgomery, erecting a pile of smaller packages on a low-wheeled truck. The llama was still on the launch with the rabbit hutches; the staghounds were still lashed to the thwarts. The pile of things completed, all three men laid hold of the truck and began shoving the ton-weight or so upon it after the puma. Presently Montgomery left them, and coming back to me held out his hand.

'I'm glad,' said he, 'for my own part. That captain was a silly ass. He'd have made things lively for you.'

'It was you,' said I, 'that saved me again.'

'That depends. You'll find this island an infernally rum place, I promise you. I'd watch my goings carefully, if I were you. *He* – ' He hesitated, and seemed to alter his mind about what was on his lips. 'I wish you'd help me with these rabbits,' he said.

His procedure with the rabbits was singular. I waded in with him, and helped him lug one of the hutches ashore. No sooner was that done than he opened the door of it, and tilting the thing on one end turned its living contents out on the ground. They fell in a struggling heap, one on the top of the other. He clapped his hands, and forthwith they went off with that hopping run of theirs, fifteen or twenty of them I should think, up the beach.

'Increase and multiply, my friends,' said Montgomery. 'Replenish the island. Hitherto we've had a certain lack of meat here.'

As I watched them disappearing, the white-haired man returned with a brandy-flask and some biscuits. 'Something to go on with, Prendick,' said he, in a far more familiar tone than before. I made no ado, but set to work on the biscuits at once, while the white-haired man helped Montgomery to release about a score more of the rabbits. Three big hutches, however, went up to the house with the puma. The brandy I did not touch, for I have been an abstainer from my birth.

CHAPTER 7

The Locked Door

The reader will perhaps understand that at first everything was so strange about me, and my position was the outcome of such unexpected adventures, that I had no discernment of the relative strangeness of this or that thing. I followed the llama up the beach, and was overtaken by Montgomery, who asked me not to enter the stone enclosure. I noticed then that the puma in its cage and the pile of packages had been placed outside the entrance to this quadrangle.

I turned and saw that the launch had now been unloaded, run out again, and was being beached, and the white-haired man was walking towards us. He addressed Montgomery.

'And now comes the problem of this uninvited guest. What are we to do with him?'

'He knows something of science,' said Montgomery.

'I'm itching to get to work again – with this new stuff,' said the white-haired man, nodding towards the enclosure. His eyes grew brighter.

'I dare say you are,' said Montgomery, in anything but a cordial tone.

'We can't send him over there, and we can't spare the time to build him a new shanty; and we certainly can't take him into our confidence just yet.'

'I'm in your hands,' said I. I had no idea of what he meant by 'over there'.

'I've been thinking of the same things,' Montgomery answered. 'There's my room with the outer door – '

'That's it,' said the elder man, promptly, looking at Montgomery; and all three of us went towards the enclosure. 'I'm sorry to make a mystery, Mr Prendick; but you'll remember you're uninvited. Our little establishment here contains a secret or so, is a kind of Blue-Beard's chamber, in fact. Nothing very dreadful, really, to a sane man; but just now, as we don't know you – '

'Decidedly,' said I, 'I should be a fool to take offence at any want of confidence.'

He twisted his heavy mouth into a faint smile – he was one of those saturnine people who smile with the corners of the mouth down – and bowed his acknowledgement of my complaisance. The main entrance to the enclosure we passed; it was a heavy wooden gate, framed in iron and locked, with the cargo of the launch piled outside it; and at the corner we came to a small doorway I had not previously observed. The white-haired man produced a bundle of keys from the pocket of his greasy blue jacket, opened this door, and entered. His keys, and the elaborate locking-up of the place even while it was still under his eye, struck me as peculiar. I followed him, and found myself in a small apartment, plainly but not uncomfortably furnished and with its inner door, which was slightly ajar, opening into a paved courtyard. This inner door Montgomery at once closed. A hammock was slung across the darker corner of the room, and a small unglazed window defended by an iron bar looked out towards the sea.

This the white-haired man told me was to be my apartment; and the inner door, which 'for fear of accidents', he said, he would lock on the other side, was my limit inward. He called my attention to a convenient deckchair before the window, and to an array of old books, chiefly, I found, surgical works and editions of the Latin and Greek classics (languages I cannot read with any comfort), on a shelf near the hammock. He left the room by the outer door, as if to avoid opening the inner one again.

'We usually have our meals in here,' said Montgomery, and then, as if in doubt, went out after the other. 'Moreau!' I heard him call, and for the moment I do not think I noticed. Then as I handled the books on the shelf it came up in consciousness. Where had I heard the name of Moreau before? I sat down before the window, took out the biscuits that still remained to me, and ate them with an excellent appetite. Moreau!

Through the window I saw one of those unaccountable men in white lugging a packing-case along the beach. Presently the window-frame hid him. Then I heard a key inserted and turned in the lock behind me. After a little while I heard through the locked door the noise of the staghounds that had now been brought up from the beach. They were not barking, but sniffing and growling in a curious fashion. I could hear the rapid patter of their feet, and Montgomery's voice soothing them.

I was very much impressed by the elaborate secrecy of these two men regarding the contents of the place, and for some time I was thinking of that and of the unaccountable familiarity of the name of Moreau; but so odd is the human memory that I could not then recall that well-known name in its proper connection. From that my thoughts went to the indefinable queerness of the deformed man on the beach. I never saw such a gait, such odd motions as he pulled at the box. I recalled that none of these men had spoken to me, though most of them I had found looking at me at one time or another in a peculiarly furtive manner, quite unlike the frank stare of your unsophisticated savage. Indeed, they had all seemed remarkably taciturn, and when they did speak, endowed with very uncanny voices. What was wrong with them? Then I recalled the eyes of Montgomery's ungainly attendant.

Just as I was thinking of him he came in. He was now dressed in white, and carried a little tray with some coffee and boiled vegetables thereon. I could hardly repress a shuddering recoil as he came, bending amiably, and placed the tray before me on the table. Then astonishment paralysed me. Under his stringy black locks I saw his ear; it jumped upon me suddenly close to my face. The man had pointed ears, covered with a fine brown fur!

'Your breakfast, sair,' he said.

I stared at his face without attempting to answer him. He turned and went towards the door, regarding me oddly over his shoulder. I followed him out with my eyes; and as I did so, by some odd trick of unconscious cerebration, there came surging into my head the phrase, 'The Moreau Hollows' – was it? 'The Moreau – ' Ah! It sent my memory back ten years. 'The Moreau Horrors!' The phrase drifted loose in my mind for a moment, and then I saw it in red lettering on a little buff-coloured pamphlet, to read which made one shiver and creep. Then I remembered distinctly all about it. That long-forgotten pamphlet came back with startling vividness to my mind. I had been a mere lad then, and Moreau was, I suppose, about fifty, a prominent and masterful physiologist, well-known in scientific circles for his extraordinary imagination and his brutal directness in discussion.

Was this the same Moreau? He had published some very astonishing facts in connection with the transfusion of blood, and in addition was known to be doing valuable work on morbid growths. Then suddenly his career was closed. He had to leave England. A journalist obtained access to his laboratory in the capacity of laboratory-assistant, with the deliberate intention of making sensational exposures; and by the help of a shocking accident (if it was an accident), his gruesome pamphlet became notorious. On the day of its publication, a wretched dog, flayed and otherwise mutilated, escaped from Moreau's house. It was in the silly season, and a prominent editor, a cousin of the temporary laboratory-assistant, appealed to the conscience of the nation. It was not the first time that conscience has turned against the methods of research. The doctor was simply howled out of the country. It may be that he deserved to be; but I still think that the tepid support of his fellow-investigators and his desertion by the great body of scientific workers was a shameful thing. Yet some of his experiments, by the journalist's account, were wantonly cruel. He might perhaps have purchased his social peace by abandoning his investigations; but he apparently preferred the latter, as most men would who have once fallen under the overmastering spell of research. He was unmarried, and had indeed nothing but his own interest to consider.

I felt convinced that this must be the same man. Everything pointed to it. It dawned upon me to what end the puma and the other animals – which had now been brought with other luggage into the enclosure behind the house – were destined; and a curious faint odour, the halitus of something familiar, an odour that had been in the background of my consciousness hitherto, suddenly came forward into the forefront of my thoughts. It was the antiseptic odour of the dissecting-room. I heard the puma growling through the wall, and one of the dogs yelped as though it had been struck.

Yet surely, and especially to another scientific man, there was nothing so horrible in vivisection as to account for this secrecy; and by some odd leap in my thoughts the pointed ears and luminous eyes of Montgomery's attendant came back again before me with the sharpest definition. I stared before me out at the green sea, frothing under a freshening breeze, and let these and other strange memories of the last few days chase one another through my mind.

What could it all mean? A locked enclosure on a lonely island, a notorious vivisector, and these crippled and distorted men?

CHAPTER 8

The Crying of the Puma

Montgomery interrupted my tangle of mystification and suspicion about one o'clock, and his grotesque attendant followed him with a tray bearing bread, some herbs and other eatables, a flask of whisky, a jug of water, and three glasses and knives. I glanced askance at this strange creature, and found him watching me with his queer, restless eyes. Montgomery said he would lunch with me, but that Moreau was too preoccupied with some work to come.

'Moreau!' said I. 'I know that name.'

'The devil you do!' said he. 'What an ass I was to mention it to you! I might have thought. Anyhow, it will give you an inkling of our – mysteries. Whisky?'

'No, thanks; I'm an abstainer.'

'I wish I'd been. But it's no use locking the door after the steed is stolen. It was that infernal stuff which led to my coming here – that, and a foggy night. I thought myself in luck at the time, when Moreau offered to get me off. It's queer – '

'Montgomery,' said I, suddenly, as the outer door closed, 'why has your man pointed ears?'

'Damn!' he said, over his first mouthful of food. He stared at me for a moment, and then repeated, 'Pointed ears?'

'Little points to them,' said I, as calmly as possible, with a catch in my breath; 'and a fine black fur at the edges?'

He helped himself to whisky and water with great deliberation. 'I was under the impression – that his hair covered his ears.'

'I saw them as he stooped by me to put that coffee you sent to me on the table. And his eyes shine in the dark.'

By this time Montgomery had recovered from the surprise of my question. 'I always thought,' he said deliberately, with a certain accentuation of his flavouring of lisp, 'that there *was* something the matter with his ears, from the way he covered them. What were they like?'

I was persuaded from his manner that this ignorance was a pretence. Still, I could hardly tell the man that I thought him a liar. 'Pointed,' I said; 'rather small and furry – distinctly furry. But the whole man is one of the strangest beings I ever set eyes on.'

A sharp, hoarse cry of animal pain came from the enclosure behind us. Its depth and volume testified to the puma. I saw Montgomery wince.

'Yes?' he said.

'Where did you pick up the creature?'

'San Francisco. He's an ugly brute, I admit. Half-witted, you know. Can't remember where he came from. But I'm used to him, you know. We both are. How does he strike you?'

'He's unnatural,' I said. 'There's something about him – don't think me fanciful, but it gives me a nasty little sensation, a tightening of my muscles, when he comes near me. It's a touch – of the diabolical, in fact.'

Montgomery had stopped eating while I told him this. 'Rum!' he said. 'I can't see it.' He resumed his meal. 'I had no idea of it,' he said, and masticated. 'The crew of the schooner must have felt it the same. Made a dead set at the poor devil. You saw the captain?'

Suddenly the puma howled again, this time more painfully. Montgomery swore under his breath. I had half a mind to attack him about the men on the beach. Then the poor brute within gave vent to a series of short, sharp cries.

'Your men on the beach,' said I; 'what race are they?'

'Excellent fellows, aren't they?' said he, absent-mindedly, knitting his brows as the animal yelled out sharply.

I said no more. There was another outcry worse than the former. He looked at me with his dull grey eyes, and then took some more whisky. He tried to draw me into a discussion about alcohol, professing to have saved my life with it. He seemed anxious to lay stress on the fact that I owed my life to him. I answered him distractedly.

Presently our meal came to an end; the misshapen monster with the pointed ears cleared the remains away, and Montgomery left me alone in the room again. All the time he had been in a state of ill-concealed irritation at the noise of the vivisected puma. He had spoken of his odd want of nerve, and left me to the obvious application.

I found myself that the cries were singularly irritating, and they grew in depth and intensity as the afternoon wore on. They were painful at first, but their constant resurgence at last altogether upset my balance. I flung aside a crib of Horace[32] I had been reading, and began to clench my fists, to bite my lips, and to pace the room. Presently I got to stopping my ears with my fingers.

The emotional appeal of those yells grew upon me steadily, grew at last to such an exquisite expression of suffering that I could stand it in

that confined room no longer. I stepped out of the door into the
slumberous heat of the late afternoon, and walking past the main
entrance – locked again, I noticed – turned the corner of the wall

The crying sounded even louder out of doors. It was as if all the pain
in the world had found a voice. Yet had I known such pain was in the
next room, and had it been dumb, I believe – I have thought since – I
could have stood it well enough. It is when suffering finds a voice and
sets our nerves quivering that this pity comes troubling us. But in spite
of the brilliant sunlight and the green fans of the trees waving in the
soothing sea-breeze, the world was a confusion, blurred with drifting
black and red phantasms, until I was out of earshot of the house in the
chequered wall.

CHAPTER 9

The Thing in the Forest

I strode through the undergrowth that clothed the ridge behind the house, scarcely heeding whither I went; passed on through the shadow of a thick cluster of straight-stemmed trees beyond it, and so presently found myself some way on the other side of the ridge, and descending towards a streamlet that ran through a narrow valley. I paused and listened. The distance I had come, or the intervening masses of thicket, deadened any sound that might be coming from the enclosure. The air was still. Then with a rustle a rabbit emerged, and went scampering up the slope before me. I hesitated, and sat down in the edge of the shade.

The place was a pleasant one. The rivulet was hidden by the luxuriant vegetation of the banks save at one point, where I caught a triangular patch of its glittering water. On the farther side I saw through a bluish haze a tangle of trees and creepers, and above these again the luminous blue of the sky. Here and there a splash of white or crimson marked the blooming of some trailing epiphyte.[33] I let my eyes wander over this scene for a while, and then began to turn over in my mind again the strange peculiarities of Montgomery's man. But it was too hot to think elaborately, and presently I fell into a tranquil state midway between dozing and waking.

From this I was aroused, after I know not how long, by a rustling amidst the greenery on the other side of the stream. For a moment I could see nothing but the waving summits of the ferns and reeds. Then suddenly upon the bank of the stream appeared Something – at first I could not distinguish what it was. It bowed its round head to the water, and began to drink. Then I saw it was a man, going on all-fours like a beast. He was clothed in bluish cloth, and was of a copper-coloured hue, with black hair. It seemed that grotesque ugliness was an invariable character of these islanders. I could hear the suck of the water at his lips as he drank.

I leant forward to see him better, and a piece of lava, detached by my hand, went pattering down the slope. He looked up guiltily, and his eyes met mine. Forthwith he scrambled to his feet, and stood wiping his clumsy hand across his mouth and regarding me. His legs were scarcely half the length of his body. So, staring one another out of countenance, we remained for perhaps the space of a minute. Then, stopping to look back once or twice, he slunk off among the bushes to the right of me, and I heard the swish of the fronds grow faint in the distance and die away. Long after he had disappeared, I remained sitting up staring in the direction of his retreat. My drowsy tranquillity had gone.

I was startled by a noise behind me, and turning suddenly saw the flapping white tail of a rabbit vanishing up the slope. I jumped to my feet. The apparition of this grotesque, half-bestial creature had suddenly populated the stillness of the afternoon for me. I looked around me rather nervously, and regretted that I was unarmed. Then I thought that the man I had just seen had been clothed in bluish cloth, had not been naked as a savage would have been; and I tried to persuade myself from that fact that he was after all probably a peaceful character, that the dull ferocity of his countenance belied him.

Yet I was greatly disturbed at the apparition. I walked to the left along the slope, turning my head about and peering this way and that among the straight stems of the trees. Why should a man go on all-fours and drink with his lips? Presently I heard an animal wailing again, and taking it to be the puma, I turned about and walked in a direction diametrically opposite to the sound. This led me down to the stream, across which I stepped and pushed my way up through the undergrowth beyond.

I was startled by a great patch of vivid scarlet on the ground, and going up to it found it to be a peculiar fungus, branched and corrugated like a foliaceous lichen, but deliquescing into slime at the touch; and then in the shadow of some luxuriant ferns I came upon an unpleasant thing – the dead body of a rabbit covered with shining flies, but still warm and with the head torn off. I stopped aghast at the sight of the scattered blood. Here at least was one visitor to the island disposed of! There were no traces of other violence about it. It looked as though it had been suddenly snatched up and killed; and as I stared at the little furry body came the difficulty of how the thing had been done. The vague dread that had been in my mind since I had seen the inhuman face of the man at the stream grew distincter as I stood there. I began to realise the hardihood of my expedition among these unknown people. The thicket about me became altered to my imagination. Every shadow became something more than a shadow – became an ambush; every rustle became a threat. Invisible things seemed watching me. I resolved to go back to the enclosure on the beach. I suddenly turned away and thrust myself violently, possibly even frantically, through the bushes, anxious to get a clear space about me again.

I stopped just in time to prevent myself emerging upon an open space. It was a kind of glade in the forest, made by a fall; seedlings were already starting up to struggle for the vacant space; and beyond, the dense growth of stems and twining vines and splashes of fungus and flowers closed in again. Before me, squatting together upon the fungoid ruins of a huge fallen tree and still unaware of my approach, were three grotesque human figures. One was evidently a female; the other two were men. They were naked, save for swathings of scarlet cloth about the middle; and their skins were of a dull pinkish-drab colour, such as I had seen in no savages before. They had fat, heavy, chinless faces, retreating foreheads, and a scant bristly hair upon their heads. I never saw such bestial-looking creatures.

They were talking, or at least one of the men was talking to the other two, and all three had been too closely interested to heed the rustling of my approach. They swayed their heads and shoulders from side to side. The speaker's words came thick and sloppy, and though I could hear them distinctly I could not distinguish what he said. He seemed to me to be reciting some complicated gibberish. Presently his articulation became shriller, and spreading his hands he rose to his feet. At that the others began to gibber in unison, also rising to their feet, spreading their hands and swaying their bodies in rhythm with their chant. I noticed then the abnormal shortness of their legs, and their lank, clumsy feet. All three began slowly to circle round, raising and stamping their feet and waving their arms; a kind of tune crept into their rhythmic recitation, and a refrain – 'Aloola,' or 'Balloola,' it sounded like. Their eyes began to sparkle, and their ugly faces to brighten, with an expression of strange pleasure. Saliva dripped from their lipless mouths.

Suddenly, as I watched their grotesque and unaccountable gestures, I perceived clearly for the first time what it was that had offended me, what had given me the two inconsistent and conflicting impressions of utter strangeness and yet of the strangest familiarity. The three creatures engaged in this mysterious rite were human in shape, and yet human beings with the strangest air about them of some familiar animal. Each of these creatures, despite its human form, its rag of clothing and the rough humanity of its bodily form, had woven into it – into its movements, into the expression of its countenance, into its whole presence – some now irresistible suggestion of a hog, a swinish taint, the unmistakable mark of the beast.

I stood overcome by this amazing realisation and then the most horrible questionings came rushing into my mind. They began leaping in the air, first one and then the other, whooping and grunting. Then one slipped, and for a moment was on all-fours – to recover, indeed, forthwith. But that transitory gleam of the true animalism of these monsters was enough.

I turned as noiselessly as possible, and becoming every now and then rigid with the fear of being discovered, as a branch cracked or a leaf rustled, I pushed back into the bushes. It was long before I grew bolder and dared to move freely. My only idea for the moment was to get away from these foul beings, and I scarcely noticed that I had emerged upon a faint pathway amidst the trees. Then suddenly traversing a little glade, I saw with an unpleasant start two clumsy legs among the trees, walking with noiseless footsteps parallel with my course, and perhaps thirty yards away from me. The head and upper part of the body were hidden by a tangle of creeper. I stopped abruptly, hoping the creature did not see me. The feet stopped as I did. So nervous was I that I controlled an impulse to headlong flight with the utmost difficulty. Then looking hard, I distinguished through the interlacing network the head and body of the brute I had seen drinking. He moved his head. There was an emerald flash in his eyes as he glanced at me from the shadow of the trees, a half-luminous colour that vanished as he turned his head again. He was motionless for a moment, and then with a noiseless tread began running through the green confusion. In another moment he had vanished behind some bushes. I could not see him, but I felt that he had stopped and was watching me again.

What on earth was he – man or beast? What did he want with me? I had no weapon, not even a stick. Flight would be madness. At any rate the Thing, whatever it was, lacked the courage to attack me. Setting my teeth hard, I walked straight towards him. I was anxious not to show the fear that seemed chilling my backbone. I pushed through a tangle of tall white-flowered bushes, and saw him twenty paces beyond, looking over his shoulder at me and hesitating. I advanced a step or two, looking steadfastly into his eyes.

'Who are you?' said I.

He tried to meet my gaze. 'No!' he said suddenly, and turning went bounding away from me through the undergrowth. Then he turned and stared at me again. His eyes shone brightly out of the dusk under the trees.

My heart was in my mouth; but I felt my only chance was bluff, and walked steadily towards him. He turned again, and vanished into the dusk. Once more I thought I caught the glint of his eyes, and that was all.

For the first time I realised how the lateness of the hour might affect me. The sun had set some minutes since, the swift dusk of the tropics was already fading out of the eastern sky, and a pioneer moth fluttered silently by my head. Unless I would spend the night among the unknown dangers of the mysterious forest, I must hasten back to the enclosure. The thought of a return to that pain-haunted refuge was extremely disagreeable, but still more so was the idea of being overtaken in the open by darkness and all that darkness might conceal. I gave one more look into the blue shadows that had swallowed up this odd creature, and then retraced my way down the slope towards the stream, going as I judged in the direction from which I had come.

I walked eagerly, my mind confused with many things, and presently found myself in a level place among scattered trees. The colourless clearness that comes after the sunset flush was darkling; the blue sky above grew momentarily deeper, and the little stars one by one pierced the attenuated light; the interspaces of the trees, the gaps in the farther vegetation, that had been hazy blue in the daylight, grew black and mysterious. I pushed on. The colour vanished from the world. The tree-tops rose against the luminous blue sky in inky silhouette, and all below that outline melted into one formless blackness. Presently the trees grew thinner, and the shrubby undergrowth more abundant. Then there was a desolate space covered with a white sand, and then another expanse of tangled bushes. I did not remember crossing the sand-opening before. I began to be tormented by a faint rustling upon my right hand. I thought at first it was fancy, for whenever I stopped there was silence, save for the evening breeze in the tree-tops. Then when I turned to hurry on again there was an echo to my footsteps.

I turned away from the thickets, keeping to the more open ground, and endeavouring by sudden turns now and then to surprise something in the act of creeping upon me. I saw nothing, and nevertheless my sense of another presence grew steadily. I increased my pace, and after some time came to a slight ridge, crossed it, and turned sharply, regarding it steadfastly from the farther side. It came out black and clear-cut against the darkling sky; and presently a shapeless lump heaved up momentarily against the skyline and vanished again. I felt assured now that my tawny-faced antagonist was stalking me once more; and coupled with that was another unpleasant realisation, that I had lost my way.

For a time I hurried on hopelessly perplexed, and pursued by that stealthy approach. Whatever it was, the Thing either lacked the courage to attack me, or it was waiting to take me at some disadvantage. I kept studiously to the open. At times I would turn and listen; and presently I had half persuaded myself that my pursuer had abandoned the chase, or was a mere creation of my disordered imagination. Then I heard the sound of the sea. I quickened my footsteps almost into a run, and immediately there was a stumble in my rear.

I turned suddenly, and stared at the uncertain trees behind me. One black shadow seemed to leap into another. I listened, rigid, and heard nothing but the creep of the blood in my ears. I thought that my nerves were unstrung, and that my imagination was tricking me, and turned resolutely towards the sound of the sea again.

In a minute or so the trees grew thinner, and I emerged upon a bare, low headland running out into the sombre water. The night was calm and clear, and the reflection of the growing multitude of the stars shivered in the tranquil heaving of the sea. Some way out, the wash upon an irregular band of reef shone with a pallid light of its own. Westward I saw the zodiacal light mingling with the yellow brilliance of the evening star. The coast fell away from me to the east, and westward it was hidden by the shoulder of the cape. Then I recalled the fact that Moreau's beach lay to the west.

A twig snapped behind me, and there was a rustle. I turned, and stood facing the dark trees. I could see nothing – or else I could see too much. Every dark form in the dimness had its ominous quality, its peculiar suggestion of alert watchfulness. So I stood for perhaps a minute, and then, with an eye to the trees still, turned westward to cross the headland; and as I moved, one among the lurking shadows moved to follow me.

My heart beat quickly. Presently the broad sweep of a bay to the westward became visible, and I halted again. The noiseless shadow halted a dozen yards from me. A little point of light shone on the farther bend of the curve, and the grey sweep of the sandy beach lay faint under the starlight. Perhaps two miles away was that little point of light. To get to the beach I should have to go through the trees where the shadows lurked and down a bushy slope.

I could see the Thing rather more distinctly now. It was no animal, for it stood erect. At that I opened my mouth to speak, and found a hoarse phlegm choked my voice. I tried again, and shouted, 'Who is there?' There was no answer. I advanced a step. The Thing did not move, only gathered itself together. My foot struck a stone. That gave me an idea. Without taking my eyes off the black form before me, I stooped and picked up this lump of rock; but at my motion the Thing turned abruptly as a dog might have done, and slunk obliquely into the farther darkness. Then I recalled a schoolboy expedient against big dogs, and twisted the rock into my handkerchief, and gave this a turn round my wrist. I heard a movement farther off among the shadows, as if the Thing was in retreat. Then suddenly my tense excitement gave way; I broke into a profuse perspiration and fell a-trembling, with my adversary routed and this weapon in my hand.

It was some time before I could summon resolution to go down through the trees and bushes upon the flank of the headland to the beach. At last I did it at a run; and as I emerged from the thicket upon the sand, I heard some other body come crashing after me. At that I completely lost my head with fear, and began running along the sand. Forthwith there came the swift patter of soft feet in pursuit. I gave a wild cry, and redoubled my pace. Some dim, black things about three or four times the size of rabbits went running or hopping up from the beach towards the bushes as I passed.

So long as I live, I shall remember the terror of that chase. I ran near the water's edge, and heard every now and then the splash of the feet that gained upon me. Far away, hopelessly far, was the yellow light. All the night about us was black and still. Splash, splash, came the pursuing feet, nearer and nearer. I felt my breath going, for I was quite out of training; it whooped as I drew it, and I felt a pain like a knife at my side. I perceived the Thing would come up with me long before I reached the enclosure, and, desperate and sobbing for my breath, I wheeled round upon it and struck at it as it came up to me – struck with all my strength. The stone came out of the sling of the handkerchief as I did so. As I turned, the Thing, which had been running on all-fours, rose to its feet, and the missile fell fair on its left temple. The skull rang loud, and the animal-man blundered into me, thrust me back with its hands, and went staggering past me to fall headlong upon the sand with its face in the water; and there it lay still.

I could not bring myself to approach that black heap. I left it there, with the water rippling round it, under the still stars, and giving it a wide berth pursued my way towards the yellow glow of the house; and presently, with a positive effect of relief, came the pitiful moaning of the puma, the sound that had originally driven me out to explore this mysterious island. At that, though I was faint and horribly fatigued, I gathered together all my strength, and began running again towards the light. I thought I heard a voice calling me.

CHAPTER 10

The Crying of the Man

As I drew near the house I saw that the light shone from the open door of my room; and then I heard coming from out of the darkness at the side of that orange oblong of light, the voice of Montgomery shouting, 'Prendick!' I continued running. Presently I heard him again. I replied by a feeble 'Hello!' and in another moment had staggered up to him.

'Where have you been?' said he, holding me at arm's length, so that the light from the door fell on my face. 'We have both been so busy that we forgot you until about half an hour ago.' He led me into the room and set me down in the deckchair. For awhile I was blinded by the light. 'We did not think you would start to explore this island of ours without telling us,' he said; and then, 'I was afraid – But – what – Hello!'

My last remaining strength slipped from me, and my head fell forward on my chest. I think he found a certain satisfaction in giving me brandy.

'For God's sake,' said I, 'fasten that door.'

'You've been meeting some of our curiosities, eh?' said he.

He locked the door and turned to me again. He asked me no questions, but gave me some more brandy and water and pressed me to eat. I was in a state of collapse. He said something vague about his forgetting to warn me, and asked me briefly when I left the house and what I had seen.

I answered him as briefly, in fragmentary sentences. 'Tell me what it all means,' said I, in a state bordering on hysterics.

'It's nothing so very dreadful,' said he. 'But I think you have had about enough for one day.' The puma suddenly gave a sharp yell of pain. At that he swore under his breath. 'I'm damned,' said he, 'if this place is not as bad as Gower Street, with its cats.'

'Montgomery,' said I, 'what was that thing that came after me? Was it a beast or was it a man?'

'If you don't sleep tonight,' he said, 'you'll be off your head tomorrow.'

I stood up in front of him. 'What was that thing that came after me?' I asked.

He looked me squarely in the eyes, and twisted his mouth askew. His eyes, which had seemed animated a minute before, went dull. 'From your account,' said he, 'I'm thinking it was a bogle.'

I felt a gust of intense irritation, which passed as quickly as it came. I flung myself into the chair again, and pressed my hands on my forehead. The puma began once more.

Montgomery came round behind me and put his hand on my shoulder. 'Look here, Prendick,' he said, 'I had no business to let you drift out into this silly island of ours. But it's not so bad as you feel, man. Your nerves are worked to rags. Let me give you something that will make you sleep. *That* – will keep on for hours yet. You must simply get to sleep, or I won't answer for it.'

I did not reply. I bowed forward, and covered my face with my hands. Presently he returned with a small measure containing a dark liquid. This he gave me. I took it unresistingly, and he helped me into the hammock.

When I awoke, it was broad day. For a little while I lay flat, staring at the roof above me. The rafters, I observed, were made out of the timbers of a ship. Then I turned my head, and saw a meal prepared for me on the table. I perceived that I was hungry, and prepared to clamber out of the hammock, which, very politely anticipating my intention, twisted round and deposited me upon all-fours on the floor.

I got up and sat down before the food. I had a heavy feeling in my head, and only the vaguest memory at first of the things that had happened over night. The morning breeze blew very pleasantly through the unglazed window, and that and the food contributed to the sense of animal comfort which I experienced. Presently the door behind me – the door inward towards the yard of the enclosure – opened. I turned and saw Montgomery's face.

'All right?' said he. 'I'm frightfully busy.' And he shut the door.

Afterwards I discovered that he forgot to re-lock it. Then I recalled the expression of his face the previous night, and with that the memory of all I had experienced reconstructed itself before me. Even as that fear came back to me, there came a cry from within; but this time it was not the cry of a puma. I put down the mouthful that hesitated upon my lips, and listened. Silence, save for the whisper of the morning breeze. I began to think my ears had deceived me.

After a long pause I resumed my meal, but with my ears still vigilant. Presently I heard something else, very faint and low. I sat as if frozen in my attitude. Though it was faint and low, it moved me more profoundly than all that I had hitherto heard of the abominations behind the wall. There was no mistake this time in the quality of the dim, broken sounds; no doubt at all of their source. For it was groaning, broken by sobs and gasps of anguish. It was no brute this time; it was a human being in torment!

As I realised this I rose, and in three steps had crossed the room, seized the handle of the door into the yard, and flung it open before me.

'Prendick, man! Stop!' cried Montgomery, intervening.

A startled deerhound yelped and snarled. There was blood, I saw, in the sink – brown, and some scarlet – and I smelt the peculiar smell of carbolic acid. Then through an open doorway beyond, in the dim light of the shadow, I saw something bound painfully upon a framework, scarred, red and bandaged; and then blotting this out appeared the face of old Moreau, white and terrible. In a moment he had gripped me by the shoulder with a hand that was smeared red, had twisted me off my feet, and flung me headlong back into my own room. He lifted me as though I was a little child. I fell at full length upon the floor, and the door slammed and shut out the passionate intensity of his face. Then I heard the key turn in the lock, and Montgomery's voice in expostulation.

'Ruin the work of a lifetime,' I heard Moreau say.

'He does not understand,' said Montgomery, with other things that were inaudible.

'I can't spare the time yet,' said Moreau.

The rest I did not hear. I picked myself up and stood trembling, my mind a chaos of the most horrible misgivings. Could it be possible, I thought, that such a thing as the vivisection of men was carried on here? The question shot like lightning across a tumultuous sky; and suddenly the clouded horror of my mind condensed into a vivid realisation of my own danger.

CHAPTER 11

The Hunting of the Man

It came before my mind with an unreasonable hope of escape that the outer door of my room was still open to me. I was convinced now, absolutely assured, that Moreau had been vivisecting a human being. All the time since I had heard his name, I had been trying to link in my mind in some way the grotesque animalism of the islanders with his abominations; and now I thought I saw it all. The memory of his work on the transfusion of blood recurred to me. These creatures I had seen were the victims of some hideous experiment. These sickening scoundrels had merely intended to keep me back, to fool me with their display of confidence, and presently to fall upon me with a fate more horrible than death – with torture; and after torture the most hideous degradation it is possible to conceive – to send me off a lost soul, a beast, to the rest of their Comus rout.[34]

I looked round for some weapon. Nothing. Then with an inspiration I turned over the deckchair, put my foot on the side of it, and tore away the side rail. It happened that a nail came away with the wood, and projecting, gave a touch of danger to an otherwise petty weapon. I heard a step outside, and incontinently flung open the door and found Montgomery within a yard of it. He meant to lock the outer door! I raised this nailed stick of mine and cut at his face; but he sprang back. I hesitated a moment, then turned and fled, round the corner of the house. 'Prendick, man!' I heard his astonished cry, 'don't be a silly ass, man!'

Another minute, thought I, and he would have had me locked in, and as ready as a hospital rabbit for my fate. He emerged behind the corner, for I heard him shout, 'Prendick!' Then he began to run after me, shouting things as he ran. This time running blindly, I went north-eastward in a direction at right angles to my previous expedition. Once, as I went running headlong up the beach, I glanced over my shoulder and saw his attendant with him. I ran furiously up the slope, over it, then turning eastward along a rocky valley fringed on either side with jungle I ran for perhaps a mile altogether, my chest straining, my heart beating in my ears; and then hearing nothing of Montgomery or his man, and feeling upon the verge of exhaustion, I doubled sharply back towards the beach as I judged, and lay down in the shelter of a canebrake.[35] There I remained for a long time, too fearful to move, and indeed too fearful even to plan a course of action. The wild scene about me lay sleeping silently under the sun, and the only sound near me was the thin hum of some small gnats that had discovered me. Presently I became aware of a drowsy breathing sound, the soughing of the sea upon the beach.

After about an hour I heard Montgomery shouting my name, far away to the north. That set me thinking of my plan of action. As I interpreted it then, this island was inhabited only by these two vivisectors and their animalised victims. Some of these no doubt they could press into their service against me if need arose. I knew both Moreau and Montgomery carried revolvers; and, save for a feeble bar of deal[36] spiked with a small nail, the merest mockery of a mace, I was unarmed.

So I lay still there, until I began to think of food and drink; and at that thought the real hopelessness of my position came home to me. I knew no way of getting anything to eat. I was too ignorant of botany to discover any resort of root or fruit that might lie about me; I had no means of trapping the few rabbits upon the island. It grew blanker the more I turned the prospect over. At last, in the desperation of my position, my mind turned to the animal men I had encountered. I tried to find some hope in what I remembered of them. In turn I recalled each one I had seen, and tried to draw some augury of assistance from my memory.

Then suddenly I heard a staghound bay, and at that realised a new danger. I took little time to think, or they would have caught me then, but snatching up my nailed stick, rushed headlong from my hiding-place towards the sound of the sea. I remember a growth of thorny plants, with spines that stabbed like penknives. I emerged bleeding and with torn clothes upon the lip of a long creek opening northward. I went straight into the water without a minute's hesitation, wading up the creek, and presently finding myself knee deep in a little stream. I scrambled out at last on the westward bank, and with my heart beating loudly in my ears, crept into a tangle of ferns to await the issue. I heard the dog (there was only one) draw nearer, and yelp when it came to the thorns. Then I heard no more, and presently began to think I had escaped.

The minutes passed; the silence lengthened out, and at last after an hour of security my courage began to return to me. By this time I was no longer very much terrified or very miserable. I had, as it were, passed the limit of terror and despair. I felt now that my life was practically lost, and that persuasion made me capable of daring anything. I had even a certain wish to encounter Moreau face to face; and as I had waded into the water, I remembered that if I were too hard pressed at least one path of escape from torment still lay open to me – they could not very well prevent my drowning myself. I had half a mind to drown myself then; but an odd wish to see the whole adventure out, a queer, impersonal, spectacular interest in myself, restrained me. I stretched my limbs, sore and painful from the pricks of the spiny plants, and stared around me at the trees; and, so suddenly that it seemed to jump out of the green tracery about it, my eyes lit upon a black face watching me. I saw that it was the simian creature who had met the launch upon the beach. He was clinging to the oblique stem of a palm tree. I gripped my stick, and stood up facing him. He began chattering. 'You, you, you,' was all I could distinguish at first. Suddenly he dropped from the tree, and in another moment was holding the fronds apart and staring curiously at me.

I did not feel the same repugnance towards this creature which I had experienced in my encounters with the other Beast Men. 'You,' he said, 'in the boat.' He was a man, then – at least as much of a man as Montgomery's attendant – for he could talk.

'Yes,' I said, 'I came in the boat. From the ship.'

'Oh!' he said, and his bright, restless eyes travelled over me, to my hands, to the stick I carried, to my feet, to the tattered places in my coat, and the cuts and scratches I had received from the thorns. He seemed puzzled at something. His eyes came back to my hands. He held his own hand out and counted his digits slowly, 'One, two, three, four, five – eight?'

I did not grasp his meaning then; afterwards I was to find that a great proportion of these Beast People had malformed hands, lacking sometimes even three digits. But guessing this was in some way a greeting, I did the same thing by way of reply. He grinned with immense satisfaction. Then his swift roving glance went round again; he made a swift movement – and vanished. The fern fronds he had stood between came swishing together,

I pushed out of the brake after him, and was astonished to find him swinging cheerfully by one lank arm from a rope of creeper that looped down from the foliage overhead. His back was to me.

'Hello!' said I.

He came down with a twisting jump, and stood facing me.

'I say,' said I, 'where can I get something to eat?'

'Eat!' he said. 'Eat Man's food, now.' And his eye went back to the swing of ropes. 'At the huts.'

'But where are the huts?'

'Oh!'

'I'm new, you know.'

At that he swung round, and set off at a quick walk. All his motions were curiously rapid. 'Come along,' said he.

I went with him to see the adventure out. I guessed the huts were some rough shelter where he and some more of these Beast People lived. I might perhaps find them friendly, find some handle in their minds to take hold of. I did not know how far they had forgotten their human heritage.

My apelike companion trotted along by my side, with his hands hanging down and his jaw thrust forward. I wondered what memory he might have in him. 'How long have you been on this island?' said I.

'How long?' he asked; and after having the question repeated, he held up three fingers.

The creature was little better than an idiot. I tried to make out what he meant by that, and it seems I bored him. After another question or two he suddenly left my side and went leaping at some fruit that hung from a tree. He pulled down a handful of prickly husks and went on, eating the contents. I noted this with satisfaction, for here at least was a hint for feeding. I tried him with some other questions, but his chattering, prompt responses were as often as not quite at cross purposes with my question. Some few were appropriate, others quite parrot-like.

I was so intent upon these peculiarities that I scarcely noticed the path we followed. Presently we came to trees, all charred and brown, and so to a bare place covered with a yellow-white encrustation, across which a drifting smoke, pungent in whiffs to nose and eyes, went drifting. On our right, over a shoulder of bare rock, I saw the level blue of the sea. The path coiled down abruptly into a narrow ravine between two tumbled and knotty masses of blackish scoriae.[37] Into this we plunged.

It was extremely dark, this passage, after the blinding sunlight reflected from the sulphurous ground. Its walls grew steep, and approached each other. Blotches of green and crimson drifted across my eyes. My conductor stopped suddenly. 'Home!' said he, and I stood on the floor of a chasm that was at first absolutely dark to me. I heard some strange noises, and thrust the knuckles of my left hand into my eyes. I became aware of a disagreeable odour, like that of a monkey's cage ill-cleaned. Beyond, the rock opened again upon a gradual slope of sunlit greenery, and on either hand the light smote down through narrow ways into the central gloom.

CHAPTER 12

The Sayers of the Law

Then something cold touched my hand. I started violently, and saw close to me a dim pinkish thing, looking more like a flayed child than anything else in the world. The creature had exactly the mild but repulsive features of a sloth, the same low forehead and slow gestures.

As the first shock of the change of light passed, I saw about me more distinctly. The little sloth-like creature was standing and staring at me. My conductor had vanished. The place was a narrow passage between high walls of lava, a crack in the knotted rock, and on either side interwoven heaps of sea-mat, palm-fans and reeds leaning against the rock formed rough and impenetrably dark dens. The winding way up the ravine between these was scarcely three yards wide, and was disigured by lumps of decaying fruit-pulp and other refuse, which accounted for the disagreeable stench of the place.

The little pink sloth-creature was still blinking at me when my Ape-man reappeared at the aperture of the nearest of these dens, and beckoned me in. As he did so a slouching monster wriggled out of one of the places, farther up this strange street, and stood up in featureless silhouette against the bright green beyond, staring at me. I hesitated, having half a mind to bolt the way I had come; and then, determined to go through with the adventure, I gripped my nailed stick about the middle and crawled into the little evil-smelling lean-to after my conductor.

It was a semicircular space, shaped like the half of a beehive; and against the rocky wall that formed the inner side of it was a pile of variegated fruits, coconuts among others. Some rough vessels of lava and wood stood about the floor, and one on a rough stool. There was no fire. In the darkest corner of the hut sat a shapeless mass of darkness that grunted 'Hey!' as I came in, and my Ape-man stood in the dim light of the doorway and held out a split coconut to me as I crawled into the other corner and squatted down. I took it, and began gnawing it, as serenely as possible, in spite of a certain trepidation and the nearly intolerable closeness of the den. The little pink sloth-creature stood in the aperture of the hut, and something else with a drab face and bright eyes came staring over its shoulder.

'Hey!' came out of the lump of mystery opposite. 'It is a man.'

'It is a man,' gabbled my conductor, 'a man, a man, a five-man, like me.'

'Shut up!' said the voice from the dark, and grunted. I gnawed my coconut amid an impressive stillness.

I peered hard into the blackness, but could distinguish nothing.

'It is a man,' the voice repeated. 'He comes to live with us?'

It was a thick voice, with something in it – a kind of whistling overtone – that struck me as peculiar; but the English accent was strangely good.

The Ape-man looked at me as though he expected something. I perceived the pause was interrogative. 'He comes to live with you,' I said.

'It is a man. He must learn the Law.'

I began to distinguish now a deeper blackness in the black, a vague outline of a hunched-up figure. Then I noticed the opening of the place was darkened by two more black heads. My hand tightened on my stick.

The thing in the dark repeated in a louder tone, 'Say the words.' I had missed its last remark. 'Not to go on all-fours; that is the Law,' it repeated in a kind of sing-song.

I was puzzled.

'Say the words,' said the Ape-man, repeating, and the figures in the doorway echoed this, with a threat in the tone of their voices.

I realised that I had to repeat this idiotic formula; and then began the insanest ceremony. The voice in the dark began intoning a mad litany, line by line, and I and the rest to repeat it. As they did so, they swayed from side to side in the oddest way, and beat their hands upon their knees; and I followed their example. I could have imagined I was already dead and in another world. That dark hut, these grotesque dim figures, just flecked here and there by a glimmer of light, and all of them swaying in unison and chanting,

'Not to go on All-Fours; *that* is the Law. Are we not Men?
Not to suck up Drink; *that* is the Law. Are we not Men?
Not to eat Fish or Flesh; *that* is the Law. Are we not Men?
Not to claw the Bark of Trees; *that* is the Law. Are we not Men?
Not to chase other Men; *that* is the Law. Are we not Men?'

And so from the prohibition of these acts of folly, on to the prohibition of what I thought then were the maddest, most impossible, and most indecent things one could well imagine. A kind of rhythmic fervour fell on all of us; we gabbled and swayed faster and faster, repeating this amazing Law. Superficially the contagion of these brutes was upon me, but deep down within me the laughter and disgust struggled together. We ran through a long list of prohibitions, and then the chant swung round to a new formula.

> '*His* is the House of Pain.
> *His* is the Hand that makes.
> *His* is the Hand that wounds.
> *His* is the Hand that heals.'

And so on for another long series, mostly quite incomprehensible gibberish to me about *Him*, whoever he might be. I could have fancied it was a dream, but never before have I heard chanting in a dream.

'*His* is the lightning flash,' we sang. '*His* is the deep, salt sea.'

A horrible fancy came into my head that Moreau, after animalising these men, had infected their dwarfed brains with a kind of deification of himself. However, I was too keenly aware of white teeth and strong claws about me to stop my chanting on that account.

'*His* are the stars in the sky.'

At last that song ended. I saw the Ape-man's face shining with perspiration; and my eyes being now accustomed to the darkness, I saw more distinctly the figure in the corner from which the voice came. It was the size of a man, but it seemed covered with a dull grey hair almost like a Skye terrier. What was it? What were they all? Imagine yourself surrounded by all the most horrible cripples and maniacs it is possible to conceive, and you may understand a little of my feelings with these grotesque caricatures of humanity about me.

'He is a five-man, a five-man, a five-man – like me,' said the Ape-man.

I held out my hands. The grey creature in the corner leant forward.

'Not to run on All-Fours; that is the Law. Are we not Men?' he said.

He put out a strangely distorted talon and gripped my fingers. The thing was almost like the hoof of a deer produced into claws. I could have yelled with surprise and pain. His face came forward and peered at my nails, came forward into the light of the opening of the hut and I saw with a quivering disgust that it was like the face of neither man nor beast, but a mere shock of grey hair, with three shadowy over-archings to mark the eyes and mouth.

'He has little nails,' said this grisly creature in his hairy beard. 'It is well.'

He threw my hand down, and instinctively I gripped my stick.

'Eat roots and herbs; it is His will,' said the Ape-man.

'I am the Sayer of the Law,' said the grey figure. 'Here come all that be new to learn the Law. I sit in the darkness and say the Law.'

'It is even so,' said one of the beasts in the doorway.

'Evil are the punishments for those who break the Law. None escape.'

'None escape,' said the Beast Folk, glancing furtively at one another.

'None, none,' said the Ape-man, 'none escape. See! I did a little thing, a wrong thing, once. I jabbered, jabbered, stopped talking. None could understand. I am burnt, branded in the hand. He is great. He is good!'

'None escape,' said the grey creature in the corner.

'None escape,' said the Beast People, looking askance at one another.

'For everyone the want is bad,' said the grey Sayer of the Law. 'What you will want we do not know; we shall know. Some want to follow things that move, to watch and slink and wait and spring; to kill and bite, bite deep and rich, sucking the blood. It is bad. "Not to chase other Men; that is the Law. *Are we not Men?* Not to eat Flesh or Fish; that is the Law. *Are we not Men?*" '

'None escape,' said a dappled brute standing in the doorway.

'For everyone the want is bad,' said the grey Sayer of the Law. 'Some want to go tearing with teeth and hands into the roots of things, snuffling into the earth. It is bad.'

'None escape,' said the men in the door.

'Some go clawing trees; some go scratching at the graves of the dead; some go fighting with foreheads or feet or claws; some bite suddenly, none giving occasion; some love uncleanness.'

'None escape,' said the Ape-man, scratching his calf.

'None escape,' said the little pink sloth-creature.

'Punishment is sharp and sure. Therefore learn the Law. Say the words.'

And incontinently he began again the strange litany of the Law, and again I and all these creatures began singing and swaying. My head reeled with this jabbering and the close stench of the place; but I kept on, trusting to find presently some chance of a new development.

'Not to go on All-Fours; that is the Law. *Are we not Men?*'

We were making such a noise that I noticed nothing of a tumult outside, until someone, who I think was one of the two Swine Men I had seen, thrust his head over the little pink sloth-creature and shouted something excitedly, something that I did not catch. Incontinently those at the opening of the hut vanished; my Ape-man rushed out; the thing that had sat in the dark followed him (I only observed that it was big and clumsy, and covered with silvery hair), and I was left alone. Then before I reached the aperture I heard the yelp of a staghound.

In another moment I was standing outside the hovel, my chair-rail in my hand, every muscle of me quivering. Before me were the clumsy backs of perhaps a score of these Beast People, their misshapen heads half hidden by their shoulder-blades. They were gesticulating excitedly. Other half-animal faces glared interrogation out of the hovels. Looking in the direction in which they faced, I saw coming through the haze under the trees beyond the end of the passage of dens the dark figure and awful white face of Moreau. He was holding the leaping staghound back, and close behind him came Montgomery revolver in hand.

For a moment I stood horror-struck. I turned and saw the passage behind me blocked by another heavy brute, with a huge grey face and twinkling little eyes, advancing towards me. I looked round and saw to the right of me and a half-dozen yards in front of me a narrow gap in the wall of rock through which a ray of light slanted into the shadows.

'Stop!' cried Moreau as I strode towards this, and then, 'Hold him!'

At that, first one face turned towards me and then others. Their bestial minds were happily slow. I dashed my shoulder into a clumsy monster who was turning to see what Moreau meant, and flung him forward into another. I felt his hands fly round, clutching at me and missing me. The little pink sloth-creature dashed at me, and I gashed down its ugly face with the nail in my stick and in another minute was scrambling up a steep side pathway, a kind of sloping chimney, out of the ravine. I heard a howl behind me, and cries of, 'Catch him!' 'Hold him!' and the grey-faced creature appeared behind me and jammed his huge bulk into the cleft. 'Go on! go on!' they howled. I clambered up the narrow cleft in the rock and came out upon the sulphur on the westward side of the village of the Beast Men.

That gap was altogether fortunate for me, for the narrow chimney, slanting obliquely upward, must have impeded the nearer pursuers. I ran over the white space and down a steep slope, through a scattered growth of trees, and came to a low-lying stretch of tall reeds, through which I pushed into a dark, thick undergrowth that was black and succulent underfoot. As I plunged into the reeds, my foremost pursuers emerged from the gap. I broke my way through this undergrowth for some minutes. The air behind me and about me was soon full of threatening cries. I heard the tumult of my pursuers in the gap up the slope, then the crashing of the reeds, and every now and then the crackling crash of a branch. Some of the creatures roared like excited beasts of prey. The staghound yelped to the left. I heard Moreau and Montgomery shouting in the same direction. I turned sharply to the right. It seemed to me even then that I heard Montgomery shouting for me to run for my life.

Presently the ground gave rich and oozy under my feet; but I was desperate and went headlong into it, struggled through knee deep, and so came to a winding path among tall canes. The noise of my pursuers passed away to my left. In one place three strange, pink, hopping animals, about the size of cats, bolted before my footsteps. This pathway ran uphill, across another open space covered with white encrustation, and plunged into a cane-brake again. Then suddenly it turned parallel with the edge of a steep-walled gap, which came without warning, like the ha-ha of an English park[38] – turned with an unexpected abruptness. I was still running with all my might, and I never saw this drop until I was flying headlong through the air.

I fell on my forearms and head, among thorns, and rose with a torn ear and bleeding face. I had fallen into a precipitous ravine, rocky and thorny, full of a hazy mist which drifted about me in wisps, and with a narrow streamlet, from which this mist came meandering, down the centre. I was astonished at this thin fog in the full blaze of daylight; but I had no time to stand wondering then. I turned to my right, down-stream, hoping to come to the sea in that direction, and so have my way open to drown myself. It was only later I found that I had dropped my nailed stick in my fall.

Presently the ravine grew narrower for a space, and carelessly I stepped into the stream. I jumped out again pretty quickly, for the water was almost boiling. I noticed too there was a thin sulphurous scum drifting upon its coiling water. Almost immediately came a turn in the ravine, and the indistinct blue horizon. The nearer sea was flashing the sun from myriad facets. I saw my death before me; but I was hot and panting, with the warm blood oozing out on my face and running pleasantly through my veins. I felt more than a touch of exultation too, at having distanced my pursuers. It was not in me then to go out and drown myself yet. I stared back the way I had come.

I listened. Save for the hum of the gnats and the chirp of some small insects that hopped among the thorns, the air was absolutely still. Then came the yelp of a dog, very faint, and a chattering and gibbering, the snap of a whip, and voices. They grew louder, then fainter again. The noise receded up the stream and faded away. For a while the chase was over; but I knew now how much hope of help for me lay in the Beast People.

CHAPTER 13

A Parley

I turned again and went on down towards the sea. I found the hot stream broadened out to a shallow, weedy sand, in which an abundance of crabs and long-bodied, many-legged creatures started from my footfall. I walked to the very edge of the salt water, and then I felt I was safe. I turned and stared, arms akimbo, at the thick green behind me, into which the steamy ravine cut like a smoking gash. But, as I say, I was too full of excitement and (a true saying, though those who have never known danger may doubt it) too desperate to die.

Then it came into my head that there was one chance before me yet. While Moreau and Montgomery and their bestial rabble chased me through the island, might I not go round the beach until I came to their enclosure – make a flank march upon them, in fact, and then with a rock lugged out of their loosely-built wall, perhaps, smash in the lock of the smaller door and see what I could find (knife, pistol or what not) to fight them with when they returned? It was at any rate something to try.

So I turned to the westward and walked along by the water's edge. The setting sun flashed his blinding heat into my eyes. The slight Pacific tide was running in with a gentle ripple. Presently the shore fell away southward, and the sun came round upon my right hand. Then suddenly, far in front of me, I saw first one and then several figures emerging from the bushes – Moreau, with his grey staghound, then Montgomery and two others. At that I stopped.

They saw me, and began gesticulating and advancing. I stood watching them approach. The two Beast Men came running forward to cut me off from the undergrowth, inland. Montgomery came, running also, but straight towards me. Moreau followed more slowly with the dog.

At last I roused myself from my inaction, and turning seaward walked straight into the water. The water was very shallow at first. I was thirty yards out before the waves reached to my waist. Dimly I could see the intertidal creatures darting away from my feet.

'What are you doing, man?' cried Montgomery.

I turned, standing waist deep, and stared at them. Montgomery stood panting at the margin of the water. His face was bright-red with exertion, his long flaxen hair blown about his head, and his dropping nether lip showed his irregular teeth. Moreau was just coming up, his face pale and firm, and the dog at his hand barked at me. Both men had heavy whips. Farther up the beach stared the Beast Men.

'What am I doing? I am going to drown myself,' said I.

Montgomery and Moreau looked at each other. 'Why?' asked Moreau.

'Because that is better than being tortured by you.'

'I told you so,' said Montgomery, and Moreau said something in a low tone.

'What makes you think I shall torture you?' asked Moreau.

'What I saw,' I said. 'And those – yonder.'

'Hush!' said Moreau, and held up his hand.

'I will not,' said I. 'They were men: what are they now? I at least will not be like them.'

I looked past my interlocutors. Up the beach were M'ling, Montgomery's attendant, and one of the white-swathed brutes from the boat. Farther up, in the shadow of the trees, I saw my little Ape-man, and behind him some other dim figures.

'Who are these creatures?' said I, pointing to them and raising my voice more and more that it might reach them. 'They were men, men like yourselves, whom you have infected with some bestial taint – men whom you have enslaved, and whom you still fear. 'You who listen,' I cried, pointing now to Moreau and shouting past him to the Beast Men, 'You who listen! Do you not see these men still fear you, go in dread of you? Why, then, do you fear them? You are many – '

'For God's sake,' cried Montgomery, 'stop that, Prendick!'

'Prendick!' cried Moreau.

They both shouted together, as if to drown my voice; and behind them lowered the staring faces of the Beast Men, wondering, their deformed hands hanging down, their shoulders hunched up. They seemed, as I fancied, to be trying to understand me, to remember, I thought, something of their human past.

I went on shouting, I scarcely remember what – that Moreau and Montgomery could be killed, that they were not to be feared: that was the burden of what I put into the heads of the Beast People. I saw the green-eyed man in the dark rags, who had met me on the evening of my arrival, come out from among the trees, and others followed him, to hear me better. At last, for want of breath, I paused.

'Listen to me for a moment,' said the steady voice of Moreau; 'and then say what you will.'

'Well?' said I.

He coughed, thought, then shouted: 'Latin, Prendick! bad Latin, schoolboy Latin; but try and understand. *Hi non sunt homines; sunt animalia qui nos habemus*[39] – vivisected. A humanising process. I will explain. Come ashore.'

I laughed. 'A pretty story,' said I. 'They talk, build houses. They *were* men. It's likely I'll come ashore!'

'The water just beyond where you stand is deep – and full of sharks.'

'That's my way,' said I. 'Short and sharp. Presently.'

'Wait a minute.' He took something out of his pocket that flashed back the sun, and dropped the object at his feet. 'That's a loaded revolver,' said he. 'Montgomery here will do the same. Now we are going up the beach until you are satisfied the distance is safe. Then come and take the revolvers.'

'Not I! You have a third between you.'

'I want you to think over things, Prendick. In the first place, I never asked you to come upon this island. If we vivisected men, we should import men, not beasts. In the next, we had you drugged last night, had we wanted to work you any mischief; and in the next, now your first panic is over and you can think a little, is Montgomery here quite up to the character you give him? We have chased you for your good. Because this island is full of inimical phenomena. Besides, why should we want to shoot you when you have just offered to drown yourself?'

'Why did you set – your people on to me when I was in the hut?'

'We felt sure of catching you, and bringing you out of danger. Afterwards we drew away from the scent, for your good.'

I mused. It seemed just possible. Then I remembered something again. 'But I saw,' said I, 'in the enclosure – '

'That was the puma.'

'Look here, Prendick,' said Montgomery, 'you're a silly ass! Come out of the water and take these revolvers, and talk. We can't do anything more than we could do now.'

I will confess that then, and indeed always, I distrusted and dreaded Moreau; but Montgomery was a man I felt I understood.

'Go up the beach,' said I, after thinking, and added, 'holding your hands up.'

'Can't do that,' said Montgomery, with an explanatory nod over his shoulder. 'Undignified.'

'Go up to the trees, then,' said I, 'as you please.'

'It's a damned silly ceremony,' said Montgomery.

Both turned and faced the six or seven grotesque creatures, who stood there in the sunlight, solid, casting shadows, moving, and yet so incredibly unreal. Montgomery cracked his whip at them, and forth-with they all turned and fled helter-skelter into the trees; and when Montgomery and Moreau were at a distance I judged sufficient, I waded ashore, and picked up and examined the revolvers. To satisfy myself against the subtlest trickery, I discharged one at a round lump of lava, and had the satisfaction of seeing the stone pulverised and the beach splashed with lead. Still I hesitated for a moment.

'I'll take the risk,' said I, at last; and with a revolver in each hand I walked up the beach towards them.

'That's better,' said Moreau, without affectation. 'As it is, you have wasted the best part of my day with your confounded imagination.' And with a touch of contempt which humiliated me, he and Montgomery turned and went on in silence before me.

The knot of Beast Men, still wondering, stood back among the trees. I passed them as serenely as possible. One started to follow me, but retreated again when Montgomery cracked his whip. The rest stood silent – watching. They may once have been animals; but I never before saw an animal trying to think.

CHAPTER 14

Doctor Moreau Explains

'And now, Prendick, I will explain,' said Dr Moreau, so soon as we had eaten and drunk. 'I must confess that you are the most dictatorial guest I ever entertained. I warn you that this is the last I shall do to oblige you. The next thing you threaten to commit suicide about, I shan't do – even at some personal inconvenience.'

He sat in my deckchair, a cigar half consumed in his white, dexterous-looking fingers. The light of the swinging lamp fell on his white hair; he stared through the little window out at the starlight. I sat as far away from him as possible, the table between us and the revolvers to hand. Montgomery was not present. I did not care to be with the two of them in such a little room.

'You admit that the vivisected human being, as you called it, is, after all, only the puma?' said Moreau. He had made me visit that horror in the inner room, to assure myself of its inhumanity.

'It is the puma,' I said, 'still alive, but so cut and mutilated as I pray I may never see living flesh again. Of all vile – '

'Never mind that,' said Moreau; 'at least, spare me those youthful horrors. Montgomery used to be just the same. You admit that it is the puma. Now be quiet, while I reel off my physiological lecture to you.'

And forthwith, beginning in the tone of a man supremely bored, but presently warming a little, he explained his work to me. He was very simple and convincing. Now and then there was a touch of sarcasm in his voice. Presently I found myself hot with shame at our mutual positions.

The creatures I had seen were not men, had never been men. They were animals, humanised animals – triumphs of vivisection.

'You forget all that a skilled vivisector can do with living things,' said Moreau. 'For my own part, I'm puzzled why the things I have done here have not been done before. Small efforts, of course, have been made – amputation, tongue-cutting, excisions. Of course you know a squint may be induced or cured by surgery? Then in the case of excisions you have all kinds of secondary changes, pigmentary disturbances, modifications of the passions, alterations in the secretion of fatty tissue. I have no doubt you have heard of these things?'

'Of course,' said I. 'But these foul creatures of yours – '

'All in good time,' said he, waving his hand at me; 'I am only beginning. Those are trivial cases of alteration. Surgery can do better things than that. There is building up as well as breaking down and changing. You have heard, perhaps, of a common surgical operation resorted to in cases where the nose has been destroyed: a flap of skin is cut from the forehead, turned down on the nose, and heals in the new position. This is a kind of grafting in a new position of part of an animal upon itself. Grafting of freshly obtained material from another animal is also possible – the case of teeth, for example. The grafting of skin and bone is done to facilitate healing: the surgeon places in the middle of the wound pieces of skin snipped from another animal, or fragments of bone from a victim freshly killed. Hunter's cock-spur[40] – possibly you have heard of that – flourished on the bull's neck; and the rhinoceros rats of the Algerian zouaves[41] are also to be thought of – monsters manufactured by transferring a slip from the tail of an ordinary rat to its snout, and allowing it to heal in that position.'

'Monsters manufactured!' said I. 'Then you mean to tell me – '

'Yes. These creatures you have seen are animals carven and wrought into new shapes. To that, to the study of the plasticity of living forms, my life has been devoted. I have studied for years, gaining in knowledge as I go. I see you look horrified, and yet I am telling you nothing new. It all lay in the surface of practical anatomy years ago, but no one had the temerity to touch it. It is not simply the outward form of an animal which I can change. The physiology, the chemical rhythm of the creature, may also be made to undergo an enduring modification – of which vaccination and other methods of inoculation with living or dead matter are examples that will, no doubt, be familiar to you. A similar operation is the transfusion of blood – with which subject, indeed, I began. These are all familiar cases. Less so, and probably far more extensive, were the operations of those mediaeval practitioners who made dwarfs and beggar-cripples, show-monsters – some vestiges of whose art still remain in the preliminary manipulation of the young mountebank or contortionist. Victor Hugo gives an account of them in *L'Homme qui Rit* . . . [42] But perhaps my meaning grows plain now. You begin to see that it is a possible thing to transplant tissue from one part of an animal to another, or from one animal to another; to alter its chemical reactions and methods of growth; to modify the articulations of its limbs; and, indeed, to change it in its most intimate structure.

'And yet this extraordinary branch of knowledge has never been sought as an end, and systematically, by modern investigators until I took it up! Some of such things have been hit upon in the last resort of surgery; most of the kindred evidence that will recur to your mind has been demonstrated as it were by accident – by tyrants, by criminals, by the breeders of horses and dogs, by all kinds of untrained clumsy-handed men working for their own immediate ends. I was the first man to take up this question armed with antiseptic surgery, and with a really scientific knowledge of the laws of growth. Yet one would imagine it must have been practised in secret before. Such creatures as the Siamese Twins . . . And in the vaults of the Inquisition. No doubt their chief aim was artistic torture, but some at least of the inquisitors must have had a touch of scientific curiosity.'

'But,' said I, 'these things – these animals *talk*!'

He said that was so, and proceeded to point out that the possibility of vivisection does not stop at a mere physical metamorphosis. A pig may be educated. The mental structure is even less determinate than the bodily. In our growing science of hypnotism we find the promise of a possibility of superseding old inherent instincts by new suggestions, grafting upon or replacing the inherited fixed ideas. Very much indeed of what we call moral education, he said, is such an artificial modification and perversion of instinct; pugnacity is trained into courageous self-sacrifice, and suppressed sexuality into religious emotion. And the great difference between man and monkey is in the larynx, he continued, – in the incapacity to frame delicately different sound-symbols by which thought could be sustained. In this I failed to agree with him, but with a certain incivility he declined to notice my objection. He repeated that the thing was so, and continued his account of his work.

I asked him why he had taken the human form as a model. There seemed to me then, and there still seems to me now, a strange wickedness in that choice.

He confessed that he had chosen that form by chance. 'I might just as well have worked to form sheep into llamas and llamas into sheep. I suppose there is something in the human form that appeals to the artistic turn of mind more powerfully than any animal shape can. But I've not confined myself to man-making. Once or twice – ' He was silent, for a minute perhaps. 'These years! How they have slipped by! And here I have wasted a day saving your life, and am now wasting an hour explaining myself!'

'But,' said I, 'I still do not understand. Where is your justification for inflicting all this pain? The only thing that could excuse vivisection to me would be some application – '

'Precisely,' said he. 'But, you see, I am differently constituted. We are on different platforms. You are a materialist.'

'I am *not* a materialist,' I began hotly.

'In my view – in my view. For it is just this question of pain that parts us. So long as visible or audible pain turns you sick, so long as your own pains drive you, so long as pain underlies your propositions about sin, so long, I tell you, you are an animal, thinking a little less obscurely what an animal feels. This pain – '

I gave an impatient shrug at such sophistry.

'Oh, but it is such a little thing! A mind truly opened to what science has to teach must see that it is a little thing. It may be that save in this little planet, this speck of cosmic dust, invisible long before the nearest star could be attained – it may be, I say, that nowhere else does this thing called *pain* occur. But the laws we feel our way towards . . . Why, even on this earth, even among living things, what pain is there?'

As he spoke he drew a little penknife from his pocket, opened the smaller blade, and moved his chair so that I could see his thigh. Then, choosing the place deliberately, he drove the blade into his leg and withdrew it.

'No doubt,' he said, 'you have seen that before. It does not hurt a pinprick. But what does it show? The capacity for pain is not needed in the muscle, and it is not placed there; it is but little needed in the skin, and only here and there over the thigh is a spot capable of feeling pain. Pain is simply our intrinsic medical adviser to warn us and stimulate us. Not all living flesh is painful; nor is all nerve, not even all sensory nerve. There's no taint of pain, real pain, in the sensations of the optic nerve. If you wound the optic nerve, you merely see flashes of light, just as disease of the auditory nerve merely means a humming in our ears. Plants do not feel pain, nor the lower animals; it's possible that such animals as the starfish and crayfish do not feel pain at all. Then with men, the more intelligent they become, the more intelligently they will see after their own welfare, and the less they will need the goad to keep them out of danger. I never yet heard of a useless thing that was not ground out of existence by evolution sooner or later. Did you? And pain gets needless.

'Then I am a religious man, Prendick, as every sane man must be. It may be, I fancy, that I have seen more of the ways of this world's Maker than you - for I have sought his laws, in *my* way, all my life, while you, I understand, have been collecting butterflies. And I tell you, pleasure and pain have nothing to do with heaven or hell. Pleasure and pain – bah! What is your theologian's ecstasy but Mahomet's houri[43] in the dark? This store which men and women set on pleasure and pain, Prendick, is the mark of the beast upon them, the mark of the beast from which they came! Pain, pain and pleasure, they are for us only so long as we wriggle in the dust.

'You see, I went on with this research just the way it led me. That is the only way I ever heard of true research going. I asked a question, devised some method of obtaining an answer, and got a fresh question. Was this possible or that possible? You cannot imagine what this means to an investigator, what an intellectual passion grows upon him! You cannot imagine the strange, colourless delight of these intellectual desires! The thing before you is no longer an animal, a fellow-creature, but a problem! Sympathetic pain – all I know of it I remember as a thing I used to suffer from years ago. I wanted – it was the one thing I wanted – to find out the extreme limit of plasticity in a living shape.'

'But,' said I, 'the thing is an abomination – '

'To this day I have never troubled about the ethics of the matter,' he continued. 'The study of Nature makes a man at last as remorseless as Nature. I have gone on, not heeding anything but the question I was pursuing; and the material has – dripped into the huts yonder . . . It is nearly eleven years since we came here, I and Montgomery and six Kanakas.[44] I remember the green stillness of the island and the empty ocean about us as though it was yesterday. The place seemed waiting for me.

'The stores were landed and the house was built. The Kanakas founded some huts near the ravine. I went to work here upon what I had brought with me. There were some disagreeable things happened at first. I began with a sheep, and killed it after a day and a half by a slip of the scalpel. I took another sheep, and made a thing of pain and fear and left it bound up to heal. It looked quite human to me when I had finished it; but when I went to it I was discontented with it. It remembered me, and was terrified beyond imagination; and it had no more than the wits of a sheep. The more I looked at it the clumsier it seemed, until at last I put the monster out of its misery. These animals without courage, these fear-haunted, pain-driven things, without a spark of pugnacious energy to face torment – they are no good for man-making.

'Then I took a gorilla I had; and upon that, working with infinite care and mastering difficulty after difficulty, I made my first man. All the week, night and day, I moulded him. With him it was chiefly the brain that needed moulding; much had to be added, much changed. I thought him a fair specimen of the negroid type when I had finished him, and he lay bandaged, bound, and motionless before me. It was only when his life was assured that I left him and came into this room again, and found

Montgomery much as you are. He had heard some of the cries as the thing grew human – cries like those that disturbed *you* so. I didn't take him completely into my confidence at first. And the Kanakas, too, had realised something of it. They were scared out of their wits by the sight of me. I got Montgomery over to me – in a way; but I and he had the hardest job to prevent the Kanakas deserting. Finally they did; and so we lost the yacht. I spent many days educating the brute – altogether I had him for three or four months. I taught him the rudiments of English; gave him ideas of counting; even made the thing read the alphabet. But at that he was slow, though I've met with idiots slower. He began with a clean sheet, mentally; had no memories left in his mind of what he had been. When his scars were quite healed, and he was no longer anything but painful and stiff, and able to converse a little, I took him yonder and introduced him to the Kanakas as an interesting stowaway.

'They were horribly afraid of him at first, somehow – which offended me rather, for I was conceited about him; but his ways seemed so mild, and he was so abject, that after a time they received him and took his education in hand. He was quick to learn, very imitative and adaptive, and built himself a hovel rather better, it seemed to me, than their own shanties. There was one among the boys a bit of a missionary, and he taught the thing to read, or at least to pick out letters, and gave him some rudimentary ideas of morality; but it seems the beast's habits were not all that is desirable.

'I rested from work for some days after this, and was in a mind to write an account of the whole affair to wake up English physiology. Then I came upon the creature squatting up in a tree and gibbering at two of the Kanakas who had been teasing him. I threatened him, told him the inhumanity of such a proceeding, aroused his sense of shame, and came home resolved to do better before I took my work back to England. I have been doing better. But somehow the things drift back again: the stubborn beast-flesh grows day by day back again. But I mean to do better things still. I mean to conquer that. This puma. . .

'But that's the story. All the Kanaka boys are dead now; one fell overboard from the launch, and one died of a wounded heel that he poisoned in some way with plant-juice. Three went away in the yacht, and I suppose and hope were drowned. The other one – was killed. Well, I have replaced them. Montgomery went on much as you are disposed to do at first, and then – '

'What became of the other one?' said I, sharply, 'the other Kanaka who was killed?'

'The fact is, after I had made a number of human creatures I made a thing – ' He hesitated.

'Yes,' said I.

'It was killed.'

'I don't understand,' said I; 'do you mean to say – '

'It killed the Kanaka – yes. It killed several other things that it caught. We chased it for a couple of days. It only got loose by accident. I never meant it to get away. It wasn't finished. It was purely an experiment. It was a limbless thing with a horrible face that writhed along the ground in a serpentine fashion. It was immensely strong, and in infuriating pain. It lurked in the woods for some days, until we hunted it; and then it wriggled into the northern part of the island, and we divided the party to close in upon it. Montgomery insisted upon coming with me. The man had a rifle; and when his body was found, one of the barrels was curved into the shape of an S and very nearly bitten through. Montgomery shot the thing. After that I stuck to the ideal of humanity – except for little things.'

He became silent. I sat in silence watching his face.

'So for twenty years altogether – counting nine years in England – I have been going on; and there is still something in everything I do that defeats me, makes me dissatisfied, challenges me to further effort. Sometimes I rise above my level, sometimes I fall below it; but always I fall short of the things I dream. The human shape I can get now, almost with ease, so that it is lithe and graceful, or thick and strong; but often there is trouble with the hands and the claws – painful things, that I dare not shape too freely. But it is in the subtle grafting and reshaping one must needs do to the brain that my trouble lies. The intelligence is often oddly low, with unaccountable blank ends, unexpected gaps. And least satisfactory of all is something that I cannot touch, somewhere – I cannot determine where – in the seat of the emotions. Cravings, instincts, desires that harm humanity, a strange hidden reservoir liable to burst forth suddenly and inundate the whole being of the creature with anger, hate or fear. These creatures of mine seemed strange and uncanny to you as soon as you began to observe them; but to me, just after I make them, they seem to be indisputably human beings. It's afterwards, as I observe them, that the persuasion fades. First one animal trait, then another, creeps to the surface and stares out at me. But I will conquer yet! Each time I dip a living creature into the bath of burning pain, I say, "This time I will burn out all the animal; this time I will make a rational creature of my own!" After all, what is ten years? Men have been a hundred thousand in the making.'

He thought darkly. 'But I am drawing near the fastness. This puma of mine – '

After a silence, 'And they revert. As soon as my hand is taken from them the beast begins to creep back, begins to assert itself again.'

Another long silence.

'Then you take the things you make into those dens?' said I.

'They go. I turn them out when I begin to feel the beast in them, and presently they wander there. They all dread this house and me. There is a kind of travesty of humanity over there. Montgomery knows about it, for he interferes in their affairs. He has trained one or two of them to our service. He's ashamed of it, but I believe he half likes some of those beasts. It's his business, not mine. They only sicken me with a sense of failure. I take no interest in them. I fancy they follow in the lines the Kanaka missionary marked out, and have a kind of mockery of a rational life, poor beasts! There's something they call the Law. Sing hymns about "all thine". They build themselves their dens, gather fruit, and pull herbs – marry even. But I can see through it all, see into their very souls, and see there nothing but the souls of beasts, beasts that perish – anger and the lust to live and gratify themselves . . . Yet they're odd; complex, like everything else alive. There is a kind of upward striving in them, part vanity, part waste sexual emotion, part waste curiosity. It only mocks me. I have some hope of this puma. I have worked hard at her head and brain.

'And now,' said he, standing up after a long gap of silence, during which we had each pursued our own thoughts, 'what do you think? Are you in fear of me still?'

I looked at him, and saw but a white-faced, white-haired man, with calm eyes. Save for his serenity, the touch almost of beauty that resulted from his set tranquillity and his magnificent build, he might have passed muster among a hundred other comfortable old gentlemen. Then I shivered. By way of answer to his second question, I handed him a revolver with either hand.

'Keep them,' he said, and snatched at a yawn. He stood up, stared at me for a moment, and smiled. 'You have had two eventful days,' said he. 'I should advise some sleep. I'm glad it's all clear. Good-night.'

He thought me over for a moment, then went out by the inner door.

I immediately turned the key in the outer one. I sat down again; sat for a time in a kind of stagnant mood, so weary, emotionally, mentally and physically, that I could not think beyond the point at which he had left me. The black window stared at me like an eye. At last with an effort I put out the light and got into the hammock. Very soon I was asleep.

CHAPTER 15

Concerning the Beast Folk

I woke early. Moreau's explanation stood before my mind, clear and definite, from the moment of my awakening. I got out of the hammock and went to the door to assure myself that the key was turned. Then I tried the window-bar, and found it firmly fixed. That these manlike creatures were in truth only bestial monsters, mere grotesque travesties of men, filled me with a vague uncertainty of their possibilities which was far worse than any definite fear.

A tapping came at the door, and I heard the glutinous accents of M'ling speaking. I pocketed one of the revolvers (keeping one hand upon it), and opened to him.

'Good-morning, sair,' he said, bringing in, in addition to the customary herb-breakfast, an ill-cooked rabbit. Montgomery followed him. His roving eye caught the position of my arm and he smiled askew.

The puma was resting to heal that day; but Moreau, who was singularly solitary in his habits, did not join us. I talked with Montgomery to clear my ideas of the way in which the Beast Folk lived. In particular, I was urgent to know how these inhuman monsters were kept from falling upon Moreau and Montgomery and from rending one another. He explained to me that the comparative safety of Moreau and himself was due to the limited mental scope of these monsters. In spite of their increased intelligence and the tendency of their animal instincts to reawaken, they had certain fixed ideas implanted by Moreau in their minds, which absolutely bounded their imaginations. They were really hypnotised; had been told that certain things were impossible, and that certain things were not to be done, and these prohibitions were woven into the texture of their minds beyond any possibility of disobedience or dispute.

Certain matters, however, in which old instinct was at war with Moreau's convenience, were in a less stable condition. A series of propositions called the Law (I had already heard them recited) battled in their minds with the deep-seated, ever-rebellious cravings of their animal natures. This Law they were ever repeating, I found, and ever breaking. Both Montgomery and Moreau displayed particular solici-tude to keep them ignorant of the taste of blood; they feared the inevitable suggestions of that flavour. Montgomery told me that the Law, especially among the feline Beast People, became oddly weakened about nightfall; that then the animal was at its strongest; that a spirit of adventure sprang up in them at the dusk, when they would dare things they never seemed to dream about by day. To that I owed my stalking by the Leopard-man, on the night of my arrival. But during these earlier days of my stay they broke the Law only furtively and after dark; in the daylight there was a general atmosphere of respect for its multifarious prohibitions.

And here perhaps I may give a few general facts about the island and the Beast People. The island, which was of irregular outline and lay low upon the wide sea, had a total area, I suppose, of seven or eight square miles.* It was volcanic in origin, and was now fringed on three sides by coral reefs; some fumaroles[45] to the northward, and a hot spring, were the only vestiges of the forces that had long since originated it. Now and then a faint quiver of earthquake would be sensible, and sometimes the ascent of the spire of smoke would be rendered tumultuous by gusts of steam; but that was all. The population of the island, Montgomery informed me, now numbered rather more than sixty of these strange creations of Moreau's art, not counting the smaller monstrosities which lived in the undergrowth and were without human form. Altogether he had made nearly a hundred and twenty; but many had died, and others – like the writhing Footless Thing of which he had told me – had come by violent ends. In answer to my question, Montgomery said that they actually bore offspring, but that these generally died. When they lived, Moreau took them and stamped the human form upon them. There was no evidence of the inheritance of their acquired human characteristics. The females were less numerous than the males, and liable to much furtive persecution in spite of the monogamy the Law enjoined.

It would be impossible for me to describe these Beast People in detail; my eye has had no training in details, and unhappily I cannot sketch. Most striking, perhaps, in their general appearance was the disproportion between the legs of these creatures and the length of their bodies; and yet – so relative is our idea of grace – my eye became habituated to their forms, and at last I even fell in with their persuasion that my own long thighs were ungainly. Another point was the forward carriage of the head and the clumsy and inhuman curvature of the spine. Even the Ape-man lacked that inward sinuous curve of the back which makes the human figure so graceful. Most had their shoulders

---

* This description corresponds in every respect to Noble's Isle – C. E. P.

hunched clumsily, and their short forearms hung weakly at their sides. Few of them were conspicuously hairy, at least until the end of my time upon the island.

The next most obvious deformity was in their faces, almost all of which were prognathous, malformed about the ears, with large and protuberant noses, very furry or very bristly hair, and often strangely-coloured or strangely-placed eyes. None could laugh, though the Ape-man had a chattering titter. Beyond these general characters their heads had little in common; each preserved the quality of its particular species: the human mark distorted but did not hide the leopard, the ox, or the sow, or other animal or animals, from which the creature had been moulded. The voices, too, varied exceedingly. The hands were always malformed; and though some surprised me by their unexpected human appearance, almost all were deficient in the number of the digits, clumsy about the fingernails and lacking any tactile sensibility.

The two most formidable animal men were my Leopard-man and a creature made of hyena and swine. Larger than these were the three bull-creatures who pulled in the boat. Then came the silvery-hairy man, who was also the Sayer of the Law, M'ling, and a satyr-like creature of ape and goat. There were three Swine-men and a Swine-woman, a mare-rhinoceros creature, and several other females whose sources I did not ascertain. There were several wolf-creatures, a bear-bull, and a St-Bernard-man. I have already described the Ape-man, and there was a particularly hateful (and evil-smelling) old woman made of vixen and bear, whom I hated from the beginning. She was said to be a passionate votary of the Law. Smaller creatures were certain dappled youths and my little sloth-creature. But enough of this catalogue.

At first I had a shivering horror of the brutes, felt all too keenly that they were still brutes; but insensibly I became a little habituated to the idea of them, and moreover I was affected by Montgomery's attitude towards them. He had been with them so long that he had come to regard them as almost normal human beings. His London days seemed a glorious, impossible past to him. Only once in a year or so did he go to Arica to deal with Moreau's agent, a trader in animals there. He hardly met the finest type of mankind in that seafaring village of Spanish mongrels. The men aboard-ship, he told me, seemed at first just as strange to him as the Beast Men seemed to me – unnaturally long in the leg, flat in the face, prominent in the forehead, suspicious, dangerous and cold-hearted. In fact, he did not like men: his heart had warmed to me, he thought, because he had saved my life. I fancied even then that he had a sneaking kindness for some of these metamorphosed brutes, a vicious sympathy with some of their ways, but that he attempted to veil it from me at first.

M'ling, the black-faced man, Montgomery's attendant, the first of the Beast Folk I had encountered, did not live with the others across the island, but in a small kennel at the back of the enclosure. The creature was scarcely so intelligent as the Ape-man, but far more docile, and the most human-looking of all the Beast Folk; and Montgomery had trained it to prepare food, and indeed to discharge all the trivial domestic offices that were required. It was a complex trophy of Moreau's horrible skill – a bear, tainted with dog and ox, and one of the most elaborately made of all his creatures. It treated Montgomery with a strange tenderness and devotion. Sometimes he would notice it, pat it, call it half-mocking, half-jocular names, and so make it caper with extraordinary delight; sometimes he would ill-treat it, especially after he had been at the whisky, kicking it, beating it, pelting it with stones or lighted fuses. But whether he treated it well or ill, it loved nothing so much as to be near him.

I say I became habituated to the Beast People, that a thousand things which had seemed unnatural and repulsive speedily became natural and ordinary to me. I suppose everything in existence takes its colour from the average hue of our surroundings. Montgomery and Moreau were too peculiar and individual to keep my general impressions of humanity well defined. I would see one of the clumsy bovine-creatures who worked the launch treading heavily through the undergrowth, and find myself asking, trying hard to recall, how he differed from some really human yokel trudging home from his mechanical labours; or I would meet the Fox-bear-woman's vulpine, shifty face, strangely human in its speculative cunning, and even imagine I had met it before in some city byway.

Yet every now and then the beast would flash out upon me beyond doubt or denial. An ugly-looking man, a hunch-backed human savage to all appearance, squatting in the aperture of one of the dens, would stretch his arms and yawn, showing with startling suddenness scissor-edged incisors and sabre-like canines, keen and brilliant as knives. Or in some narrow pathway, glancing with a transitory daring into the eyes of some lithe, white-swathed female figure, I would suddenly see (with a spasmodic revulsion) that she had slit-like pupils, or glancing down note the curving nail with which she held her shapeless wrap about her. It is a curious thing, by the by, for which I am quite unable to account, that these weird creatures – the females, I mean – had in the earlier days of my stay an instinctive sense of their own repulsive clumsiness, and displayed in consequence a more than human regard for the decency and decorum of extensive costume.

graceful

CHAPTER 16

How the Beast Folk Taste Blood

My inexperience as a writer betrays me, and I wander from the thread of my story.

After I had breakfasted with Montgomery, he took me across the island to see the fumarole and the source of the hot spring into whose scalding waters I had blundered on the previous day. Both of us carried whips and loaded revolvers. While going through a leafy jungle on our road thither, we heard a rabbit squealing. We stopped and listened, but we heard no more; and presently we went on our way, and the incident dropped out of our minds. Montgomery called my attention to certain little pink animals with long hind-legs, that went leaping through the undergrowth. He told me they were creatures made of the offspring of the Beast People, that Moreau had invented. He had fancied they might serve for meat, but a rabbit-like habit of devouring their young had defeated this intention. I had already encountered some of these creatures – once during my moonlight flight from the Leopard-man and once during my pursuit by Moreau on the previous day. By chance, one hopping to avoid us leapt into the hole caused by the uprooting of a wind-blown tree; before it could extricate itself we managed to catch it. It spat like a cat, scratched and kicked vigorously with its hind-legs, and made an attempt to bite; but its teeth were too feeble to inflict more than a painless pinch. It seemed to me rather a pretty little creature; and as Montgomery stated that it never destroyed the turf by burrowing, and was very cleanly in its habits, I should imagine it might prove a convenient substitute for the common rabbit in gentlemen's parks.

We also saw on our way the trunk of a tree barked in long strips and splintered deeply. Montgomery called my attention to this. ' "Not to claw Bark of Trees, *that* is the Law," ' he said. 'Much some of them care for it!' It was after this, I think, that we met the Satyr and the Ape-man. The Satyr was a gleam of classical memory on the part of Moreau, his face ovine in expression, like the coarser Hebrew type, his voice a harsh bleat, his nether extremities satyric. He was gnawing the husk of a pod-like fruit as he passed us. Both of them saluted Montgomery.

'Hail,' said they, 'to the Other with the Whip!'

'There's a Third with a Whip now,' said Montgomery. 'So you'd better mind!'

'Was he not made?' said the Ape-man. 'He said – he said he was made.'

The Satyr-man looked curiously at me. 'The Third with the Whip, he that walks weeping into the sea, has a thin white face.'

'He has a thin long whip,' said Montgomery.

'Yesterday he bled and wept,' said the Satyr. 'You never bleed nor weep. The Master does not bleed or weep.'

'Ollendorffian beggar!'[46] said Montgomery, 'you'll bleed and weep if you don't look out!'

'He has five fingers, he is a five-man like me,' said the Ape-man.

'Come along, Prendick,' said Montgomery, taking my arm; and I went on with him.

The Satyr and the Ape-man stood watching us and making other remarks to each other.

'He says nothing,' said the Satyr. 'Men have voices.'

'Yesterday he asked me of things to eat,' said the Ape-man. 'He did not know.'

Then they spoke inaudible things, and I heard the Satyr laughing.

It was on our way back that we came upon the dead rabbit. The red body of the wretched little beast was rent to pieces, many of the ribs stripped white, and the backbone indisputably gnawed.

At that Montgomery stopped. 'Good God!' said he, stooping down, and picking up some of the crushed vertebrae to examine them more closely. 'Good God!' he repeated, 'what can this mean?'

'Some carnivore of yours has remembered its old habits,' I said, after a pause. 'This backbone has been bitten through.'

He stood staring, with his face white and his lip pulled askew. 'I don't like this,' he said slowly.

'I saw something of the same kind,' said I, 'the first day I came here.'

'The devil you did! What was it?'

'A rabbit with its head twisted off.'

'The day you came here?'

'The day I came here. In the undergrowth at the back of the enclosure, when I went out in the evening. The head was completely wrung off.'

He gave a long, low whistle.

'And what is more, I have an idea which of your brutes did the thing. It's only a suspicion, you know. Before I came on the rabbit I saw one of your monsters drinking in the stream.'

'Sucking his drink?'

'Yes.'

' "Not to suck your Drink; *that* is the Law." Much the brutes care for the Law, eh? when Moreau's not about!'

'It was the brute who chased me.'

'Of course,' said Montgomery; 'it's just the way with carnivores. After a kill, they drink. It's the taste of blood, you know . . . What was the brute like?' he continued. 'Would you know him again?' He glanced about us, standing astride over the mess of dead rabbit, his eyes roving among the shadows and screens of greenery, the lurking-places and ambuscades of the forest that bounded us in. 'The taste of blood,' he said again.

He took out his revolver, examined the cartridges in it and replaced it. Then he began to pull at his dropping lip.

'I think I should know the brute again,' I said. 'I stunned him. He ought to have a handsome bruise on the forehead of him.'

'But then we have to *prove* that he killed the rabbit,' said Montgomery. 'I wish I'd never brought the things here.'

I should have gone on, but he stayed there thinking over the mangled rabbit in a puzzle-headed way. As it was, I went to such a distance that the rabbit's remains were hidden.

'Come on!' I said.

Presently he woke up and came towards me. 'You see,' he said, almost in a whisper, 'they are all supposed to have a fixed idea against eating anything that runs on land. If some brute has by any accident tasted blood . . . '

He went on some way in silence. 'I wonder what can have happened,' he said to himself. Then, after a pause again: 'I did a foolish thing the other day. That servant of mine – I showed him how to skin and cook a rabbit. It's odd . . . I saw him licking his hands . . . It never occurred to me – '

Then: 'We must put a stop to this. I must tell Moreau.'

He could think of nothing else on our homeward journey.

Moreau took the matter even more seriously than Montgomery, and I need scarcely say that I was affected by their evident consternation.

'We must make an example,' said Moreau. 'I've no doubt in my own mind that the Leopard-man was the sinner. But how can we prove it? I wish, Montgomery, you had kept your taste for meat in hand, and gone without these exciting novelties. We may find ourselves in a mess yet, through it.'

'I was a silly ass,' said Montgomery. 'But the thing's done now; and you said I might have them, you know.'

'We must see to the thing at once,' said Moreau. 'I suppose if anything should turn up, M'ling can take care of himself?'

'I'm not so sure of M'ling,' said Montgomery. 'I think I ought to know him.'

In the afternoon, Moreau, Montgomery, myself and M'ling went across the island to the huts in the ravine. We three were armed; M'ling carried the little hatchet he used in chopping firewood, and some coils of wire. Moreau had a huge cowherd's horn slung over his shoulder.

'You will see a gathering of the Beast People,' said Montgomery. 'It is a pretty sight!'

Moreau said not a word on the way, but the expression of his heavy, white-fringed face was grimly set.

We crossed the ravine down which smoked the stream of hot water, and followed the winding pathway through the cane-brakes until we reached a wide area covered over with a thick, powdery yellow substance which I believe was sulphur. Above the shoulder of a weedy bank the sea glittered. We came to a kind of shallow natural amphitheatre, and here the four of us halted. Then Moreau sounded the horn, and broke the sleeping stillness of the tropical afternoon. He must have had strong lungs. The hooting note rose and rose amidst its echoes to at last an ear-penetrating intensity.

'Ah!' said Moreau, letting the curved instrument fall to his side again.

Immediately there was a crashing through the yellow canes, and a sound of voices from the dense green jungle that marked the morass through which I had run on the previous day. Then at three or four points on the edge of the sulphurous area appeared the grotesque forms of the Beast People hurrying towards us. I could not help a creeping horror, as I perceived first one and then another trot out from the trees or reeds and come shambling along over the hot dust. But Moreau and Montgomery stood calmly enough; and, perforce, I stuck beside them.

First to arrive was the Satyr, strangely unreal for all that he cast a shadow and tossed the dust with his hoofs. After him from the brake came a monstrous lout, a thing of horse and rhinoceros, chewing a straw as it came; then appeared the Swine-woman and two Wolf-women; then the Fox-bear witch, with her red eyes in her peaked red face, and then others – all hurrying eagerly. As they came forward they began to cringe towards Moreau and chant, quite regardless of one another, fragments of the latter half of the litany of the Law: '*His* is the Hand that wounds; *His* is the Hand that heals,' and so forth. As soon as they had approached within a distance of perhaps thirty yards they halted, and bowing on knees and elbows began flinging the white dust upon their heads.

Imagine the scene if you can! We three blue-clad men, with our misshapen black-faced attendant, standing in a wide expanse of sunlit yellow dust under the blazing blue sky, and surrounded by this circle of crouching and gesticulating monstrosities, some almost human save in their subtle expression and gestures, some like cripples, some so strangely distorted as to resemble nothing but the denizens of our wildest dreams; and, beyond, the reedy lines of a cane-brake in one direction, a dense tangle of palm trees in the other, separating us from the ravine with the huts, and to the north the hazy horizon of the Pacific Ocean.

'Sixty-two, sixty-three,' counted Moreau. 'There are four more.'

'I do not see the Leopard-man,' said I.

Presently Moreau sounded the great horn again, and at the sound of it all the Beast People writhed and grovelled in the dust. Then, slinking out of the cane-brake, stooping near the ground and trying to join the dust-throwing circle behind Moreau's back, came the Leopard-man. The last of the Beast People to arrive was the little Ape-man. The earlier animals, hot and weary with their grovelling, shot vicious glances at him.

'Cease!' said Moreau, in his firm, loud voice; and the Beast People sat back upon their hams and rested from their worshipping.

'Where is the Sayer of the Law?' said Moreau, and the hairy-grey monster bowed his face in the dust.

'Say the words!' said Moreau.

Forthwith all in the kneeling assembly, swaying from side to side and dashing up the sulphur with their hands, – first the right hand and a puff of dust, and then the left, – began once more to chant their strange litany. When they reached, 'Not to eat Fish or Flesh, *that* is the Law,' Moreau held up his lank white hand.

'*Stop!*' he cried, and there fell absolute silence upon them all.

I think they all knew and dreaded what was coming. I looked round at their strange faces. When I saw their wincing attitudes and the furtive dread in their bright eyes, I wondered that I had ever believed them to be men.

'That Law has been broken!' said Moreau.

'None escape,' from the faceless creature with the silvery hair. 'None escape,' repeated the kneeling circle of Beast People.

'Who is he?' cried Moreau, and looked round at their faces, cracking his whip. I fancied the Hyena-swine looked dejected, so too did the Leopard-man. Moreau stopped, facing this creature, who cringed towards him with the memory and dread of infinite torment.

'Who is he?' repeated Moreau, in a voice of thunder.

'Evil is he who breaks the Law,' chanted the Sayer of the Law.

Moreau looked into the eyes of the Leopard-man, and seemed to be dragging the very soul out of the creature.

'Who breaks the Law – ' said Moreau, taking his eyes off his victim, and turning towards us. It seemed to me there was a touch of exultation in his voice.

'Goes back to the House of Pain,' they all clamoured; 'goes back to the House of Pain, O Master!'

'Back to the House of Pain, back to the House of Pain,' gabbled the Ape-man, as though the idea was sweet to him.

'Do you hear?' said Moreau, turning back to the criminal, 'my friend . . . Hello!'

For the Leopard-man, released from Moreau's eye, had risen straight from his knees, and now, with eyes aflame and his huge feline tusks flashing out from under his curling lips, leapt towards his tormentor. I am convinced that only the madness of unendurable fear could have prompted this attack. The whole circle of threescore monsters seemed to rise about us. I drew my revolver. The two figures collided. I saw Moreau reeling back from the Leopard-man's blow. There was a furious yelling and howling all about us. Everyone was moving rapidly. For a moment I thought it was a general revolt. The furious face of the Leopard-man flashed by mine, with M'ling close in pursuit. I saw the yellow eyes of the Hyena-swine blazing with excitement, his attitude as if he were half resolved to attack me. The Satyr, too, glared at me over the Hyena-swine's hunched shoulders. I heard the crack of Moreau's pistol, and saw the pink flash dart across the tumult. The whole crowd seemed to swing round in the direction of the glint of fire, and I too was swung round by the magnetism of the movement. In another second I was running, one of a tumultuous shouting crowd, in pursuit of the escaping Leopard-man.

That is all I can tell definitely. I saw the Leopard-man strike Moreau, and then everything spun about me until I was running headlong. M'ling was ahead, close in pursuit of the fugitive. Behind, their tongues already lolling out, ran the Wolf-women in great leaping strides. The Swine folk followed, squealing with excitement, and the two Bull-men in their swathings of white. Then came Moreau in a cluster of the Beast People, his wide-brimmed straw hat blown off, his revolver in hand, and his lank white hair streaming out. The Hyena-swine ran beside me, keeping pace with me and glancing furtively at me out of his feline eyes, and the others came pattering and shouting behind us.

The Leopard-man went bursting his way through the long canes, which sprang back as he passed, and rattled in M'ling's face. We others in the rear found a trampled path for us when we reached the brake. The chase lay through the brake for perhaps a quarter of a mile, and then plunged into a dense thicket, which retarded our movements exceedingly, though we went through it in a crowd together – fronds flicking into our faces, ropy creepers catching us under the chin or gripping our ankles, thorny plants hooking into and tearing cloth and flesh together.

'He has gone on all-fours through this,' panted Moreau, now just ahead of me.

'None escape,' said the Wolf-bear, laughing into my face with the exultation of hunting. We burst out again among rocks, and saw the quarry ahead running lightly on all-fours and snarling at us over his shoulder. At that the Wolf Folk howled with delight. The Thing was still clothed, and at a distance its face still seemed human; but the carriage of its four limbs was feline, and the furtive droop of its shoulder was distinctly that of a hunted animal. It leapt over some thorny yellow-flowering bushes and was hidden. M'ling was halfway across the space.

Most of us now had lost the first speed of the chase, and had fallen into a longer and steadier stride. I saw as we traversed the open that the pursuit was now spreading from a column into a line. The Hyena-swine still ran close to me, watching me as it ran, every now and then puckering its muzzle with a snarling laugh.

At the edge of the rocks the Leopard-man, realising that he was making for the projecting cape upon which he had stalked me on the night of my arrival, had doubled in the undergrowth; but Montgomery had seen the manoeuvre, and turned him again. So, panting, tumbling against rocks, torn by brambles, impeded by ferns and reeds, I helped to pursue the Leopard-man who had broken the Law, and the Hyena-swine ran, laughing savagely, by my side. I staggered on, my head reeling and my heart beating against my ribs, tired almost to death, and yet not daring to lose sight of the chase lest I should be left alone with this horrible companion. I staggered on in spite of infinite fatigue and the dense heat of the tropical afternoon.

At last the fury of the hunt slackened. We had pinned the wretched brute into a corner of the island. Moreau, whip in hand, marshalled us all into an irregular line, and we advanced now slowly, shouting to one another as we advanced and tightening the cordon about our victim. He lurked, noiseless and invisible, in the bushes through which I had run from him during that midnight pursuit.

colonial
indyle

'Steady!' cried Moreau, 'steady!' as the ends of the line crept round the tangle of undergrowth and hemmed the brute in.

' 'Ware a rush!' came the voice of Montgomery from beyond the thicket.

I was on the slope above the bushes; Montgomery and Moreau beat along the beach beneath. Slowly we pushed in among the fretted network of branches and leaves. The quarry was silent.

'Back to the House of Pain, the House of Pain, the House of Pain!' yelped the voice of the Ape-man, some twenty yards to the right.

When I heard that, I forgave the poor wretch all the fear he had inspired in me. I heard the twigs snap and the boughs swish aside before the heavy tread of the Horse-rhinoceros upon my right. Then suddenly, through a polygon of green, in the half darkness under the luxuriant growth, I saw the creature we were hunting. I halted. He was crouched together into the smallest possible compass, his luminous green eyes turned over his shoulder regarding me.

It may seem a strange contradiction in me – I cannot explain the fact – but now, seeing the creature there in a perfectly animal attitude, with the light gleaming in its eyes and its imperfectly human face distorted with terror, I realised again the fact of its humanity. In another moment other of its pursuers would see it, and it would be overpowered and captured, to experience once more the horrible tortures of the enclosure. Abruptly I slipped out my revolver, aimed between its terror-struck eyes, and fired. As I did so, the Hyena-swine saw the thing, and flung itself upon it with an eager cry, thrusting thirsty teeth into its neck. All about me the green masses of the thicket were swaying and cracking as the Beast People came rushing together. One face and then another appeared.

'Don't kill it, Prendick!' cried Moreau. 'Don't kill it!' and I saw him stooping as he pushed through the under fronds of the big ferns.

In another moment he had beaten off the Hyena-swine with the handle of his whip, and he and Montgomery were keeping away the excited carnivorous Beast People, and particularly M'ling, from the still quivering body. The hairy-grey thing came sniffing at the corpse under my arm. The other animals, in their animal ardour, jostled me to get a nearer view.

'Confound you, Prendick!' said Moreau. 'I wanted him.'

'I'm sorry,' said I, though I was not. 'It was the impulse of the moment.' I felt sick with exertion and excitement. Turning, I pushed my way out of the crowding Beast People and went on alone up the slope towards the higher part of the headland. Under the shouted directions of Moreau, I heard the three white-swathed Bull-men begin dragging the victim down towards the water.

It was easy now for me to be alone. The Beast People manifested a quite human curiosity about the dead body, and followed it in a thick knot, sniffing and growling at it as the Bull-men dragged it down the beach. I went to the headland and watched the Bull-men, black against the evening sky, as they carried the weighted dead body out to sea; and like a wave across my mind came the realisation of the unspeakable aimlessness of things upon the island. Upon the beach among the rocks beneath me were the Ape-man, the Hyena-swine and several other of the Beast People standing about Montgomery and Moreau. They were all still intensely excited, and all overflowing with noisy expressions of their loyalty to the Law; yet I felt an absolute assurance in my own mind that the Hyena-swine was implicated in the rabbit-killing. A strange persuasion came upon me, that, save for the grossness of the line, the grotesqueness of the forms, I had here before me the whole balance of human life in miniature, the whole interplay of instinct, reason and fate in its simplest form. The Leopard-man had happened to go under: that was all the difference. Poor brute!

Poor brutes! I began to see the viler aspect of Moreau's cruelty. I had not thought before of the pain and trouble that came to these poor victims after they had passed from Moreau's hands. I had shivered only at the days of actual torment in the enclosure. But now that seemed to me the lesser part. Before, they had been beasts, their instincts fitly adapted to their surroundings, and happy as living things may be. Now they stumbled in the shackles of humanity, lived in a fear that never died, fretted by a law they could not understand; their mock-human existence, begun in an agony, was one long internal struggle, one long dread of Moreau – and for what? It was the wantonness of it that stirred me.

Had Moreau had any intelligible object, I could have sympathised at least a little with him. I am not so squeamish about pain as that. I could have forgiven him a little even had his motive been only hate. But he was so irresponsible, so utterly careless! His curiosity, his mad, aimless investigations, drove him on; and the Things were thrown out to live a year or so, to struggle and blunder and suffer, and at last to die painfully. They were wretched in themselves; the old animal hate moved them to trouble one another; the Law held them back from a brief hot struggle and a decisive end to their natural animosities.

In those days my fear of the Beast People went the way of my personal fear of Moreau. I fell indeed into a morbid state, deep and enduring, and alien to fear, which has left permanent scars upon my mind. I must confess that I lost faith in the sanity of the world when I saw it suffering the painful disorder of this island. A blind fate, a vast pitiless mechanism, seemed to cut and shape the fabric of existence, and I, Moreau (by his passion for research), Montgomery (by his passion for drink) and the Beast People with their instincts and mental restrictions were torn and crushed, ruthlessly, inevitably, amid the infinite complexity of its incessant wheels. But this condition did not come all at once: I think indeed that I anticipate a little in speaking of it now.

leads him into a depression
the meaningless of life
on the edge of the world
where anything can be done
but nothing is — there is nothing
out there — It is chance and
force.

industrial?

inevitable
brutality
of the world.

image of the universe as a machine
just does what is set up to do.

existential crisis.

ruthless

CHAPTER 17

A Catastrophe

Scarcely six weeks passed before I had lost every feeling but dislike and abhorrence for this infamous experiment of Moreau's. My one idea was to get away from these horrible caricatures of my Maker's image, back to the sweet and wholesome intercourse of men. My fellow-creatures, from whom I was thus separated, began to assume idyllic virtue and beauty in my memory. My first friendship with Montgomery did not increase. His long separation from humanity, his secret vice of drunkenness, his evident sympathy with the Beast People, tainted him for me. Several times I let him go alone among them. I avoided intercourse with them in every possible way. I spent an increasing proportion of my time upon the beach, looking for some liberating sail that never appeared – until one day there fell upon us an appalling disaster, which put an altogether different aspect upon my strange surroundings.

It was about seven or eight weeks after my landing – rather more, I think, though I had not troubled to keep account of the time – when this catastrophe occurred. It happened in the early morning – I should think about six. I had risen and breakfasted early, having been aroused by the noise of three Beast Men carrying wood into the enclosure.

After breakfast I went to the open gateway of the enclosure, and stood there smoking a cigarette and enjoying the freshness of the early morning. Moreau presently came round the corner of the enclosure and greeted me. He passed by me, and I heard him behind me unlock and enter his laboratory. So indurated was I at that time to the abomination of the place, that I heard without a touch of emotion the puma victim begin another day of torture. It met its persecutor with a shriek, almost exactly like that of an angry virago.

Then suddenly something happened. I do not know what it was to this day. I heard a short, sharp cry behind me, a fall, and turning saw an awful face rushing upon me – not human, not animal, but hellish, brown, seamed with red branching scars, red drops starting out upon it, and the lidless eyes ablaze. I threw up my arm to defend myself from the blow that flung me headlong with a broken forearm; and the great monster, swathed in lint and with red-stained bandages fluttering about it, leapt over me and passed. I rolled over and over down the beach, tried to sit up, and collapsed upon my broken arm. Then Moreau appeared, his massive white face all the more terrible for the blood that trickled from his forehead. He carried a revolver in one hand. He scarcely glanced at me, but rushed off at once in pursuit of the puma.

I tried the other arm and sat up. The muffled figure in front ran in great striding leaps along the beach, and Moreau followed her. She turned her head and saw him, then doubling abruptly made for the bushes. She gained upon him at every stride. I saw her plunge into them, and Moreau, running slantingly to intercept her, fired and missed as she disappeared. Then he too vanished in the green confusion. I stared after them, and then the pain in my arm flamed up, and with a groan I staggered to my feet. Montgomery appeared in the doorway, dressed, and with his revolver in his hand.

'Great God, Prendick!' he said, not noticing that I was hurt, 'that brute's loose! Tore the fetter out of the wall! Have you seen them?' Then sharply, seeing I gripped my arm, 'What's the matter?'

'I was standing in the doorway,' said I.

He came forward and took my arm. 'Blood on the sleeve,' said he, and rolled back the flannel. He pocketed his weapon, felt my arm about painfully, and led me inside. 'Your arm is broken,' he said, and then, 'Tell me exactly how it happened – what happened?'

I told him what I had seen; told him in broken sentences, with gasps of pain between them, and very dexterously and swiftly he bound my arm meanwhile. He slung it from my shoulder, stood back and looked at me.

'You'll do,' he said. 'And now?'

He thought. Then he went out and locked the gates of the enclosure. He was absent some time.

I was chiefly concerned about my arm. The incident seemed merely one more of many horrible things. I sat down in the deckchair, and I must admit swore heartily at the island. The first dull feeling of injury in my arm had already given way to a burning pain when Montgomery reappeared. His face was rather pale, and he showed more of his lower gums than ever.

'I can neither see nor hear anything of him,' he said. 'I've been thinking he may want my help.' He stared at me with his expressionless eyes. 'That was a strong brute,' he said. 'It simply wrenched its fetter out of the wall.' He went to the window, then to the door, and there turned to me. 'I shall go after him,' he said. 'There's another revolver I can leave with you. To tell you the truth, I feel anxious somehow.'

He obtained the weapon, and put it ready to my hand on the table;

then went out, leaving a restless contagion in the air. I did not sit long after he left, but took the revolver in hand and went to the doorway.

The morning was as still as death. Not a whisper of wind was stirring; the sea was like polished glass, the sky empty, the beach desolate. In my half-excited, half-feverish state, this stillness of things oppressed me. I tried to whistle, and the tune died away. I swore again – the second time that morning. Then I went to the corner of the enclosure and stared inland at the green bush that had swallowed up Moreau and Montgomery. When would they return, and how? Then far away up the beach a little grey Beast Man appeared, ran down to the water's edge and began splashing about. I strolled back to the doorway, then to the corner again, and so began pacing to and fro like a sentinel upon duty. Once I was arrested by the distant voice of Montgomery bawling, 'Coo-ee – Moreau!' My arm became less painful, but very hot. I got feverish and thirsty. My shadow grew shorter. I watched the distant figure until it went away again. Would Moreau and Montgomery never return? Three sea-birds began fighting for some stranded treasure.

Then from far away behind the enclosure I heard a pistol-shot. A long silence, and then came another. Then a yelling cry nearer, and another dismal gap of silence. My unfortunate imagination set to work to torment me. Then suddenly a shot close by. I went to the corner, startled, and saw Montgomery, his face scarlet, his hair disordered and the knee of his trousers torn. His face expressed profound conster-nation. Behind him slouched the Beast Man, M'ling, and round M'ling's jaws were some queer dark stains.

'Has he come?' said Montgomery.

'Moreau?' said I. 'No.'

'My God!' The man was panting, almost sobbing. 'Go back in,' he said, taking my arm. 'They're mad. They're all rushing about mad. What can have happened? I don't know. I'll tell you, when my breath comes. Where's some brandy?'

Montgomery limped before me into the room and sat down in the deckchair. M'ling flung himself down just outside the doorway and began panting like a dog. I got Montgomery some brandy-and-water. He sat staring in front of him at nothing, recovering his breath. After some minutes he began to tell me what had happened.

He had followed their track for some way. It was plain enough at first on account of the crushed and broken bushes, white rags torn from the puma's bandages, and occasional smears of blood on the leaves of the shrubs and undergrowth. He lost the track, however, on the stony ground beyond the stream where I had seen the Beast Man drinking, and went wandering aimlessly westward shouting Moreau's name. Then M'ling had come to him carrying a light hatchet. M'ling had seen nothing of the puma affair; had been felling wood and heard him calling. They went on shouting together. Two Beast Men came crouching and peering at them through the undergrowth, with gestures and a furtive carriage that alarmed Montgomery by their strangeness. He hailed them, and they fled guiltily. He stopped shouting after that, and after wandering some time farther in an undecided way, determined to visit the huts.

He found the ravine deserted.

Growing more alarmed every minute, he began to retrace his steps. Then it was he encountered the two Swine-men I had seen dancing on the night of my arrival; blood-stained they were about the mouth, and intensely excited. They came crashing through the ferns, and stopped with fierce faces when they saw him. He cracked his whip in some trepidation, and forthwith they rushed at him. Never before had a Beast Man dared to do that. One he shot through the head; M'ling flung himself upon the other, and the two rolled grappling. M'ling got his brute under, with his teeth in its throat, and Montgomery shot that too as it struggled in M'ling's grip. He had some difficulty in inducing M'ling to come on with him.

Thence they had hurried back to me. On the way, M'ling had suddenly rushed into a thicket and driven out an undersized Ocelot-man, also blood-stained, and lame through a wound in the foot. This brute had run a little way and then turned savagely at bay, and Montgomery – with a certain wantonness, I thought – had shot him.

'What does it all mean?' said I.

He shook his head, and turned once more to the brandy.

CHAPTER 18

The Finding of Moreau

When I saw Montgomery swallow a third dose of brandy, I took it upon myself to interfere. He was already more than half fuddled. I told him that some serious thing must have happened to Moreau by this time, or he would have returned before this, and that it behoved us to ascertain what that catastrophe was. Montgomery raised some feeble objections, but at last agreed. We had some food, and then all three of us started.

It is possibly due to the tension of my mind at the time, but even now that start into the hot stillness of the tropical afternoon is a singularly vivid impression. M'ling went first, his shoulder hunched, his strange black head moving with quick starts as he peered first on this side of the way and then on that. He was unarmed; his axe he had dropped when he encountered the Swine-man. Teeth were *his* weapons, when it came to fighting. Montgomery followed with stumbling footsteps, his hands in his pockets, his face downcast; he was in a state of muddled sullenness with me on account of the brandy. My left arm was in a sling (it was lucky it was my left), and I carried my revolver in my right. Soon we traced a narrow path through the wild luxuriance of the island, going northwestward; and presently M'ling stopped, and became rigid with watchfulness. Montgomery almost staggered into him, and then stopped too. Then, listening intently, we heard coming through the trees the sound of voices and footsteps approaching us.

'He is dead,' said a deep, vibrating voice.

'He is not dead; he is not dead,' jabbered another.

'We saw, we saw,' said several voices.

'*Hel*-lo!' suddenly shouted Montgomery. 'Hello, there!'

'Confound you!' said I, and gripped my pistol.

There was a silence, then a crashing among the interlacing vegetation, first here, then there, and then half a dozen faces appeared, strange faces, lit by a strange light. M'ling made a growling noise in his throat. I recognised the Ape-man – I had indeed already identified his voice – and two of the white-swathed brown-featured creatures I had seen in Montgomery's boat. With these were the two dappled brutes and that grey, horribly crooked creature who said the Law, with grey hair streaming down its cheeks, heavy grey eyebrows, and grey locks pouring off from a central parting upon its sloping forehead – a heavy, faceless thing, with strange red eyes, looking at us curiously from amid the green.

For a space no one spoke. Then Montgomery hiccoughed, 'Who – said he was dead?'

The Monkey-man looked guiltily at the hairy Grey Thing. 'He is dead,' said this monster. 'They saw.'

There was nothing threatening about this detachment, at any rate. They seemed awe-stricken and puzzled.

'Where is he?' said Montgomery.

'Beyond,' and the grey creature pointed.

'Is there a Law now?' asked the Monkey-man. 'Is it still to be this and that? Is he dead indeed?'

'Is there a Law?' repeated the man in white. 'Is there a Law, thou Other with the Whip?'

'He is dead,' said the hairy Grey Thing. And they all stood watching us.

'Prendick,' said Montgomery, turning his dull eyes to me. 'He's dead, evidently.'

I had been standing behind him during this colloquy. I began to see how things lay with them. I suddenly stepped in front of Montgomery and lifted up my voice: – 'Children of the Law,' I said, 'he is *not* dead!' M'ling turned his sharp eyes on me. 'He has changed his shape; he has changed his body,' I went on. 'For a time you will not see him. He is – there,' I pointed upward, 'where he can watch you. You cannot see him, but he can see you. Fear the Law!'

I looked at them squarely. They flinched.

'He is great, he is good,' said the Ape-man, peering fearfully upward among the dense trees.

'And the other Thing?' I demanded.

'The Thing that bled, and ran screaming and sobbing – that is dead too,' said the Grey Thing, still regarding me.

'That's well,' grunted Montgomery.

'The Other with the Whip – ' began the Grey Thing.

'Well?' said I.

'Said he was dead.'

But Montgomery was still sober enough to understand my motive in denying Moreau's death. 'He is not dead,' he said slowly, 'not dead at all. No more dead than I am.'

'Some,' said I, 'have broken the Law: they will die. Some have died. Show us now where his old body lies – the body he cast away because he had no more need of it.'

'It is this way, Man who walked in the Sea,' said the Grey Thing.

And with these six creatures guiding us, we went through the tumult of ferns and creepers and tree-stems towards the north-west. Then came a yelling, a crashing among the branches, and a little pink homunculus rushed by us shrieking. Immediately after appeared a feral monster in headlong pursuit, blood-bedabbled, who was among us almost before he could stop his career. The Grey Thing leapt aside. M'ling, with a snarl, flew at it, and was struck aside. Montgomery fired and missed, bowed his head, threw up his arm, and turned to run. I fired, and the Thing still came on; fired again, point-blank, into its ugly face. I saw its features vanish in a flash: its face was driven in. Yet it passed me, gripped Montgomery, and holding him, fell headlong beside him and pulled him sprawling upon itself in its death-agony.

I found myself alone with M'ling, the dead brute and the prostrate man. Montgomery raised himself slowly and stared in a muddled way at the shattered Beast Man beside him. It more than half sobered him. He scrambled to his feet. Then I saw the Grey Thing returning cautiously through the trees.

'See,' said I, pointing to the dead brute, 'is the Law not alive? This came of breaking the Law.'

He peered at the body. 'He sends the Fire that kills,' said he, in his deep voice, repeating part of the Ritual. The others gathered round and stared for a space.

At last we drew near the westward extremity of the island. We came upon the gnawed and mutilated body of the puma, its shoulder-bone smashed by a bullet, and perhaps twenty yards farther found at last what we sought. Moreau lay face downward in a trampled space in a cane-brake. One hand was almost severed at the wrist and his silvery hair was dabbled in blood. His head had been battered in by the fetters of the puma. The broken canes beneath him were smeared with blood. His revolver we could not find. Montgomery turned him over. Resting at intervals, and with the help of the seven Beast People (for he was a heavy man), we carried Moreau back to the enclosure. The night was darkling. Twice we heard unseen creatures howling and shrieking past our little band, and once the little pink sloth-creature appeared and stared at us, and vanished again. But we were not attacked again. At the gates of the enclosure our company of Beast People left us, M'ling going with the rest. We locked ourselves in, and then took Moreau's mangled body into the yard and laid it upon a pile of brushwood. Then we went into the laboratory and put an end to all we found living there.

CHAPTER 19

Montgomery's 'Bank Holiday'

When this was accomplished, and we had washed and eaten, Montgomery and I went into my little room and seriously discussed our position for the first time. It was then near midnight. He was almost sober, but greatly disturbed in his mind. He had been strangely under the influence of Moreau's personality: I do not think it had ever occurred to him that Moreau could die. This disaster was the sudden collapse of the habits that had become part of his nature in the ten or more monotonous years he had spent on the island. He talked vaguely, answered my questions crookedly, wandered into general questions.

'This silly ass of a world,' he said; 'what a muddle it all is! I haven't had any life. I wonder when it's going to begin. Sixteen years being bullied by nurses and schoolmasters at their own sweet will; five in London grinding hard at medicine, bad food, shabby lodgings, shabby clothes, shabby vice, a blunder – *I* didn't know any better – and hustled off to this beastly island. Ten years here! What's it all for, Prendick? Are we bubbles blown by a baby?'

It was hard to deal with such ravings. 'The thing we have to think of now,' said I, 'is how to get away from this island.'

'What's the good of getting away? I'm an outcast. Where am *I* to join on? It's all very well for *you*, Prendick. Poor old Moreau! We can't leave him here to have his bones picked. As it is . . . And besides, what will become of the decent part of the Beast Folk?'

'Well,' said I, 'that will do tomorrow. I've been thinking we might make that brushwood into a pyre and burn his body – and those other things. But what will happen with the Beast Folk?'

'*I* don't know. I suppose those that were made of beasts of prey will make silly asses of themselves sooner or later. We can't massacre the lot – can we? I suppose that's what *your* humanity would suggest? But they'll change. They are sure to change.'

He talked thus inconclusively until at last I felt my temper going.

'Damnation!' he exclaimed at some petulance of mine; 'can't you see I'm in a worse hole than you are?' And he got up, and went for the brandy. 'Drink!' he said returning. 'You logic-chopping, chalky-faced saint of an atheist, drink!'

'Not I,' said I, and sat grimly watching his face under the yellow paraffin flare as he drank himself into a garrulous misery.

I have a memory of infinite tedium. He wandered into a maudlin defence of the Beast People and of M'ling. M'ling, he said, was the only thing that had ever really cared for him. And suddenly an idea came to him.

'I'm damned!' said he, staggering to his feet and clutching the brandy bottle.

By some flash of intuition I knew what it was he intended. 'You don't give drink to that beast!' I said, rising and facing him.

'Beast!' said he. 'You're the beast. He takes his liquor like a Christian. Come out of the way, Prendick!'

'For God's sake,' said I.

'*Get* – out of the way!' he roared, and suddenly whipped out his revolver.

'Very well,' said I, and stood aside, half-minded to fall upon him as he put his hand upon the latch, but deterred by the thought of my useless arm. 'You've made a beast of yourself – to the beasts you may go.'

He flung the doorway open, and stood half facing me between the yellow lamplight and the pallid glare of the moon; his eye-sockets were blotches of black under his stubbly eyebrows.

'You're a solemn prig, Prendick, a silly ass! You're always fearing and fancying. We're on the edge of things. I'm bound to cut my throat tomorrow. I'm going to have a damned Bank Holiday tonight.' He turned and went out into the moonlight. 'M'ling!' he cried; 'M'ling, old friend!'

Three dim creatures in the silvery light came along the edge of the wan beach, one a white-wrapped creature, the other two blotches of blackness following it. They halted, staring. Then I saw M'ling's hunched shoulders as he came round the corner of the house.

'Drink!' cried Montgomery, 'drink, you brutes! Drink and be men! Damme, I'm the cleverest. Moreau forgot this; this is the last touch. Drink, I tell you!' And waving the bottle in his hand he started off at a kind of quick trot to the westward, M'ling ranging himself between him and the three dim creatures who followed.

I went to the doorway. They were already indistinct in the mist of the moonlight before Montgomery halted. I saw him administer a dose of the raw brandy to M'ling, and saw the five figures melt into one vague patch.

'Sing!' I heard Montgomery shout, 'sing all together, "Confound old Prendick!" ' That's right; now again, "Confound old Prendick!" '

The black group broke up into five separate figures, and wound slowly away from me along the band of shining beach. Each went howling at his own sweet will, yelping insults at me, or giving whatever other vent this new inspiration of brandy demanded. Presently I heard Montgomery's voice shouting, 'Right turn!' and they passed with their shouts and howls into the blackness of the landward trees. Slowly, very slowly, they receded into silence.

The peaceful splendour of the night healed again. The moon was now past the meridian and travelling down the west. It was at its full, and very bright riding through the empty blue sky. The shadow of the wall lay, a yard wide and of inky blackness, at my feet. The eastward sea was a featureless grey, dark and mysterious; and between the sea and the shadow the grey sands (of volcanic glass and crystals) flashed and shone like a beach of diamonds. Behind me the paraffin lamp flared hot and ruddy.

Then I shut the door, locked it, and went into the enclosure where Moreau lay beside his latest victims – the staghounds and the llama and some other wretched brutes – with his massive face calm even after his terrible death, and with the hard eyes open, staring at the dead white moon above. I sat down upon the edge of the sink, and with my eyes upon that ghastly pile of silvery light and ominous shadows began to turn over my plans. In the morning I would gather some provisions in the dinghy, and after setting fire to the pyre before me, push out into the desolation of the high sea once more. I felt that for Montgomery there was no help; that he was, in truth, half akin to these Beast Folk, unfitted for human kindred.

I do not know how long I sat there scheming. It must have been an hour or so. Then my planning was interrupted by the return of Montgomery to my neighbourhood. I heard a yelling from many throats, a tumult of exultant cries passing down towards the beach, whooping and howling and excited shrieks that seemed to come to a stop near the water's edge. The riot rose and fell; I heard heavy blows and the splintering smash of wood, but it did not trouble me then. A discordant chanting began.

My thoughts went back to my means of escape. I got up, brought the lamp, and went into a shed to look at some kegs I had seen there. Then I became interested in the contents of some biscuit-tins, and opened one. I saw something out of the tail of my eye – a red flicker – and turned sharply.

Behind me lay the yard, vividly black and white in the moonlight, and the pile of wood and faggots on which Moreau and his mutilated victims lay, one over another. They seemed to be gripping one another in one last revengeful grapple. His wounds gaped, black as night, and the blood that had dripped lay in black patches upon the sand. Then I saw, without understanding, the cause of my phantom, a ruddy glow that came and danced and went upon the wall opposite. I misinterpreted this, fancied it was a reflection of my flickering lamp, and turned again to the stores in the shed. I went on rummaging among them, as well as a one-armed man could, finding this convenient thing and that, and putting them aside for tomorrow's launch. My movements were slow, and the time passed quickly. Insensibly the daylight crept upon me.

The chanting died down, giving place to a clamour; then it began again, and suddenly broke into a tumult. I heard cries of, 'More! more!' a sound like quarrelling, and a sudden wild shriek. The quality of the sounds changed so greatly that it arrested my attention. I went out into the yard and listened. Then cutting like a knife across the confusion came the crack of a revolver.

I rushed at once through my room to the little doorway. As I did so I heard some of the packing-cases behind me go sliding down and smash together with a clatter of glass on the floor of the shed. But I did not heed these. I flung the door open and looked out.

Up the beach by the boathouse a bonfire was burning, raining up sparks into the indistinctness of the dawn. Around this struggled a mass of black figures. I heard Montgomery call my name. I began to run at once towards this fire, revolver in hand. I saw the pink tongue of Montgomery's pistol lick out once, close to the ground. He was down. I shouted with all my strength and fired into the air. I heard someone cry, 'The Master!' The knotted black struggle broke into scattering units, the fire leapt and sank down. The crowd of Beast People fled in sudden panic before me, up the beach. In my excitement I fired at their retreating backs as they disappeared among the bushes. Then I turned to the black heaps upon the ground.

Montgomery lay on his back, with the hairy Grey Thing sprawling across his body. The brute was dead, but still gripping Montgomery's throat with its curving claws. Near by lay M'ling on his face and quite still, his neck bitten open and the upper part of the smashed brandy-bottle in his hand. Two other figures lay near the fire – the one motionless, the other groaning fitfully, every now and then raising its head slowly, then dropping it again.

I caught hold of the Grey Thing and pulled it off Montgomery's body; its claws drew down the torn coat reluctantly as I dragged it away. Montgomery was dark in the face and scarcely breathing. I splashed sea-water on his face and pillowed his head on my rolled-up coat. M'ling was dead. The wounded creature by the fire – it was a Wolf-brute with a bearded grey face – lay, I found, with the fore part of its body upon the still glowing timber. The wretched thing was injured so dreadfully that in mercy I blew its brains out at once. The other brute was one of the Bull-men swathed in white. He too was dead. The rest of the Beast People had vanished from the beach.

I went to Montgomery again and knelt beside him, cursing my ignorance of medicine. The fire beside me had sunk down, and only charred beams of timber glowing at the central ends and mixed with a grey ash of brushwood remained. I wondered casually where Montgomery had got his wood. Then I saw that the dawn was upon us. The sky had grown brighter, the setting moon was becoming pale and opaque in the luminous blue of the day. The sky to the eastward was rimmed with red.

Suddenly I heard a thud and a hissing behind me, and, looking round, sprang to my feet with a cry of horror. Against the warm dawn great tumultuous masses of black smoke were boiling up out of the enclosure, and through their stormy darkness shot flickering threads of blood-red flame. Then the thatched roof caught. I saw the curving charge of the flames across the sloping straw. A spurt of fire jetted from the window of my room.

I knew at once what had happened. I remembered the crash I had heard. When I had rushed out to Montgomery's assistance, I had overturned the lamp.

The hopelessness of saving any of the contents of the enclosure stared me in the face. My mind came back to my plan of flight, and turning swiftly I looked to see where the two boats lay upon the beach. They were gone! Two axes lay upon the sands beside me; chips and splinters were scattered broadcast, and the ashes of the bonfire were blackening and smoking under the dawn. Montgomery had burnt the boats to revenge himself upon me and prevent our return to mankind!

A sudden convulsion of rage shook me. I was almost moved to batter his foolish head in as he lay there helpless at my feet. Then suddenly his hand moved, so feebly, so pitifully, that my wrath vanished. He groaned, and opened his eyes for a minute. I knelt down beside him and raised his head. He opened his eyes again, staring silently at the dawn, and then they met mine. The lids fell.

'Sorry,' he said presently, with an effort. He seemed trying to think. 'The last,' he murmured, 'the last of this silly universe. What a mess – '

I listened. His head fell helplessly to one side. I thought some drink might revive him; but there was neither drink nor vessel in which to bring drink at hand. He seemed suddenly heavier. My heart went cold. I bent down to his face, put my hand through the rent in his blouse. He was dead; and even as he died a line of white heat, the limb of the sun, rose eastward beyond the projection of the bay, splashing its radiance across the sky and turning the dark sea into a weltering tumult of dazzling light. It fell like a glory upon his death-shrunken face.

I let his head fall gently upon the rough pillow I had made for him, and stood up. Before me was the glittering desolation of the sea, the awful solitude upon which I had already suffered so much; behind me the island, hushed under the dawn, its Beast People silent and unseen. The enclosure, with all its provisions and ammunition, burnt noisily, with sudden gusts of flame, a fitful crackling, and now and then a crash. The heavy smoke drove up the beach away from me, rolling low over the distant tree-tops towards the huts in the ravine. Beside me were the charred vestiges of the boats and these four dead bodies.

Then out of the bushes came three Beast People, with hunched shoulders, protruding heads, misshapen hands awkwardly held, and inquisitive, unfriendly eyes, and advanced towards me with hesitating gestures.

CHAPTER 20

Alone with the Beast Folk

I faced these people, facing my fate in them, single-handed now – literally single-handed, for I had a broken arm. In my pocket was a revolver with two empty chambers. Among the chips scattered about the beach lay the two axes that had been used to chop up the boats. The tide was creeping in behind me. There was nothing for it but courage. I looked squarely into the faces of the advancing monsters. They avoided my eyes, and their quivering nostrils investigated the bodies that lay beyond me on the beach. I took half a dozen steps, picked up the blood-stained whip that lay beneath the body of the Wolf-man, and cracked it. They stopped and stared at me.

'Salute!' said I. 'Bow down!'

They hesitated. One bent his knees. I repeated my command, with my heart in my mouth, and advanced upon them. One knelt, then the other two.

I turned and walked towards the dead bodies, keeping my face towards the three kneeling Beast Men, very much as an actor passing up the stage faces the audience.

'They broke the Law,' said I, putting my foot on the Sayer of the Law. 'They have been slain – even the Sayer of the Law; even the Other with the Whip. Great is the Law! Come and see.'

'None escape,' said one of them, advancing and peering.

'None escape,' said I. 'Therefore hear and do as I command.' They stood up, looking questioningly at one another.

'Stand there,' said I.

I picked up the hatchets and swung them by their heads from the sling of my arm; I turned Montgomery over, picked up his revolver still loaded in two chambers, and bending down to rummage, found half a dozen cartridges in his pocket.

'Take him,' said I, standing up again and pointing with the whip; 'take him, and carry him out and cast him into the sea.'

They came forward, evidently still afraid of Montgomery, but still more afraid of my cracking red whiplash; and after some fumbling and hesitation, some whip-cracking and shouting, they lifted him gingerly, carried him down to the beach, and went splashing into the dazzling welter of the sea.

'On!' said I, 'on! Carry him far.'

They went in up to their armpits and stood regarding me.

'Let go,' said I; and the body of Montgomery vanished with a splash. Something seemed to tighten across my chest.

'Good!' said I, with a break in my voice; and they came back, hurrying and fearful, to the margin of the water, leaving long wakes of black in the silver. At the water's edge they stopped, turning and glaring into the sea as though they presently expected Montgomery to arise therefrom and exact vengeance.

'Now these,' said I, pointing to the other bodies.

They took care not to approach the place where they had thrown Montgomery into the water, but instead, carried the four dead Beast People slantingly along the beach for perhaps a hundred yards before they waded out and cast them away.

As I watched them disposing of the mangled remains of M'ling, I heard a light footfall behind me, and turning quickly saw the big Hyena-swine perhaps a dozen yards away. His head was bent down, his bright eyes were fixed upon me, his stumpy hands clenched and held close by his sides. He stopped in this crouching attitude when I turned, his eyes a little averted.

For a moment we stood eye to eye. I dropped the whip and snatched at the pistol in my pocket; for I meant to kill this brute, the most formidable of any left now upon the island, at the first excuse. It may seem treacherous, but so I was resolved. I was far more afraid of him than of any other two of the Beast Folk. His continued life was I knew a threat against mine.

I was perhaps a dozen seconds collecting myself. Then cried I, 'Salute! Bow down!'

His teeth flashed upon me in a snarl. 'Who are *you* that I should – '

Perhaps a little too spasmodically I drew my revolver, aimed quickly and fired. I heard him yelp, saw him run sideways and turn, knew I had missed, and clicked back the cock with my thumb for the next shot. But he was already running headlong, jumping from side to side, and I dared not risk another miss. Every now and then he looked back at me over his shoulder. He went slanting along the beach, and vanished beneath the driving masses of dense smoke that were still pouring out from the burning enclosure. For some time I stood staring after him. I turned to my three obedient Beast Folk again and signalled them to drop the body they still carried. Then I went back to the place by the fire where the bodies had fallen and kicked the sand until all the brown bloodstains were absorbed and hidden.

I dismissed my three serfs with a wave of the hand, and went up the beach into the thickets. I carried my pistol in my hand, my whip thrust with the hatchets in the sling of my arm. I was anxious to be alone, to think out the position in which I was now placed. A dreadful thing that I was only beginning to realise was that over all this island there was now no safe place where I could be alone and secure to rest or sleep. I had recovered strength amazingly since my landing, but I was still inclined to be nervous and to break down under any great stress. I felt that I ought to cross the island and establish myself with the Beast People, and make myself secure in their confidence. But my heart failed me. I went back to the beach, and turning eastward past the burning enclosure, made for a point where a shallow spit of coral sand ran out towards the reef. Here I could sit down and think, my back to the sea and my face against any surprise. And there I sat, chin on knees, the sun beating down upon my head and unspeakable dread in my mind, plotting how I could live on against the hour of my rescue (if ever rescue came). I tried to review the whole situation as calmly as I could, but it was difficult to clear the thing of emotion.

I began turning over in my mind the reason of Montgomery's despair. 'They will change,' he said; 'they are sure to change.' And Moreau, what was it that Moreau had said? 'The stubborn beast-flesh grows day by day back again.' Then I came round to the Hyena-swine. I felt sure that if I did not kill that brute, he would kill me. The Sayer of the Law was dead: worse luck. They knew now that we of the Whips could be killed even as they themselves were killed. Were they peering at me already out of the green masses of ferns and palms over yonder, watching until I came within their spring? Were they plotting against me? What was the Hyena-swine telling them? My imagination was running away with me into a morass of insubstantial fears.

My thoughts were disturbed by a crying of sea-birds hurrying towards some black object that had been stranded by the waves on the beach near the enclosure. I knew what that object was, but I had not the heart to go back and drive them off. I began walking along the beach in the opposite direction, designing to come round the eastward corner of the island and so approach the ravine of the huts, without traversing the possible ambuscades of the thickets.

Perhaps half a mile along the beach I became aware of one of my three Beast Folk advancing out of the landward bushes towards me. I was now so nervous with my own imaginings that I immediately drew my revolver. Even the propitiatory gestures of the creature failed to disarm me. He hesitated as he approached.

'Go away!' cried I.

There was something very suggestive of a dog in the cringing attitude of the creature. It retreated a little way, very like a dog being sent home, and stopped, looking at me imploringly with canine brown eyes.

'Go away,' said I. 'Do not come near me.'

'May I not come near you?' it said.

'No; go away,' I insisted, and snapped my whip. Then putting my whip in my teeth, I stooped for a stone, and with that threat drove the creature away.

So in solitude I came round by the ravine of the Beast People, and hiding among the weeds and reeds that separated this crevice from the sea I watched such of them as appeared, trying to judge from their gestures and appearance how the death of Moreau and Montgomery and the destruction of the House of Pain had affected them. I know now the folly of my cowardice. Had I kept my courage up to the level of the dawn, had I not allowed it to ebb away in solitary thought, I might have grasped the vacant sceptre of Moreau and ruled over the Beast People. As it was I lost the opportunity, and sank to the position of a mere leader among my fellows.

Towards noon certain of them came and squatted basking in the hot sand. The imperious voices of hunger and thirst prevailed over my dread. I came out of the bushes, and, revolver in hand, walked down towards these seated figures. One, a Wolf-woman, turned her head and stared at me, and then the others did the same. None attempted to rise or salute me. I felt too faint and weary to insist, and I let the moment pass.

'I want food,' said I, almost apologetically, and drawing near.

'There is food in the huts,' said an Ox-boar-man, drowsily, and looking away from me.

I passed them, and went down into the shadow and odours of the almost deserted ravine. In an empty hut I feasted on some specked and half-decayed fruit; and then after I had propped some branches and sticks about the opening, and placed myself with my face towards it and my hand upon my revolver, the exhaustion of the last thirty hours claimed its own, and I let myself fall into a light slumber, trusting that the flimsy barricade I had erected would cause sufficient noise in its removal to save me from surprise.

CHAPTER 21

The Reversion of the Beast Folk

In this way I became one among the Beast People on the Island of Doctor Moreau. When I awoke, it was dark about me. My arm ached in its bandages. I sat up, wondering at first where I might be. I heard coarse voices talking outside. Then I saw that my barricade had gone, and that the opening of the hut stood clear. My revolver was still in my hand.

I heard something breathing, saw something crouched together close beside me. I held my breath, trying to see what it was. It began to move slowly, interminably. Then something soft and warm and moist passed across my hand. All my muscles contracted. I snatched my hand away. A cry of alarm began and was stifled in my throat. Then I just realised what had happened sufficiently to stay my fingers on the revolver.

'Who is that?' I said in a hoarse whisper, the revolver still pointed.

'I – Master.'

'Who are you?'

'They say there is no Master now. But I know, I know. I carried the bodies into the sea, O Walker in the Sea! the bodies of those you slew. I am your slave, Master.'

'Are you the one I met on the beach?' I asked.

'The same, Master.'

The Thing was evidently faithful enough, for it might have fallen upon me as I slept. 'It is well,' I said, extending my hand for another licking kiss. I began to realise what its presence meant, and the tide of my courage flowed. 'Where are the others?' I asked.

'They are mad; they are fools,' said the Dog-man. 'Even now they talk together beyond there. They say, "The Master is dead. The Other with the Whip is dead. That Other who walked in the Sea is as we are. We have no Master, no Whips, no House of Pain, any more. There is an end. We love the Law, and will keep it; but there is no Pain, no Master, no Whips for ever again." So they say. But I know, Master, I know.'

I felt in the darkness, and patted the Dog-man's head. 'It is well,' I said again.

'Presently you will slay them all,' said the Dog-man.

'Presently,' I answered, 'I will slay them all – after certain days and certain things have come to pass. Every one of them save those you spare, every one of them shall be slain.'

'What the Master wishes to kill, the Master kills,' said the Dog-man with a certain satisfaction in his voice.

'And that their sins may grow,' I said, 'let them live in their folly until their time is ripe. Let them not know that I am the Master.'

'The Master's will is sweet,' said the Dog-man, with the ready tact of his canine blood.

'But one has sinned,' said I. 'Him I will kill, whenever I may meet him. When I say to you, "*That is he*," see that you fall upon him. And now I will go to the men and women who are assembled together.'

For a moment the opening of the hut was blackened by the exit of the Dog-man. Then I followed and stood up almost in the exact spot where I had been when I had heard Moreau and his staghound pursuing me. But now it was night, and all the miasmatic ravine about me was black; and beyond, instead of a green, sunlit slope, I saw a red fire, before which hunched, grotesque figures moved to and fro. Farther were the thick trees, a bank of darkness, fringed above with the black lace of the upper branches. The moon was just riding up on the edge of the ravine, and like a bar across its face drove the spire of vapour that was forever streaming from the fumaroles of the island.

'Walk by me,' said I, nerving myself; and side by side we walked down the narrow way, taking little heed of the dim Things that peered at us out of the huts.

None about the fire attempted to salute me. Most of them disregarded me – ostentatiously. I looked round for the Hyena-swine, but he was not there. Altogether, perhaps twenty of the Beast Folk squatted, staring into the fire or talking to one another.

'He is dead, he is dead! the Master is dead!' said the voice of the Ape-man to the right of me. 'The House of Pain – there is no House of Pain!'

'He is not dead,' said I, in a loud voice. 'Even now he watches us!'

This startled them. Twenty pairs of eyes regarded me.

'The House of Pain is gone,' said I. 'It will come again. The Master you cannot see; yet even now he listens among you.'

'True, true!' said the Dog-man.

They were staggered at my assurance. An animal may be ferocious and cunning enough, but it takes a real man to tell a lie.

'The Man with the Bandaged Arm speaks a strange thing,' said one of the Beast Folk.

'I tell you it is so,' I said. 'The Master and the House of Pain will come again. Woe be to him who breaks the Law!'

They looked curiously at one another. With an affectation of indifference I began to chop idly at the ground in front of me with my hatchet. They looked, I noticed, at the deep cuts I made in the turf.

Then the Satyr raised a doubt. I answered him. Then one of the dappled things objected, and an animated discussion sprang up round the fire. Every moment I began to feel more convinced of my present security. I talked now without the catching in my breath, due to the intensity of my excitement, that had troubled me at first. In the course of about an hour I had really convinced several of the Beast Folk of the truth of my assertions, and talked most of the others into a dubious state. I kept a sharp eye for my enemy the Hyena-swine, but he never appeared. Every now and then a suspicious movement would startle me, but my confidence grew rapidly. Then, as the moon crept down from the zenith, one by one the listeners began to yawn (showing the oddest teeth in the light of the sinking fire), and first one and then another retired towards the dens in the ravine; and I, dreading the silence and darkness, went with them, knowing I was safer with several of them than with one alone.

In this manner began the longer part of my sojourn upon this Island of Doctor Moreau. But from that night until the end came, there was but one thing happened to tell save a series of innumerable small unpleasant details and the fretting of an incessant uneasiness. So that I prefer to make no chronicle for that gap of time, to tell only one cardinal incident of the ten months I spent as an intimate of these half-humanised brutes. There is much that sticks in my memory that I could write, things that I would cheerfully give my right hand to forget; but they do not help the telling of the story.

In the retrospect it is strange to remember how soon I fell in with these monsters' ways, and gained my confidence again. I had my quarrels with them of course, and could show some of their teethmarks still; but they soon gained a wholesome respect for my trick of throwing stones and for the bite of my hatchet. And my St-Bernard-man's loyalty was of infinite service to me. I found their simple scale of honour was based mainly on the capacity for inflicting trenchant wounds. Indeed, I may say – without vanity, I hope – that I held something like pre-eminence among them. One or two, whom in a rare access of high spirits I had scarred rather badly, bore me a grudge; but it vented itself chiefly behind my back, and at a safe distance from my missiles, in grimaces.

The Hyena-swine avoided me, and I was always on the alert for him.

My inseparable Dog-man hated and dreaded him intensely. I really believe that was at the root of the brute's attachment to me. It was soon evident to me that the former monster had tasted blood, and gone the way of the Leopard-man. He formed a lair somewhere in the forest, and became solitary. Once I tried to induce the Beast Folk to hunt him, but I lacked the authority to make them co-operate for one end. Again and again I tried to approach his den and come upon him unawares; but always he was too acute for me, and saw or winded me and got away. He too made every forest pathway dangerous to me and my ally with his lurking ambuscades. The Dog-man scarcely dared to leave my side.

In the first month or so the Beast Folk, compared with their latter condition, were human enough, and for one or two besides my canine friend I even conceived a friendly tolerance. The little pink sloth-creature displayed an odd affection for me, and took to following me about. The Monkey-man bored me, however; he assumed, on the strength of his five digits, that he was my equal, and was forever jabbering at me – jabbering the most arrant nonsense. One thing about him entertained me a little: he had a fantastic trick of coining new words. He had an idea, I believe, that to gabble about names that meant nothing was the proper use of speech. He called it 'Big Thinks' to distinguish it from 'Little Thinks', the sane everyday interests of life. If ever I made a remark he did not understand, he would praise it very much, ask me to say it again, learn it by heart, and go off repeating it, with a word wrong here or there, to all the milder of the Beast People. He thought nothing of what was plain and comprehensible. I invented some very curious 'Big Thinks' for his especial use. I think now that he was the silliest creature I ever met; he had developed in the most wonderful way the distinctive silliness of man without losing one jot of the natural folly of a monkey.

This, I say, was in the earlier weeks of my solitude among these brutes. During that time they respected the usage established by the Law, and behaved with general decorum. Once I found another rabbit torn to pieces – by the Hyena-swine, I am assured – but that was all. It was about May when I first distinctly perceived a growing difference in their speech and carriage, a growing coarseness of articulation, a growing disinclination to talk. My Monkey-man's jabber multiplied in volume but grew less and less comprehensible, more and more simian. Some of the others seemed altogether slipping their hold upon speech, though they still understood what I said to them at that time. (Can you imagine language, once clear-cut and exact, softening and guttering, losing shape and import, becoming mere limps of sound again?) And they walked erect with an increasing difficulty. Though they evidently felt ashamed of themselves, every now and then I would come upon one or another running on toes and fingertips, and quite unable to recover the vertical attitude. They held things more clumsily; drinking by suction, feeding by gnawing, grew commoner every day. I realised more keenly than ever what Moreau had told me about the 'stubborn beast-flesh'. They were reverting, and reverting very rapidly.

Some of them – the pioneers in this, I noticed with some surprise, were all females – began to disregard the injunction of decency, deliberately for the most part. Others even attempted public outrages upon the institution of monogamy. The tradition of the Law was clearly losing its force. I cannot pursue this disagreeable subject.

My Dog-man imperceptibly slipped back to the dog again; day by day he became dumb, quadrupedal, hairy. I scarcely noticed the transition from the companion on my right hand to the lurching dog at my side.

As the carelessness and disorganisation increased from day to day, the lane of dwelling places, at no time very sweet, became so loathsome that I left it, and going across the island made myself a hovel of boughs amid the black ruins of Moreau's enclosure. Some memory of pain, I found, still made that place the safest from the Beast Folk.

It would be impossible to detail every step of the lapsing of these monsters – to tell how, day by day, the human semblance left them; how they gave up bandagings and wrappings, abandoned at last every stitch of clothing; how the hair began to spread over the exposed limbs; how their foreheads fell away and their faces projected; how the quasi-human intimacy I had permitted myself with some of them in the first month of my loneliness became a shuddering horror to recall.

The change was slow and inevitable. For them and for me it came without any definite shock. I still went among them in safety, because no jolt in the downward glide had released the increasing charge of explosive animalism that ousted the human day by day. But I began to fear that soon now that shock must come. My St-Bernard-brute followed me to the enclosure every night, and his vigilance enabled me to sleep at times in something like peace. The little pink sloth-thing became shy and left me, to crawl back to its natural life once more among the tree-branches. We were in just the state of equilibrium that would remain in one of those 'Happy Family' cages which animal-tamers exhibit, if the tamer were to leave it for ever.

Of course these creatures did not decline into such beasts as the reader has seen in zoological gardens – into ordinary bears, wolves,

tigers, oxen, swine and apes. There was still something strange about
each; in each Moreau had blended this animal with that. One perhaps
was ursine chiefly, another feline chiefly, another bovine chiefly; but
each was tainted with other creatures – a kind of generalised animalism
appearing through the specific dispositions. And the dwindling shreds
of the humanity still startled me every now and then – a momentary
recrudescence of speech perhaps, an unexpected dexterity of the fore-
feet, a pitiful attempt to walk erect.

I too must have undergone strange changes. My clothes hung about
me as yellow rags, through whose rents showed the tanned skin. My
hair grew long, and became matted together. I am told that even now
my eyes have a strange brightness, a swift alertness of movement.

At first I spent the daylight hours on the southward beach watching
for a ship, hoping and praying for a ship. I counted on the *Ipecacuanha*
returning as the year wore on; but she never came. Five times I saw
sails, and thrice smoke; but nothing ever touched the island. I always
had a bonfire ready, but no doubt the volcanic reputation of the island
was taken to account for that.

It was only about September or October that I began to think of
making a raft. By that time my arm had healed, and both my hands were
at my service again. At first, I found my helplessness appalling. I had
never done any carpentry or suchlike work in my life, and I spent day
after day in experimental chopping and binding among the trees. I had
no ropes, and could hit on nothing wherewith to make ropes; none of
the abundant creepers seemed limber or strong enough, and with all my
litter of scientific education I could not devise any way of making them
so. I spent more than a fortnight grubbing among the black ruins of the
enclosure and on the beach where the boats had been burnt, looking for
nails and other stray pieces of metal that might prove of service. Now
and then some Beast-creature would watch me, and go leaping off when
I called to it. There came a season of thunderstorms and heavy rain,
which greatly retarded my work; but at last the raft was completed.

I was delighted with it. But with a certain lack of practical sense which
has always been my bane, I had made it a mile or more from the sea;
and before I had dragged it down to the beach the thing had fallen to
pieces. Perhaps it is as well that I was saved from launching it; but at the
time my misery at my failure was so acute that for some days I simply
moped on the beach, and stared at the water and thought of death.

I did not, however, mean to die, and an incident occurred that warned
me unmistakably of the folly of letting the days pass so – for each fresh
day was fraught with increasing danger from the Beast People.

I was lying in the shade of the enclosure wall, staring out to sea, when I was startled by something cold touching the skin of my heel, and starting round found the little pink sloth-creature blinking into my face. He had long since lost speech and active movement, and the lank hair of the little brute grew thicker every day and his stumpy claws more askew. He made a moaning noise when he saw he had attracted my attention, went a little way towards the bushes and looked back at me.

At first I did not understand, but presently it occurred to me that he wished me to follow him; and this I did at last – slowly, for the day was hot. When we reached the trees he clambered into them, for he could travel better among their swinging creepers than on the ground. And suddenly in a trampled space I came upon a ghastly group. My St-Bernard-creature lay on the ground, dead; and near his body crouched the Hyena-swine, gripping the quivering flesh with its misshapen claws, gnawing at it, and snarling with delight. As I approached, the monster lifted its glaring eyes to mine, its lips went trembling back from its red-stained teeth, and it growled menacingly. It was not afraid and not ashamed; the last vestige of the human taint had vanished. I advanced a step farther, stopped, and pulled out my revolver. At last I had him face to face.

The brute made no sign of retreat; but its ears went back, its hair bristled, and its body crouched together. I aimed between the eyes and fired. As I did so, the Thing rose straight at me in a leap, and I was knocked over like a ninepin. It clutched at me with its crippled hand, and struck me in the face. Its spring carried it over me. I fell under the hind part of its body; but luckily I had hit as I meant, and it had died even as it leapt. I crawled out from under its unclean weight and stood up trembling, staring at its quivering body. That danger at least was over; but this, I knew, was only the first of the series of relapses that must come.

I burnt both of the bodies on a pyre of brushwood; but after that I saw that unless I left the island my death was only a question of time. The Beast People by that time had, with one or two exceptions, left the ravine and made themselves lairs according to their taste among the thickets of the island. Few prowled by day, most of them slept, and the island might have seemed deserted to a newcomer; but at night the air was hideous with their calls and howling. I had half a mind to make a massacre of them; to build traps, or fight them with my knife. Had I possessed sufficient cartridges, I should not have hesitated to begin the killing. There could now be scarcely a score left of the dangerous carnivores; the braver of these were already dead. After the death of this poor dog of mine, my last friend, I too adopted to some extent the practice of slumbering in the daytime in order to be on my guard at night. I rebuilt my den in the walls of the enclosure, with such a narrow opening that anything attempting to enter must necessarily make a considerable noise. The creatures had lost the art of fire, too, and recovered their fear of it. I turned once more, almost passionately now, to hammering together stakes and branches to form a raft for my escape.

I found a thousand difficulties. I am an extremely unhandy man (my schooling was over before the days of Slöjd);[47] but most of the requirements of a raft I met at last in some clumsy circuitous way or other, and this time I took care of the strength. The only insurmountable obstacle was that I had no vessel to contain the water I should need if I floated forth upon these untravelled seas. I would have even tried pottery, but the island contained no clay. I used to go moping about the island trying with all my might to solve this one last difficulty. Sometimes I would give way to wild outbursts of rage, and hack and splinter some unlucky tree in my intolerable vexation. But I could think of nothing.

And then came a day, a wonderful day, which I spent in ecstasy. I saw a sail to the southwest, a small sail like that of a little schooner; and forthwith I lit a great pile of brushwood, and stood by it in the heat of it, and the heat of the midday sun, watching. All day I watched that sail, eating or drinking nothing, so that my head reeled; and the Beasts came and glared at me, and seemed to wonder, and went away. It was still distant when night came and swallowed it up; and all night I toiled to keep my blaze bright and high, and the eyes of the Beasts shone out of the darkness, marvelling. In the dawn the sail was nearer, and I saw it was the dirty lug-sail of a small boat. But it sailed strangely. My eyes were weary with watching, and I peered and could not believe them. Two men were in the boat, sitting low down – one by the bows, the other at the rudder. The head was not kept to the wind; it yawed and fell away.

As the day grew brighter, I began waving the last rag of my jacket to them; but they did not notice me, and sat still, facing each other. I went to the lowest point of the low headland and gesticulated and shouted. There was no response, and the boat kept on her aimless course, making slowly, very slowly, for the bay. Suddenly a great white bird flew up out of the boat, and neither of the men stirred nor noticed it; it circled round, and then came sweeping overhead with its strong wings outspread.

Then I stopped shouting, and sat down on the headland and rested my chin on my hands and stared. Slowly, slowly, the boat drove past towards the west. I would have swum out to it, but something – a cold, vague fear – kept me back. In the afternoon the tide stranded the boat, and left it a hundred yards or so to the westward of the ruins of the enclosure. The men in it were dead, had been dead so long that they fell to pieces when I tilted the boat on its side and dragged them out. One had a shock of red hair, like the captain of the *Ipecacuanha*, and a dirty white cap lay in the bottom of the boat.

As I stood beside the boat, three of the Beasts came slinking out of the bushes and sniffing towards me. One of my spasms of disgust came upon me. I thrust the little boat down the beach and clambered on board her. Two of the brutes were Wolf-beasts, and came forward with quivering nostrils and glittering eyes; the third was the horrible nondescript of bear and bull. When I saw them approaching those wretched remains, heard them snarling at one another and caught the gleam of their teeth, a frantic horror succeeded my repulsion. I turned my back upon them, struck the lug and began paddling out to sea. I could not bring myself to look behind me.

I lay, however, between the reef and the island that night, and the next morning went round to the stream and filled the empty keg aboard with water. Then, with such patience as I could command, I collected a quantity of fruit, and waylaid and killed two rabbits with my last three cartridges. While I was doing this I left the boat moored to an inward projection of the reef, for fear of the Beast People.

CHAPTER 22

The Man Alone

In the evening I started, and drove out to sea before a gentle wind from the southwest, slowly, steadily; and the island grew smaller and smaller, and the lank spire of smoke dwindled to a finer and finer line against the hot sunset. The ocean rose up around me, hiding that low, dark patch from my eyes. The daylight, the trailing glory of the sun, went streaming out of the sky, was drawn aside like some luminous curtain, and at last I looked into the blue gulf of immensity which the sunshine hides, and saw the floating hosts of the stars. The sea was silent, the sky was silent. I was alone with the night and silence.

So I drifted for three days, eating and drinking sparingly, and meditating upon all that had happened to me, not desiring very greatly then to see men again. One unclean rag was about me, my hair a black tangle: no doubt my discoverers thought me a madman.

It is strange, but I felt no desire to return to mankind. I was only glad to be quit of the foulness of the Beast People. And on the third day I was picked up by a brig from Apia[48] to San Francisco. Neither the captain nor the mate would believe my story, judging that solitude and danger had made me mad; and fearing their opinion might be that of others, I refrained from telling my adventure further, and professed to recall nothing that had happened to me between the loss of the *Lady Vain* and the time when I was picked up again – the space of a year.

I had to act with the utmost circumspection to save myself from the suspicion of insanity. My memory of the Law, of the two dead sailors, of the ambuscades of the darkness, of the body in the cane-brake, haunted me; and, unnatural as it seems, with my return to mankind came, instead of that confidence and sympathy I had expected, a strange enhancement of the uncertainty and dread I had experienced during my stay upon the island. No one would believe me; I was almost as queer to men as I had been to the Beast People. I may have caught something of the natural wildness of my companions. They say that terror is a disease, and anyhow I can witness that for several years now a restless fear has dwelt in my mind – such a restless fear as a half-tamed lion cub may feel.

My trouble took the strangest form. I could not persuade myself that the men and women I met were not also another, still passably human,

Beast People, animals half wrought into the outward image of human
souls, and that they would presently begin to revert – to show first this
bestial mark and then that. But I have confided my case to a strangely
able man – a man who had known Moreau, and seemed half to credit
my story; a mental specialist – and he has helped me mightily, though I
do not expect that the terror of that island will ever altogether leave
me. At most times it lies far in the back of my mind, a mere distant
cloud, a memory and a faint distrust; but there are times when the little
cloud spreads until it obscures the whole sky. Then I look about me at
my fellow men; and I go in fear. I see faces keen and bright; others dull
or dangerous; others unsteady, insincere – none that have the calm
authority of a reasonable soul. I feel as though the animal was surging
up through them; that presently the degradation of the Islanders will
be played over again on a larger scale. I know this is an illusion; that
these seeming men and women about me are indeed men and women,
men and women for ever, perfectly reasonable creatures, full of human
desires and tender solicitude, emancipated from instinct and the slaves
of no fantastic Law – beings altogether different from the Beast Folk.
Yet I shrink from them, from their curious glances, their enquiries and
assistance, and long to be away from them and alone. For that reason I
live near the broad free downland, and can escape thither when this
shadow is over my soul; and very sweet is the empty downland then,
under the windswept sky.

When I lived in London the horror was well-nigh insupportable. I
could not get away from men: their voices came through windows;
locked doors were flimsy safeguards. I would go out into the streets to
fight with my delusion, and prowling women would mew after me;
furtive, craving men glance jealously at me; weary, pale workers go
coughing by me with tired eyes and eager paces, like wounded deer
dripping blood; old people, bent and dull, pass murmuring to themselves; and, all unheeding, a ragged tail of gibing children. Then I would
turn aside into some chapel – and even there, such was my disturbance,
it seemed that the preacher gibbered 'Big Thinks', even as the Ape-
man had done; or into some library, and there the intent faces over
the books seemed but patient creatures waiting for prey. Particularly
nauseous were the blank, expressionless faces of people in trains and
omnibuses; they seemed no more my fellow-creatures than dead bodies
would be, so that I did not dare to travel unless I was assured of being
alone. And even it seemed that I too was not a reasonable creature, but
only an animal tormented with some strange disorder in its brain which
sent it to wander alone, like a sheep stricken with gid.[49]

This is a mood, however, that comes to me now, I thank God, more rarely. I have withdrawn myself from the confusion of cities and multitudes, and spend my days surrounded by wise book – bright windows in this life of ours, lit by the shining souls of men. I see few strangers, and have but a small household. My days I devote to reading and to experiments in chemistry, and I spend many of the clear nights in the study of astronomy. There is – though I do not know how there is or why there is – a sense of infinite peace and protection in the glittering hosts of heaven. There it must be, I think, in the vast and eternal laws of matter, and not in the daily cares and sins and troubles of men, that whatever is more than animal within us must find its solace and its hope. I hope, or I could not live.

And so, in hope and solitude, my story ends.

EDWARD PRENDICK

NOTE[50] The substance of the chapter entitled 'Doctor Moreau Explains', which contains the essential idea of the story, appeared as a middle article in the *Saturday Review* in January 1895. This is the only portion of this story that has been previously published, and it has been entirely recast to adapt it to the narrative form.

Aepyornis Island

THE MAN WITH THE SCARRED FACE leant over the table and looked at my bundle.

'Orchids?' he asked.

'A few,' I said.

'Cypripediums,'[51] he said.

'Chiefly,' said I.

'Anything new? I thought not. *I* did these islands twenty-five – twenty-seven years ago. If you find anything new here – well, it's brand new. I didn't leave much.'

'I'm not a collector,' said I.

'I was young then,' he went on. 'Lord! how I used to fly round.' He seemed to take my measure. 'I was in the East Indies two years, and in Brazil seven. Then I went to Madagascar.'

'I know a few explorers by name,' I said, anticipating a yarn. 'Whom did you collect for?'

'Dawson's. I wonder if you've heard the name of Butcher ever?'

'Butcher – Butcher?' The name seemed vaguely present in my memory; then I recalled *Butcher* v. *Dawson*. 'Why!' said I, 'you are the man who sued them for four years' salary – got cast away on a desert island . . . '

'Your servant,' said the man with the scar, bowing. 'Funny case, wasn't it? Here was me, making a little fortune on that island, doing nothing for it neither, and them quite unable to give me notice. It often used to amuse me thinking over it while I was there. I did calculations of it – big – all over the blessed atoll[52] in ornamental figuring.'

'How did it happen?' said I. 'I don't rightly remember the case.'

'Well . . . You've heard of the Aepyornis?'[53]

'Rather. Andrews was telling me of a new species he was working on only a month or so ago. Just before I sailed. They've got a thigh bone, it seems, nearly a yard long. Monster the thing must have been!'

'I believe you,' said the man with the scar. 'It *was* a monster. Sinbad's roc[54] was just a legend of 'em. But when did they find these bones?'

'Three or four years ago – '91, I fancy. Why?'

'Why? Because *I* found 'em – Lord! – it's nearly twenty years ago. If Dawson's hadn't been silly about that salary they might have made a perfect ring in 'em. . . . *I* couldn't help the infernal boat going adrift.'

He paused, 'I suppose it's the same place. A kind of swamp about

ninety miles north of Antananarivo.[55] Do you happen to know? You
have to go to it along the coast by boats. You don't happen to remember,
perhaps?'

'I don't. I fancy Andrews said something about a swamp.'

'It must be the same. It's on the east coast. And somehow there's
something in the water that keeps things from decaying. Like creosote
it smells. It reminded me of Trinidad. Did they get any more eggs?
Some of the eggs I found were a foot and a half long. The swamp goes
circling round, you know, and cuts off this bit. It's mostly salt, too.
Well . . . What a time I had of it! I found the things quite by accident.
We went for eggs, me and two native chaps, in one of those rum
canoes all tied together, and found the bones at the same time. We had
a tent and provisions for four days, and we pitched on one of the firmer
places. To think of it brings that odd tarry smell back even now. It's
funny work. You go probing into the mud with iron rods, you know.
Usually the egg gets smashed. I wonder how long it is since these
Aepyornises really lived. The missionaries say the natives have legends
about when they were alive, but I never heard any such stories myself.*
But certainly those eggs we got were as fresh as if they had been new
laid. Fresh! Carrying them down to the boat one of my chaps dropped
one on a rock and it smashed. How I lammed into the beggar! But
sweet it was, as if it was new laid, not even smelly, and its mother dead
these four hundred years, perhaps. Said a centipede had bit him. However, I'm getting off the straight with the story. It had taken us all day
to dig into the slush and get these eggs out unbroken, and we were all
covered with beastly black mud, and naturally I was cross. So far as I
knew they were the only eggs that have ever been got out not even
cracked. I went afterwards to see the ones they have at the Natural
History Museum in London; all of them were cracked and just stuck
together like a mosaic, and bits missing. Mine were perfect, and I
meant to blow them when I got back. Naturally I was annoyed at the
silly duffer dropping three hours' work just on account of a centipede. I
hit him about rather.'

The man with the scar took out a clay pipe. I placed my pouch before
him. He filled up absent-mindedly.

'How about the others? Did you get those home? I don't remember – '

'That's the queer part of the story. I had three others. Perfectly fresh
eggs. Well, we put 'em in the boat, and then I went up to the tent to

* No European is known to have seen a live Aepyornis, with the doubtful
  exception of MacAndrew, who visited Madagascar in 1745.   H. G .W.

make some coffee, leaving my two heathens down by the beach – the one fooling about with his sting and the other helping him. It never occurred to me that the beggars would take advantage of the peculiar position I was in to pick a quarrel. But I suppose the centipede poison and the kicking I had given him had upset the one – he was always a cantankerous sort – and he persuaded the other.

'I remember I was sitting and smoking and boiling up the water over a spirit-lamp[56] business I used to take on these expeditions. Incidentally I was admiring the swamp under the sunset. All black and blood-red it was, in streaks – a beautiful sight. And up beyond the land rose grey and hazy to the hills, and the sky behind them red, like a furnace mouth. And fifty yards behind the back of me was these blessed heathen – quite regardless of the tranquil air of things – plotting to cut off with the boat and leave me all alone with three days' provisions and a canvas tent, and nothing to drink whatsoever, beyond a little keg of water. I heard a kind of yelp behind me, and there they were in this canoe affair – it wasn't properly a boat – perhaps twenty yards from land. I realised what was up in a moment. My gun was in the tent, and, besides, I had no bullets – only duck shot.[57] They knew that. But I had a little revolver in my pocket, and I pulled that out as I ran down to the beach.

' "Come back!" says I, flourishing it.

'They jabbered something at me, and the man that broke the egg jeered. I aimed at the other – because he was unwounded and had the paddle, and I missed. They laughed. However, I wasn't beat. I knew I had to keep cool, and I tried him again and made him jump with the whang[58] of it. He didn't laugh that time. The third time I got his head, and over he went, and the paddle with him. It was a precious lucky shot for a revolver. I reckon it was fifty yards. He went right under. I don't know if he was shot, or simply stunned and drowned. Then I began to shout to the other chap to come back, but he huddled up in the canoe and refused to answer. So I fired out my revolver at him and never got near him.

'I felt a precious fool, I can tell you. There I was on this rotten, black beach, flat swamp all behind me, and the flat sea, cold after the sunset, and just this black canoe drifting steadily out to sea. I tell you I damned Dawson's and Jamrach's[59] and museums and all the rest of it just to rights. I bawled to this blighter to come back, until my voice went up into a scream.

'There was nothing for it but to swim after him and take my luck with the sharks. So I opened my clasp-knife and put it in my mouth, and took off my clothes and waded in. As soon as I was in the water I lost sight of the canoe, but I aimed, as I judged, to head it off. I hoped the man in it was too bad to navigate it, and that it would keep on drifting in the same direction. Presently it came up over the horizon again to the south-westward about. The afterglow of sunset was well over now and the dim of night creeping up. The stars were coming through the blue. I swum like a champion, though my legs and arms were soon aching.

'However, I came up to him by the time the stars were fairly out. As it got darker I began to see all manner of glowing things in the water – phosphorescence,[60] you know. At times it made me giddy. I hardly knew which was stars and which was phosphorescence, and whether I was swimming on my head or my heels. The canoe was as black as sin, and the ripple under the bows like liquid fire. I was naturally chary of clambering up into it. I was anxious to see what he was up to first. He seemed to be lying cuddled up in a lump in the bows, and the stern was all out of the water. The thing kept turning round slowly as it drifted – kind of waltzing, don't you know. I went to the stern, and pulled it down, expecting him to wake up. Then I began to clamber in with my knife in my hand, and ready for a rush. But he never stirred. So there I sat in the stern of the little canoe, drifting away over the calm phosphorescent sea, and with all the host of the stars above me, waiting for something to happen.

'After a long time I called him by name, but he never answered. I was too tired to take any risks by going along to him. So we sat there. I fancy I dozed once or twice. When the dawn came I saw he was as dead as a doornail and all puffed up and purple. My three eggs and the bones were lying in the middle of the canoe, and the keg of water and some coffee and biscuits wrapped in a *Cape Argus*[61] by his feet, and a tin of methylated spirit underneath him. There was no paddle, nor, in fact, anything except the spirit-tin that one could use as one, so I settled to drift until I was picked up. I held an inquest on him, brought in a verdict against some snake, scorpion or centipede unknown, and sent him overboard.

'After that I had a drink of water and a few biscuits, and took a look round. I suppose a man low down as I was don't see very far; leastways, Madagascar was clean out of sight, and any trace of land at all. I saw a sail going south-westward – looked like a schooner, but her hull never came up. Presently the sun got high in the sky and began to beat down upon me. Lord! It pretty near made my brains boil. I tried dipping my head in the sea, but after a while my eye fell on the Cape *Argus*, and I lay down flat in the canoe and spread this over me. Wonderful things these newspapers! I never read one through thoroughly before, but it's odd what you get up to when you're alone, as I was. I suppose I read that blessed old Cape *Argus* twenty times. The pitch in the canoe simply reeked with the heat and rose up into big blisters.

'I drifted ten days,' said the man with the scar. 'It's a little thing in the telling, isn't it? Every day was like the last. Except in the morning and the evening I never kept a look-out even – the blaze was so infernal. I didn't see a sail after the first three days, and those I saw took no notice of me. About the sixth night a ship went by scarcely half a mile away from me, with all its lights ablaze and its ports open, looking like a big firefly. There was music aboard. I stood up and shouted and screamed at it. The second day I broached one of the Aepyornis eggs, scraped the shell away at the end bit by bit, and tried it, and I was glad to find it was good enough to eat. A bit flavoury – not bad, I mean – but with something of the taste of a duck's egg. There was a kind of circular patch, about six inches across, on one side of the yolk, and with streaks of blood and a white mark like a ladder in it that I thought queer, but I did not understand what this meant at the time, and I wasn't inclined to be particular. The egg lasted me three days, with biscuits and a drink of water. I chewed coffee berries too – invigorating stuff. The second egg I opened about the eighth day, and it scared me.'

The man with the scar paused. 'Yes,' he said, 'developing . . . '

'I dare say you find it hard to believe. *I* did, with the thing before me. There the egg had been, sunk in that cold black mud, perhaps three hundred years. But there was no mistaking it. There was the – what is it? – embryo, with its big head and curved back, and its heart beating under its throat, and the yolk shrivelled up and great membranes spreading inside of the shell and all over the yolk. Here was I hatching out the eggs of the biggest of all extinct birds, in a little canoe in the midst of the Indian Ocean. If old Dawson had known that! It was worth four years' salary. What do *you* think?

'However, I had to eat that precious thing up, every bit of it, before I sighted the reef, and some of the mouthfuls were beastly unpleasant. I left the third one alone. I held it up to the light, but the shell was too thick for me to get any notion of what might be happening inside; and though I fancied I heard blood pulsing, it might have been the rustle in my own ears, like what you listen to in a seashell.

'Then came the atoll. Came out of the sunrise, as it were, suddenly, close up to me. I drifted straight towards it until I was about half a mile from shore, not more, and then the current took a turn, and I had to paddle as hard as I could with my hands and bits of the Aepyornis shell to make the place. However, I got there. It was just a common atoll about four miles round, with a few trees growing and a spring in one place, and the lagoon full of parrot-fish.[62] I took the egg ashore and put it in a good place well above the tide lines and in the sun, to give it all the chance I could, and pulled the canoe up safe, and loafed about prospecting. It's rum how dull an atoll is. As soon as I had found a spring all the interest seemed to vanish. When I was a kid I thought nothing could be finer or more adventurous than the Robinson Crusoe[63] business, but that place was as monotonous as a book of sermons. I went round finding eatable things and generally thinking; but I tell you I was bored to death before the first day was out. It shows my luck – the very day I landed the weather changed. A thunderstorm went by to the north and flicked its wing over the island, and in the night there came a drencher and a howling wind slap over us. It wouldn't have taken much, you know, to upset that canoe.

'I was sleeping under the canoe, and the egg was luckily among the sand higher up the beach, and the first thing I remember was a sound like a hundred pebbles hitting the boat at once, and a rush of water over my body. I'd been dreaming of Antananarivo, and I sat up and hallooed to Intoshi to ask her what the devil was up, and clawed out at the chair where the matches used to be. Then I remembered where I was. There were phosphorescent waves rolling up as if they meant to eat me, and all the rest of the night as black as pitch. The air was simply yelling. The clouds seemed down on your head almost, and the rain fell as if heaven was sinking and they were baling out the waters above the firmament. One great roller came writhing at me, like a fiery serpent, and I bolted. Then I thought of the canoe, and ran down to it as the water went hissing back again; but the thing had gone. I wondered about the egg then, and felt my way to it. It was all right and well out of reach of the maddest waves, so I sat down beside it and cuddled it for company. Lord! what a night that was!

'The storm was over before the morning. There wasn't a rag of cloud left in the sky when the dawn came, and all along the beach there were bits of plank scattered – which was the disarticulated skeleton, so to speak, of my canoe. However, that gave me something to do, for, taking advantage of two of the trees being together, I rigged up a kind of storm-shelter with these vestiges. And that day the egg hatched.

'Hatched, sir, when my head was pillowed on it and I was asleep. I heard a whack and felt a jar and sat up, and there was the end of the egg pecked out and a rum little brown head looking out at me. "Lord!" I said, "you're welcome" – and with a little difficulty he came out.

'He was a nice friendly little chap, at first, about the size of a small hen – very much like most other young birds, only bigger. His plumage was a dirty brown to begin with, with a sort of grey scab that fell off it very soon, and scarcely feathers – a kind of downy hair. I can hardly express how pleased I was to see him. I tell you, Robinson Crusoe don't make near enough of his loneliness. But here was interesting company. He looked at me and winked his eye from the front backwards, like a hen, and gave a chirp and began to peck about at once, as though being hatched three hundred years too late was just nothing. "Glad to see you, Man Friday!" says I, for I had naturally settled he was to be called Man Friday if ever he was hatched, as soon as ever I found the egg in the canoe had developed. I was a bit anxious about his feed, so I gave him a lump of raw parrot-fish at once. He took it, and opened his beak for more. I was glad of that, for, under the circumstances, if he'd been at all fanciful, I should have had to eat him after all. You'd be surprised what an interesting bird that Aepyornis chick was. He followed me about from the very beginning. He used to stand by me and watch while I fished in the lagoon, and go shares in anything I caught. And he was sensible, too. There were nasty green warty things, like pickled gherkins, used to lie about on the beach, and he tried one of these and it upset him. He never even looked at any of them again.

'And he grew. You could almost see him grow. And as I was never much of a society man his quiet, friendly ways suited me to a T. For nearly two years we were as happy as we could be on that island. I had no business worries, for I knew my salary was mounting up at Dawson's. We would see a sail now and then, but nothing ever came near us. I amused myself, too, by decorating the island with designs worked in sea-urchins and fancy shells of various kinds. I put 'Aepyornis Island' all round the place very nearly, in big letters, like what you see done with coloured stones at railway stations in the old country, and mathematical calculations and drawings of various sorts. And I used to lie watching the blessed bird stalking round and growing, growing; and think how I could make a living out of him by showing him about if I ever got taken off. After his first moult he began to get handsome, with a crest and a blue wattle,[64] and a lot of green feathers at the behind of him. And then I used to puzzle whether Dawson's had any right to claim him or not. Stormy weather and in the rainy season we lay snug under the shelter I had made out of the old canoe, and I used to tell him lies about my friends at home. And after a storm we would go round the island together to see if there was any drift. It was a kind of idyll, you might say. If only I had had some tobacco it would have been simply just like heaven.

'It was about the end of the second year our little paradise went wrong. Friday was then about fourteen feet high to the bill of him, with a big, broad head like the end of a pickaxe, and two huge brown eyes with yellow rims, set together like a man's – not out of sight of each other like a hen's. His plumage was fine – none of the half-mourning style of your ostrich – more like a cassowary[65] as far as colour and texture go. And then it was he began to cock his comb at me and give himself airs, and show signs of a nasty temper . . .

'At last came a time when my fishing had been rather unlucky, and he began to hang about me in a queer, meditative way. I thought he might have been eating sea-cucumbers[66] or something, but it was really just discontent on his part. I was hungry too, and when at last I landed a fish I wanted it for myself. Tempers were short that morning on both sides. He pecked at it and grabbed it, and I gave him a whack on the head to make him leave go. And at that he went for me. Lord! . . .

'He gave me this in the face.' The man indicated his scar. 'Then he kicked me. It was like a carthorse. I got up, and seeing he hadn't finished, I started off full tilt with my arms doubled up over my face. But he ran on those gawky legs of his faster than a racehorse, and kept landing out at me with sledge-hammer kicks, and bringing his pickaxe down on the back of my head. I made for the lagoon, and went in up to my neck. He stopped at the water, for he hated getting his feet wet, and began to make a shindy,[67] something like a peacock's, only hoarser. He started strutting up and down the beach. I'll admit I felt small to see this blessed fossil lording it there. And my head and face were all bleeding, and – well, my body was just one jelly of bruises.

'I decided to swim across the lagoon and leave him alone for a bit, until the affair blew over. I shinned up the tallest palm tree, and sat there thinking of it all. I don't suppose I ever felt so hurt by anything before or since. It was the brutal ingratitude of the creature. I'd been more than a brother to him. I'd hatched him, educated him. A great gawky, out-of-date bird! And me a human being – heir of the ages and all that.

'I thought after a time he'd begin to see things in that light himself, and feel a little sorry for his behaviour. I thought if I was to catch some nice little bits of fish, perhaps, and go to him presently in a casual kind of way, and offer them to him, he might do the sensible thing. It took me some time to learn how unforgiving and cantankerous an extinct bird can be. Malice!

'I won't tell you all the little devices I tried to get that bird round again. I simply can't. It makes my cheek burn with shame even now to think of the snubs and buffets I had from this infernal curiosity. I tried violence. I chucked lumps of coral at him from a safe distance, but he only swallowed them. I shied my open knife at him and almost lost it, though it was too big for him to swallow. I tried starving him out and struck fishing, but he took to picking along the beach at low water after worms, and rubbed along on that. Half my time I spent up to my neck in the lagoon, and the rest up the palm trees. One of them was scarcely high enough, and when he caught me up it he had a regular Bank Holiday with the calves of my legs. It got unbearable. I don't know if you have ever tried sleeping up a palm tree. It gave me the most horrible nightmares. Think of the shame of it, too! Here was this extinct animal mooning about my island like a sulky duke, and me not allowed to rest the sole of my foot on the place. I used to cry with weariness and vexation. I told him straight that I didn't mean to be chased about a desert island by any damned anachronisms. I told him to go and peck a navigator of his own age. But he only snapped his beak at me. Great ugly bird – all legs and neck!

'I shouldn't like to say how long that went on altogether. I'd have killed him sooner if I'd known how. However, I hit on a way of settling him at last. It is a South American dodge. I joined all my fishing-lines together with stems of seaweed and things and made a stoutish string, perhaps twelve yards in length or more, and I fastened two lumps of coral rock to the ends of this. It took me some time to do, because every now and then I had to go into the lagoon or up a tree as the fancy took me. This I whirled rapidly round my head, and then let it go at him. The first time I missed, but the next time the string caught his legs beautifully, and wrapped round them again and again. Over he went. I threw it standing waist-deep in the lagoon, and as soon as he went down I was out of the water and sawing at his neck with my knife . . .

'I don't like to think of that even now. I felt like a murderer while I did it, though my anger was hot against him. When I stood over him and saw him bleeding on the white sand, and his beautiful great legs and neck writhing in his last agony . . . Pah!

'With that tragedy loneliness came upon me like a curse. Good Lord! you can't imagine how I missed that bird. I sat by his corpse and sorrowed over him, and shivered as I looked round the desolate, silent reef. I thought of what a jolly little bird he had been when he was hatched, and of a thousand pleasant tricks he had played before he went wrong. I thought if I'd only wounded him I might have nursed him round into a better understanding. If I'd had any means of digging into the coral rock I'd have buried him. I felt exactly as if he was human. As it was, I couldn't think of eating him, so I put him in the lagoon, and the little fishes picked him clean. I didn't even save the feathers. Then one day a chap cruising about in a yacht had a fancy to see if my atoll still existed.

'He didn't come a moment too soon, for I was about sick enough of the desolation of it, and only hesitating whether I should walk out into the sea and finish up the business that way, or fall back on the green things . . .

'I sold the bones to a man named Winslow – a dealer near the British Museum, and he says he sold them to old Havers. It seems Havers didn't understand they were extra large, and it was only after his death they attracted attention. They called 'em *Aepyornis* – what was it?'

'*Aepyornis vastus*,' said I. 'It's funny, the very thing was mentioned to me by a friend of mine. When they found an Aepyornis, with a thigh a yard long, they thought they had reached the top of the scale and called him *Aepyornis maximus*. Then someone turned up another thighbone four feet six or more, and that they called *Aepyornis titan*. Then your *vastus* was found after old Havers died, in his collection, and then a *vastissimus* turned up.'

'Winslow was telling me as much,' said the man with the scar. 'If they get any more Aepyornises, he reckons some scientific swell will go and burst a blood vessel. But it was a queer thing to happen to a man; wasn't it – altogether?'

The Sea Raiders

1

UNTIL THE EXTRAORDINARY affair at Sidmouth, the peculiar species *Haploteuthis ferox*[68] was known to science only generically, on the strength of a half-digested tentacle obtained near the Azores and a decaying body, pecked by birds and nibbled by fish, found early in 1896 by Mr Jennings, near Land's End.

In no department of zoological science, indeed, are we quite so much in the dark as with regard to the deep-sea cephalopods.[69] A mere accident, for instance, it was that led to the Prince of Monaco's discovery[70] of nearly a dozen new forms in the summer of 1895, a discovery in which the before-mentioned tentacle was included. It chanced that a cachalot[71] was killed off Terceira by some sperm whalers and in its last struggles charged almost to the Prince's yacht, missed it, rolled under and died within twenty yards of his rudder. And in its agony it threw up a number of large objects, which the Prince, dimly perceiving they were strange and important, was, by a happy expedient, able to secure before they sank. He set his screws in motion, and kept them circling in the vortices thus created until a boat could be lowered. And these specimens were whole cephalopods and fragments of cephalopods, some of gigantic proportions, and almost all of them unknown to science!

It would seem, indeed, that these large and agile creatures, living in the middle depths of the sea, must, to a large extent, for ever remain unknown to us, since under water they are too nimble for nets, and it is only by such rare, unlooked-for accidents that specimens can be obtained. In the case of *Haploteuthis ferox*, for instance, we are still altogether ignorant of its habitat, as ignorant as we are of the breeding-ground of the herring or the seaways of the salmon. And zoologists are altogether at a loss to account for its sudden appearance on our coast. Possibly it was the stress of a hunger migration that drove it hither out of the deep. But it will be, perhaps, better to avoid necessarily inconclusive discussion, and to proceed at once with our narrative.

The first human being to set eyes upon a living *Haploteuthis* – the first human being to survive, that is, for there can be little doubt now that the wave of bathing fatalities and boating accidents that travelled along the coast of Cornwall and Devon in early May was due to this cause –

was a retired tea-dealer by the name of Fison, who was stopping at a Sidmouth boarding-house. It was in the afternoon, and he was walking along the cliff path between Sidmouth and Ladram Bay.[72] The cliffs in this direction are very high, but down the red face of them in one place a kind of ladder staircase has been made. He was near this when his attention was attracted by what at first he thought to be a cluster of birds struggling over a fragment of food, that caught the sunlight and glistened pinkish-white. The tide was right out, and this object was not only far below him, but remote across a broad waste of rock reefs covered with dark seaweed and interspersed with silvery shining tidal pools. And he was, moreover, dazzled by the brightness of the farther water.

In a minute, regarding this again, he perceived that his judgement was in fault, for over this struggle circled a number of birds, jackdaws and gulls for the most part, the latter gleaming blindingly when the sunlight smote their wings, and they seemed minute in comparison with it. And his curiosity was, perhaps, aroused all the more strongly because of his first insufficient explanations.

As he had nothing better to do than amuse himself, he decided to make this object, whatever it was, the goal of his afternoon walk, instead of Ladram Bay, conceiving it might perhaps be a great fish of some sort, stranded by some chance, and flapping about in its distress. And so he hurried down the long steep ladder, stopping at intervals of thirty feet or so to take breath and scan the mysterious movement.

At the foot of the cliff he was, of course, nearer his object than he had been; but, on the other hand, it now came up against the incandescent sky, beneath the sun, so as to seem dark and indistinct. Whatever was pinkish of it was now hidden by a skerry[73] of weedy boulders. But he perceived that it was made up of seven rounded bodies, distinct or connected, and that the birds kept up a constant croaking and screaming, but seemed afraid to approach it too closely.

Mr Fison, torn by curiosity, began picking his way across the wave-worn rocks, and finding the wet seaweed that covered them thickly rendered them extremely slippery, he stopped, removed his shoes and socks, and rolled his trousers above his knees. His object was, of course, merely to avoid stumbling into the rocky pools about him, and perhaps he was rather glad, as all men are, of an excuse to resume, even for a moment, the sensations of his boyhood. At any rate, it is to this, no doubt, that he owes his life.

He approached his mark with all the assurance which the absolute security of this country against all forms of animal life gives its inhabitants. The round bodies moved to and fro, but it was only when he surmounted the skerry of boulders I have mentioned that he realised the horrible nature of the discovery. It came upon him with some suddenness.

The rounded bodies fell apart as he came into sight over the ridge, and displayed the pinkish object to be the partially devoured body of a human being, but whether of a man or woman he was unable to say. And the rounded bodies were new and ghastly-looking creatures, each in shape somewhat resembling an octopus, with huge and very long and flexible tentacles, coiled copiously on the ground. The skin had a glistening texture, unpleasant to see, like shiny leather. The downward bend of the tentacle-surrounded mouth, the curious excrescence at the bend, the tentacles, and the large intelligent eyes, gave the creatures a grotesque suggestion of a face. They were the size of a fair-sized swine about the body, and the tentacles seemed to him to be many feet in length. There were, he thinks, seven or eight at least of the creatures. Twenty yards beyond them, amid the surf of the now returning tide, two others were emerging from the sea.

Their bodies lay flatly on the rocks, and their eyes regarded him with evil interest; but it does not appear that Mr Fison was afraid, or that he realised that he was in any danger. Possibly his confidence is to be ascribed to the limpness of their attitudes. But he was horrified, of course, and intensely excited and indignant at such revolting creatures preying upon human flesh. He thought they had chanced upon a drowned body. He shouted to them, with the idea of driving them off, and finding they did not budge, cast about him, picked up a big rounded lump of rock, and flung it at one.

And then, slowly uncoiling their tentacles, they all began moving towards him – creeping at first deliberately, and making a soft purring sound to each other.

In a moment Mr Fison realised that he was in danger. He shouted again, threw both his boots, and started off, with a leap, forthwith. Twenty yards off he stopped and faced about, judging them slow, and behold! The tentacles of their leader were already pouring over the rocky ridge on which he had just been standing!

At that he shouted again, but this time not threatening, but a cry of dismay, and began jumping, striding, slipping, wading across the uneven expanse between him and the beach. The tall red cliffs seemed suddenly at a vast distance, and he saw, as though they were creatures in another world, two minute workmen engaged in the repair of the ladder-way, little suspecting the race for life that was beginning below them. At one time he could hear the creatures splashing in the pools not a dozen feet behind him, and once he slipped and almost fell.

They chased him to the very foot of the cliffs, and desisted only when he had been joined by the workmen at the foot of the ladder-way up the cliff. All three of the men pelted them with stones for a time, and then hurried to the cliff top and along the path towards Sidmouth, to secure assistance and a boat, and to rescue the desecrated body from the clutches of these abominable creatures.

2

And, as if he had not already been in sufficient peril that day, Mr Fison went with the boat to point out the exact spot of his adventure.

As the tide was down, it required a considerable detour to reach the spot, and when at last they came off the ladder-way, the mangled body had disappeared. The water was now running in, submerging first one slab of slimy rock and then another, and the four men in the boat – the workmen, that is, the boatman and Mr Fison – now turned their attention from the bearings off shore to the water beneath the keel.

At first they could see little below them, save a dark jungle of laminaria,[74] with an occasional darting fish. Their minds were set on adventure, and they expressed their disappointment freely. But presently they saw one of the monsters swimming through the water seaward, with a curious rolling motion that suggested to Mr Fison the spinning roll of a captive balloon. Almost immediately after, the waving streamers of laminaria were extraordinarily perturbed, parted for a moment, and three of these beasts became darkly visible, struggling for what was probably some fragment of the drowned man. In a moment the copious olive-green ribbons had poured again over this writhing group.

At that all four men, greatly excited, began beating the water with oars and shouting, and immediately they saw a tumultuous movement among the weeds. They desisted to see more clearly, and as soon as the water was smooth, they saw, as it seemed to them, the whole sea bottom among the weeds set with eyes.

'Ugly swine!' cried one of the men. 'Why, there's dozens!'

And forthwith the things began to rise through the water about them. Mr Fison has since described to the writer this startling eruption out of the waving laminaria meadows. To him it seemed to occupy a considerable time, but it is probable that really it was an affair of a few seconds only. For a time nothing but eyes, and then he speaks of tentacles streaming out and parting the weed fronds this way and that. Then these things, growing larger, until at last the bottom was hidden by their intercoiling forms, and the tips of tentacles rose darkly here and there into the air above the swell of the waters.

One came up boldly to the side of the boat, and clinging to this with three of its sucker-set tentacles, threw four others over the gunwale, as if with an intention either of oversetting the boat or of clambering into it. Mr Fison at once caught up the boat-hook, and jabbing furiously at the soft tentacles, forced it to desist. He was struck in the back and almost pitched overboard by the boatman, who was using his oar to resist a similar attack on the other side of the boat. But the tentacles on either side at once relaxed their hold, slid out of sight, and splashed into the water.

'We'd better get out of this,' said Mr Fison, who was trembling violently. He went to the tiller, while the boatman and one of the workmen seated themselves and began rowing. The other workman stood up in the fore part of the boat, with the boat-hook, ready to strike any more tentacles that might appear. Nothing else seems to have been said. Mr Fison had expressed the common feeling beyond amendment. In a hushed, scared mood, with faces white and drawn, they set about escaping from the position into which they had so recklessly blundered.

But the oars had scarcely dropped into the water before dark, tapering, serpentine ropes had bound them, and were about the rudder; and creeping up the sides of the boat with a looping motion came the suckers again. The men gripped their oars and pulled, but it was like trying to move a boat in a floating raft of weeds. 'Help here!' cried the boatman, and Mr Fison and the second workman rushed to help lug at the oar.

Then the man with the boat-hook – his name was Ewan, or Ewen – sprang up with a curse and began striking downward over the side, as far as he could reach, at the bank of tentacles that now clustered along the boat's bottom. And, at the same time, the two rowers stood up to get a better purchase for the recovery of their oars. The boatman handed his to Mr Fison, who lugged desperately while the boatman opened a big clasp-knife, and leaning over the side of the boat, began hacking at the spiralling arms upon the oar shaft.

Mr Fison, staggering with the quivering rocking of the boat, his teeth set, his breath coming short, and the veins starting on his hands as he pulled at his oar, suddenly cast his eyes seaward. And there, not fifty yards off, across the long rollers of the incoming tide, was a large boat standing in towards them, with three women and a little child in it. A boatman was rowing, and a little man in a pink-ribboned straw hat and whites stood in the stern hailing them. For a moment, of course, Mr Fison thought of help, and then he thought of the child. He abandoned his oar forthwith, threw up his arms in a frantic gesture, and screamed to the party in the boat to keep away 'for God's sake!' It says much for the modesty and courage of Mr Fison that he does not seem to be aware that there was any quality of heroism in his action at this juncture. The oar he had abandoned was at once drawn under, and presently reappeared floating about twenty yards away.

At the same moment Mr Fison felt the boat under him lurch violently, and a hoarse scream, a prolonged cry of terror from Hill, the boatman, caused him to forget the party of excursionists altogether. He turned, and saw Hill crouching by the forward rowlock,[75] his face convulsed with terror and his right arm over the side and drawn tightly down. He gave now a succession of short, sharp cries, 'Oh! Oh! Oh – ! Oh!' Mr Fison believes that he must have been hacking at the tentacles below the water-line, and have been grasped by them, but of course, it is quite impossible to say now certainly what had happened. The boat was heeling over, so that the gunwale was within ten inches of the water, and both Ewan and the other labourer were striking down into the water, with oar and boat-hook, on either side of Hill's arm. Mr Fison instinctively placed himself to counterpoise them.

Then Hill, who was a burly, powerful man, made a strenuous effort, and rose almost to a standing position. He lifted his arm, indeed, clean out of the water. Hanging to it was a complicated tangle of brown ropes, and the eyes of one of the brutes that had hold of him, glaring straight and resolute, showed momentarily above the surface. The boat heeled more and more, and the green-brown water came pouring in a cascade over the side. Then Hill slipped and fell with his ribs across the side, and his arm and the mass of tentacles about it splashed back into the water. He rolled over; his boot kicked Mr Fison's knee as that gentleman rushed forward to seize him, and in another moment fresh tentacles had whipped about his waist and neck and, after a brief, convulsive struggle, in which the boat was nearly capsized, Hill was lugged overboard. The boat righted with a violent jerk that all but sent Mr Fison over the other side, and hid the struggle in the water from his eyes.

He stood staggering to recover his balance for a moment, and as he did so he became aware that the struggle and the inflowing tide had carried them close upon the weedy rocks again. Not four yards off a table of rock still rose in rhythmic movements above the inwash of the tide. In a moment Mr Fison seized the oar from Ewan, gave one vigorous stroke, then, dropping it, ran to the bows and leapt. He felt his feet slide over the rock, and by a frantic effort, leapt again towards a further mass. He stumbled over this, came to his knees, and rose again.

'Look out!' cried someone, and a large drab body struck him. He was knocked flat into a tidal pool by one of the workmen, and as he went down he heard smothered, choking cries, that he believed at the time came from Hill. Then he found himself marvelling at the shrillness and variety of Hill's voice. Someone jumped over him, and a curving rush of foamy water poured over him, and passed. He scrambled to his feet dripping, and without looking seaward, ran as fast as his terror would let him shoreward. Before him, over the flat space of scattered rocks, stumbled the two workmen – one a dozen yards in front of the other.

He looked over his shoulder at last, and seeing that he was not pursued, faced about. He was astonished. From the moment of the rising of the cephalopods out of the water he had been acting too swiftly to fully comprehend his actions. Now it seemed to him as if he had suddenly jumped out of an evil dream.

For there were the sky, cloudless and blazing with the afternoon sun, the sea weltering under its pitiless brightness, the soft creamy foam of the breaking water, and the low, long, dark ridges of rock. The righted boat floated, rising and falling gently on the swell about a dozen yards from shore. Hill and the monsters, all the stress and tumult of that fierce fight for life, had vanished as though they had never been.

Mr Fison's heart was beating violently; he was throbbing to the fingertips, and his breath came deep.

There was something missing. For some seconds he could not think clearly enough what this might be. Sun, sky, sea, rocks – what was it? Then he remembered the boatload of excursionists. It had vanished. He wondered whether he had imagined it. He turned, and saw the two workmen standing side by side under the projecting masses of the tall pink cliffs. He hesitated whether he should make one last attempt to save the man Hill. His physical excitement seemed to desert him suddenly, and leave him aimless and helpless. He turned shoreward, stumbling and wading towards his two companions.

He looked back again, and there were now two boats floating, and the one farthest out at sea pitched clumsily, bottom upward.

So it was that *Haploteuthis ferox* made its appearance upon the Devonshire coast. So far, this has been its most serious aggression. Mr Fison's account, taken together with the wave of boating and bathing casualties to which I have already alluded, and the absence of fish from the Cornish coasts that year, points clearly to a shoal of these voracious deep-sea monsters prowling slowly along the sub-tidal coastline. Hunger migration has, I know, been suggested as the force that drove them hither; but, for my own part, I prefer to believe the alternative theory of Hemsley.[76] Hemsley holds that a pack or shoal of these creatures may have become enamoured of human flesh by the accident of a foundered ship sinking among them, and have wandered in search of it out of their accustomed zone; first waylaying and following ships, and so coming to our shores in the wake of the Atlantic traffic. But to discuss Hemsley's cogent and admirably-stated arguments would be out of place here.

It would seem that the appetites of the shoal were satisfied by the catch of eleven people – for, so far as can be ascertained, there were ten people in the second boat, and certainly these creatures gave no further signs of their presence off Sidmouth that day. The coast between Seaton and Budleigh Salterton[77] was patrolled all that evening and night by four Preventive Service[78] boats, the men in which were armed with harpoons and cutlasses, and as the evening advanced, a number of more or less similarly equipped expeditions, organised by private individuals, joined them. Mr Fison took no part in any of these expeditions.

About midnight excited hails were heard from a boat about a couple of miles out at sea to the south-east of Sidmouth, and a lantern was seen waving in a strange manner to and fro and up and down. The nearer boats at once hurried towards the alarm. The venturesome occupants of the boat, a seaman, a curate and two schoolboys, had actually seen the monsters passing under their boat. The creatures, it seems, like most deep-sea organisms, were phosphorescent, and they had been floating, five fathoms deep or so, like creatures of moonshine through the blackness of the water, their tentacles retracted and as if asleep, rolling over and over, and moving slowly in a wedgelike formation towards the south-east.

These people told their story in gesticulated fragments, as first one boat drew alongside and then another. At last there was a little fleet of eight or nine boats collected together, and from them a tumult, like the chatter of a marketplace, rose into the stillness of the night. There was little or no disposition to pursue the shoal; the people had neither weapons nor experience for such a dubious chase, and presently – even with a certain relief, it may be – the boats turned shoreward.

And now to tell what is perhaps the most astonishing fact in this whole astonishing raid. We have not the slightest knowledge of the subsequent movements of the shoal, although the whole south-west coast was now alert for it. But it may, perhaps, be significant that a cachalot was stranded off Sark[79] on June 3. Two weeks and three days after this Sidmouth affair, a living *Haploteuthis* came ashore on Calais sands. It was alive, because several witnesses saw its tentacles moving in a convulsive way. But it is probable that it was dying. A gentleman named Pouchet obtained a rifle and shot it.

That was the last appearance of a living *Haploteuthis*. No others were seen on the French coast. On the 15th of June a dead carcass, almost complete, was washed ashore near Torquay, and a few days later a boat from the Marine Biological station, engaged in dredging off Plymouth, picked up a rotting specimen, slashed deeply with a cutlass wound. How the former had come by its death it is impossible to say. And on the last day of June, Mr Egbert Caine, an artist, bathing near Newlyn,[80] threw up his arms, shrieked, and was drawn under. A friend bathing with him made no attempt to save him, but swam at once for the shore. This is the last fact to tell of this extraordinary raid from the deeper sea. Whether it is really the last of these horrible creatures it is, as yet, premature to say. But it is believed, and certainly it is to be hoped, that they have returned now, and returned for good, to the sunless depths of the middle seas, out of which they had so strangely and so mysteriously arisen.

The Empire of the Ants

WHEN CAPTAIN GERILLEAU received instructions to take his new gunboat, the *Benjamin Constant*,[81] to Badama on the Batemo arm of the Guaramadema[82] and there assist the the inhabitants against a plague of ants, he suspected the authorities of mockery. His promotion had been romantic and irregular, the affections of a prominent Brazilian lady and the captain's liquid eyes had played a part in the process, and the *Diario* and *O Futuro*[83] had been lamentably disrespectful in their comments. He felt he was to give further occasion for disrespect.

He was a Creole,[84] his conceptions of etiquette and discipline were pure-blooded Portuguese, and it was only to Holroyd, the Lancashire engineer who had come over with the boat, and as an exercise in the use of English – his 'th' sounds were very uncertain – that he opened his heart.

'It is in effect,' he said, 'to make me absurd! What can a man do against ants? Dey come, dey go.'

'They say,' said Holroyd, 'that these don't go. That chap you said was a Sambo –'

'Zambo – it is a sort of mixture of blood.'

'Sambo. He said the people are going!'

The captain smoked fretfully for a time. 'Dese tings 'ave to happen,' he said at last. 'What is it? Plagues of ants and suchlike as God wills. Dere was a plague in Trinidad – the little ants that carry leaves. Orl der orange trees, all der mangoes! What does it matter? Sometimes ant armies come into your houses – fighting ants; a different sort. You go and they clean the house. Then you come back again – the house is clean, like new! No cockroaches, no fleas, no jiggers[85] in the floor.'

'That Sambo chap,' said Holroyd, 'says these are a different sort of ant.'

The captain shrugged his shoulders, fumed, and gave his attention to a cigarette.

Afterwards he reopened the subject. 'My dear 'Olroyd, what am I to do about dese infernal ants?'

The captain reflected. 'It is ridiculous,' he said. But in the afternoon he put on his full uniform and went ashore, and jars and boxes came back to the ship and subsequently he did. And Holroyd sat on deck in the evening coolness and smoked profoundly and marvelled at Brazil.

They were six days up the Amazon, some hundreds of miles from the ocean, and east and west of him there was a horizon like the sea, and to the south nothing but a sand-bank island with some tufts of scrub. The water was always running like a sluice, thick with dirt, animated with crocodiles and hovering birds, and fed by some inexhaustible source of tree trunks; and the waste of it, the headlong waste of it, filled his soul. The town of Alemquer,[86] with its meagre church, its thatched sheds for houses, its discoloured ruins of ampler days, seemed a little thing lost in this wilderness of nature, a sixpence dropped on the Sahara. He was a young man, this was his first sight of the tropics; he came straight from England, where nature is hedged, ditched and drained into the perfection of submission, and he had suddenly discovered the insignificance of man. For six days they had been steaming up from the sea by unfrequented channels; and man had been as rare as a rare butterfly. One saw one day a canoe, another day a distant station, the next no men at all. He began to perceive that man is indeed a rare animal, having but a precarious hold upon this land.

He perceived it more clearly as the days passed and he made his devious way to the Batemo, in the company of this remarkable commander, who ruled over one big gun, and was forbidden to waste his ammunition. Holroyd was learning Spanish industriously, but he was still in the present tense and substantive stage of speech, and the only other person who had any words of English was a negro stoker, who had them all wrong. The second in command was a Portuguese, da Cunha, who spoke French, but it was a different sort of French from the French Holroyd had learnt in Southport,[87] and their intercourse was confined to politenesses and simple propositions about the weather. And the weather, like everything else in this amazing new world, the weather had no human aspect, and was hot by night and hot by day, and the air steam, even the wind was hot steam, smelling of vegetation in decay; and the alligators and the strange birds, the flies of many sorts and sizes, the beetles, the ants, the snakes and monkeys seemed to wonder what man was doing in an atmosphere that had no gladness in its sunshine and no coolness in its night. To wear clothing was intolerable, but to cast it aside was to scorch by day, and expose an ampler area to the mosquitoes by night; to go on deck by day was to be blinded by glare and to stay below was to suffocate. And in the daytime came certain flies, extremely clever and noxious about one's wrist and ankle. Captain Gerilleau, who was Holroyd's sole distraction from these physical distresses, developed into a formidable bore, telling the simple story of his heart's affections day by day, a string of anonymous women, as if he was telling beads. Sometimes he suggested sport, and they shot at alligators, and at rare intervals they came to human aggregations in the waste of trees, and stayed for a day or so, and drank and sat about, and, one night, danced with Creole girls, who found Holroyd's poor elements of Spanish, without either past tense or future, amply sufficient for their purposes. But these were mere luminous chinks in the long grey passage of the streaming river, up which the throbbing engines beat. A certain liberal heathen deity, in the shape of a demi-john, held seductive court aft, and, it is probable, forward.

But Gerilleau learnt things about the ants, more things and more, at this stopping-place and that, and became interested in his mission.

'Dey are a new sort of ant,' he said. 'We have got to be – what do you call it? – entomologie? Big. Five centimetres! Some bigger! It is ridiculous. We are like de monkeys – sent to pick insects . . . But dey are eating up de country.'

He burst out indignantly. 'Suppose – suddenly, there are complications with Europe. Here am I – soon we shall be above de Rio Negro[88] – and my gun, useless!'

He nursed his knee and mused.

'Dose people who were dere at de dancing place, dey 'ave come down. Dey 'ave lost all dey got. De ants come to deir house one afternoon. Everyone run out. You know when de ants come one must – everyone runs out and dey go over de house. If you stayed dey'd eat you. See? Well, presently dey go back; dey say, "De ants 'ave gone." . . . De ants 'aven't gone. Dey try to go in – de son, 'e goes in. De ants fight.'

'Swarm over him?'

'Bite 'im. Presently he comes out again – screaming and running. He runs past them to de river. See? He gets into de water and drowns de ants – yes.' Gerilleau paused, brought his liquid eyes close to Holroyd's face, tapped Holroyd's knee with his knuckle. 'Dat night he dies, just as if he was stung by a snake.'

'Poisoned – by the ants?'

'Who knows?' Gerilleau shrugged his shoulders. 'Perhaps dey bit him badly . . . When I joined dis service I joined to fight men. Dese things, dese ants, dey come and go. It is no business for men.'

After that he talked frequently of the ants to Holroyd, and whenever they chanced to drift against any speck of humanity in that waste of water and sunshine and distant trees, Holroyd's improving knowledge of the language enabled him to recognise the ascendant word *Saüba* more and more completely dominating the whole.

He perceived the ants were becoming interesting, and the nearer he drew to them the more interesting they became. Gerilleau abandoned his old themes almost suddenly, and the Portuguese lieutenant became a conversational figure; he knew something about the leaf-cutting ant, and expanded his knowledge. Gerilleau sometimes rendered what he had to tell to Holroyd. He told of the little workers that swarm and fight, and the big workers that command and rule, and how these latter always crawled to the neck and how their bites drew blood. He told how they cut leaves and made fungus beds, and how their nests in Caracas[89] are sometimes a hundred yards across. Two days the three men spent disputing whether ants have eyes. The discussion grew dangerously heated on the second afternoon, and Holroyd saved the situation by going ashore in a boat to catch ants and see. He captured various specimens and returned, and some had eyes and some hadn't. Also, they argued, do ants bite or sting?

'Dese ants,' said Gerilleau, after collecting information at a rancho, 'have big eyes. Dey don't run about blind – not as most ants do. No! Dey get in corners and watch what you do.'

'And they sting?' asked Holroyd.

'Yes. Dey sting. Dere is poison in de sting.' He meditated. 'I do not see what men can do against ants. Dey come and go.'

'But these don't go.'

'They will,' said Gerilleau.

Past Tamandu[90] there is a long low coast of eighty miles without any population, and then one comes to the confluence of the main river and the Batemo arm like a great lake, and then the forest came nearer, came at last intimately near. The character of the channel changes, snags abound, and the *Benjamin Constant* moored by a cable that night, under the very shadow of dark trees. For the first time for many days came a spell of coolness, and Holroyd and Gerilleau sat late, smoking cigars and enjoying this delicious sensation. Gerilleau's mind was full of ants and what they could do. He decided to sleep at last, and lay down on a mattress on deck, a man hopelessly perplexed, his last words, when he already seemed asleep, were to ask, with a flourish of despair, 'What can one do with ants? . . . De whole thing is absurd.'

Holroyd was left to scratch his bitten wrists, and meditate alone.

He sat on the bulwark and listened to the little changes in Gerilleau's breathing until he was fast asleep, and then the ripple and lap of the stream took his mind, and brought back that sense of immensity that had been growing upon him since first he had left Pará[91] and come up the river. The monitor showed but one small light, and there was first a little talking forward and then stillness. His eyes went from the dim

black outlines of the middle works of the gunboat towards the bank, to
the black overwhelming mysteries of forest, lit now and then by a firefly,
and never still from the murmur of alien and mysterious activities . . .

It was the inhuman immensity of this land that astonished and
oppressed him. He knew the skies were empty of men, the stars were
specks in an incredible vastness of space; he knew the ocean was
enormous and untamable; but in England he had come to think of the
land as man's. In England it is indeed man's, the wild things live
by sufferance, grow on lease; everywhere are roads and fences, and
absolute security prevails. In an atlas, too, the land is man's, and all
coloured to show his claim to it – in vivid contrast to the universal
independent blueness of the sea. He had taken it for granted that a day
would come when everywhere about the earth, plough and culture,
light tramways and good roads, an ordered security, would prevail.
But now, he doubted.

This forest was interminable, it had an air of being invincible, and
man seemed at best an infrequent precarious intruder. One travelled
for miles, amidst the still, silent struggle of giant trees, of strangulating
creepers, of assertive flowers; everywhere the alligator, the turtle and
endless varieties of birds and insects seemed at home, dwelt
irreplaceably – but man, man at most held a footing upon resentful
clearings, fought weeds, fought beasts and insects for the barest
foothold, fell a prey to snake and beast, insect and fever, and was
presently carried away. In many places down the river he had been
manifestly driven back, this deserted creek or that preserved the name
of a *casa*,[92] and here and there ruinous white walls and a shattered
tower enforced the lesson. The puma, the jaguar, were more the
masters here . . .

Who were the real masters?

In a few miles of this forest there must be more ants than there are
men in the whole world! This seemed to Holroyd a perfectly new
idea. In a few thousand years men had emerged from barbarism to a
stage of civilisation that made them feel lords of the future and masters
of the earth! But what was to prevent the ants evolving also? Such ants
as one knew lived in little communities of a few thousand individuals,
made no concerted efforts against the greater world. But they had a
language, they had an intelligence! Why should things stop at that any
more than men had stopped at the barbaric stage? Suppose presently
the ants began to store knowledge, just as men had done by means of
books and records, use weapons, form great empires, sustain a planned
and organised war?

Things came back to him that Gerilleau had gathered about these ants they were approaching. They used a poison like the poison of snakes. They obeyed greater leaders even as the leaf-cutting ants do. They were carnivorous, and where they came they stayed . . .

The forest was very still. The water lapped incessantly against the side. About the lantern overhead there eddied a noiseless whirl of phantom moths.

Gerilleau stirred in the darkness and sighed. 'What can one *do*?' he murmured, and turned over and was still again.

Holroyd was roused from meditations that were becoming sinister by the hum of a mosquito.

2

The next morning Holroyd learnt they were within forty kilometres of Badama, and his interest in the banks intensified. He came up whenever an opportunity offered to examine his surroundings. He could see no signs of human occupation whatever, save for a weedy ruin of a house and the green-stained façade of the long-deserted monastery at Mojû,[93] with a forest tree growing out of a vacant window space, and great creepers netted across its vacant portals. Several flights of strange yellow butterflies with semi-transparent wings crossed the river that morning, and many alighted on the monitor and were killed by the men. It was towards afternoon that they came upon the derelict cuberta.[94]

She did not at first appear to be derelict; both her sails were set and hanging slack in the afternoon calm, and there was the figure of a man sitting on the fore planking beside the shipped sweeps. Another man appeared to be sleeping face downwards on the sort of longitudinal bridge these big canoes have in the waist. But it was presently apparent, from the sway of her rudder and the way she drifted into the course of the gunboat, that something was out of order with her. Gerilleau surveyed her through a field-glass, and became interested in the queer darkness of the face of the sitting man; a red-faced man he seemed, without a nose – crouching he was rather than sitting, and the longer the captain looked the less he liked to look at him, and the less able he was to take his glasses away.

But he did so at last, and went a little way to call up Holroyd. Then he went back to hail the cuberta. He hailed her again as she drifted past him. *Santa Rosa* stood out clearly as her name.

As she came by and into the wake of the monitor, she pitched a little, and suddenly the figure of the crouching man collapsed as though all his joints had given way. His hat fell off, his head was not nice to look at, and his body flopped lax and rolled out of sight behind the bulwarks.

'Caramba!'[95] cried Gerilleau, and resorted to Holroyd forthwith.

Holroyd was halfway up the companion. 'Did you see dat?' said the captain.

'Dead!' said Holroyd. 'Yes. You'd better send a boat aboard. There's something wrong.'

'Did you – by any chance – see his face?'

'What was it like?'

'It was – ugh! – I have no words.' And the captain suddenly turned his back on Holroyd and became an active and strident commander.

The gunboat came about, steamed parallel to the erratic course of the canoe, and dropped the boat with Lieutenant da Cunha and three sailors to board her. Then the curiosity of the captain made him draw up almost alongside as the lieutenant prepared to go aboard, so that the whole of the *Santa Rosa*, deck and hold, was visible to Holroyd.

He saw now clearly that the sole crew of the vessel was these two dead men, and though he could not see their faces, he saw by their outstretched hands, which were all of ragged flesh, that they had been subjected to some strange exceptional process of decay. For a moment his attention concentrated on those two enigmatical bundles of dirty clothes and laxly flung limbs, and then his eyes went forward to discover the open hold piled high with trunks and cases, and aft, to where the little cabin gaped inexplicably empty. Then he became aware that the planks of the middle decking were dotted with moving black specks.

His attention was riveted by these specks. They were all walking in directions radiating from the fallen man in a manner – the image came unsought to his mind – like the crowd dispersing from a bullfight.

He became aware of Gerilleau beside him. 'Capo,' he said, 'have you your glasses? Can you focus as closely as those planks there?'

Gerilleau made an effort, grunted, and handed him the glasses.

There followed a moment of scrutiny. 'It's ants,' said the Englishman, and handed the focused field-glass back to Gerilleau.

His impression of them was of a crowd of large black ants, very like ordinary ants except for their size, and for the fact that some of the larger of them bore a sort of clothing of grey. But at the time his inspection was too brief for particulars. The head of Lieutenant da Cunha peered over the side of the cuberta, and a brief colloquy ensued.

'You must go aboard,' said Gerilleau.

The lieutenant objected that the boat was full of ants.

'You have your boots,' said Gerilleau.

The lieutenant changed the subject. 'How did these men die?' he asked.

Captain Gerilleau embarked upon speculations that Holroyd could not follow, and the two men disputed with a certain increasing vehemence. Holroyd took up the field-glass and resumed his scrutiny, first of the ants and then of the dead man amidships.

He has described these ants to me very particularly.

He says they were as large as any ants he has ever seen, black and moving with a steady deliberation very different from the mechanical fussiness of the common ant. About one in twenty was much larger than its fellows, and with an exceptionally large head. These reminded him at once of the master workers who are said to rule over the leaf-cutter ants; like them they seemed to be directing and co-ordinating the general movements. They tilted their bodies back in a manner altogether singular as if they made some use of the fore feet. And he had a curious fancy, that he was too far off to verify, that most of these ants of both kinds were wearing accoutrements, had things strapped about their bodies by bright white bands like white metal threads . . .

He put down the glasses abruptly, realising that the question of discipline between the captain and his subordinate had become acute.

'It is your duty,' said the captain, 'to go aboard. These are my instructions.'

The lieutenant seemed on the verge of refusing. The head of one of the mulatto sailors appeared beside him.

'I believe these men were killed by the ants,' said Holroyd abruptly in English.

The captain burst into a rage. He made no answer to Holroyd. 'I have commanded you to go aboard,' he screamed to his subordinate in Portuguese. 'If you do not go aboard forthwith it is mutiny – rank mutiny. Mutiny and cowardice! Where is the courage that should animate us? I will have you in irons, I will have you shot like a dog.' He began a torrent of abuse and curses, he danced to and fro. He shook his fists, he behaved as if beside himself with rage, and the lieutenant, white and still, stood looking at him. The crew appeared forward, with amazed faces.

Suddenly, in a pause of this outbreak, the lieutenant came to some heroic decision, saluted, drew himself together and clambered upon the deck of the cuberta.

'Ah!' said Gerilleau, and his mouth shut like a trap. Holroyd saw the ants retreating before da Cunha's boots. The Portuguese walked slowly to the fallen man, stooped down, hesitated, clutched his coat and turned him over. A black swarm of ants rushed out of the clothes, and da Cunha stepped back very quickly and trod two or three times on the deck.

Holroyd put up the glasses. He saw the scattered ants about the invader's feet, and doing what he had never seen ants doing before. They had nothing of the blind movements of the common ant; they were looking at him – as a rallying crowd of men might look at some gigantic monster that had dispersed it.

'How did he die?' the captain shouted.

Holroyd understood the Portuguese to say the body was too much eaten to tell.

'What is there forward?' asked Gerilleau.

The lieutenant walked a few paces, and began his answer in Portuguese. He stopped abruptly and beat off something from his leg. He made some peculiar steps as if he was trying to stamp on something invisible, and went quickly towards the side. Then he controlled himself, turned about, walked deliberately forward to the hold, clambered up to the fore decking, from which the sweeps are worked, stooped for a time over the second man, groaned audibly, and made his way back and aft to the cabin, moving very rigidly. He turned and began a conversation with his captain, cold and respectful in tone on either side, contrasting vividly with the wrath and insult of a few moments before. Holroyd gathered only fragments of its purport.

He reverted to the field-glass, and was surprised to find the ants had vanished from all the exposed surfaces of the deck. He turned towards the shadows beneath the decking, and it seemed to him they were full of watching eyes.

The cuberta, it was agreed, was derelict, but too full of ants to put men aboard to sit and sleep: it must be towed. The lieutenant went forward to take in and adjust the cable, and the men in the boat stood up to be ready to help him. Holroyd's glasses searched the canoe.

He became more and more impressed by the fact that a great if minute and furtive activity was going on. He perceived that a number of gigantic ants – they seemed nearly a couple of inches in length – carrying oddly-shaped burthens for which he could imagine no use – were moving in rushes from one point of obscurity to another. They did not move in columns across the exposed places, but in open, spaced-out lines, oddly suggestive of the rushes of modern infantry advancing under fire. A number were taking cover under the dead man's clothes, and a perfect swarm was gathering along the side over which da Cunha must presently go.

He did not see them actually rush for the lieutenant as he returned, but he has no doubt they did make a concerted rush. Suddenly the lieutenant was shouting and cursing and beating at his legs. 'I'm stung!' he shouted, with a face of hate and accusation towards Gerilleau.

Then he vanished over the side, dropped into his boat, and plunged at once into the water. Holroyd heard the splash.

The three men in the boat pulled him out and brought him aboard, and that night he died.

3

Holroyd and the captain came out of the cabin in which the swollen and contorted body of the lieutenant lay and stood together at the stern of the monitor, staring at the sinister vessel they trailed behind them. It was a close, dark night that had only phantom flickerings of sheet lightning to illuminate it. The cuberta, a vague black triangle, rocked about in the steamer's wake, her sails bobbing and flapping, and the black smoke from the funnels, spark-lit ever and again, streamed over her swaying masts.

Gerilleau's mind was inclined to run on the unkind things the lieutenant had said in the heat of his last fever.

'He says I murdered ''im,' he protested. 'It is simply absurd. Someone 'ad to go aboard. Are we to run away from dese confounded ants whenever dey show up?'

Holroyd said nothing. He was thinking of a disciplined rush of little black shapes across bare sunlit planking.

'It was his place to go,' harped Gerilleau. 'He died in the execution of his duty. What has he to complain of? Murdered! ... But the poor fellow was – what is it? – demented. He was not in his right mind. The poison swelled him ... U'm.'

They came to a long silence.

'We will sink dat canoe – burn it.'

'And then?'

The enquiry irritated Gerilleau. His shoulders went up, his hands flew out at right angles from his body. 'What is one to *do*?' he said, his voice going up to an angry squeak.

'Anyhow,' he broke out vindictively, 'every ant in dat cuberta! – I will burn dem alive!'

Holroyd was not moved to conversation. A distant ululation of howling monkeys filled the sultry night with foreboding sounds, and as the gunboat drew near the black mysterious banks this was reinforced by a depressing clamour of frogs.

'What is one to *do*?' the captain repeated after a vast interval, and suddenly becoming active and savage and blasphemous, decided to burn the *Santa Rosa* without further delay. Everyone aboard was pleased by that idea, everyone helped with zest; they pulled in the cable, cut it, dropped the boat and fired her with tow and kerosene, and soon the cuberta was crackling and flaring merrily amidst the immensities of the tropical night. Holroyd watched the mounting yellow flare against the blackness, and the livid flashes of sheet lightning that came and went above the forest summits, throwing them into momentary silhouette, and his stoker stood behind him watching also.

The stoker was stirred to the depths of his linguistics. '*Saüba*[96] go pop, pop,' he said. 'Wahaw!' and laughed richly.

But Holroyd was thinking that these little creatures on the decked canoe had also eyes and brains.

The whole thing impressed him as incredibly foolish and wrong, but – what was one to *do*? This question came back enormously reinforced on the morrow, when at last the gunboat reached Badama.

This place, with its leaf-thatch-covered houses and sheds, its creeper-invaded sugar-mill, its little jetty of timber and canes, was very still in the morning heat, and showed never a sign of living men. Whatever ants there were at that distance were too small to see.

'All the people have gone,' said Gerilleau, 'but we will do one thing anyhow. We will 'oot and vissel.'

So Holroyd hooted and whistled.

Then the captain fell into a doubting fit of the worst kind. 'Dere is one thing we can do,' he said presently,

'What's that?' said Holroyd.

' 'Oot and vissel again.'

So they did.

The captain walked his deck and gesticulated to himself. He seemed to have many things on his mind. Fragments of speeches came from his lips. He appeared to be addressing some imaginary public tribunal either in Spanish or Portuguese. Holroyd's improving ear detected something about ammunition. He came out of these preoccupations suddenly into English. 'My dear 'Olroyd!' he cried, and broke off with, 'But what *can* one do?'

They took the boat and the field-glasses, and went close in to examine the place. They made out a number of big ants, whose still postures had a certain effect of watching them, dotted about the edge of the rude embarkation jetty. Gerilleau tried ineffectual pistol shots at these. Holroyd thinks he distinguished curious earthworks running between the nearer houses that may have been the work of the insect conquerors of those human habitations. The explorers pulled past the jetty, and became aware of a human skeleton wearing a loin cloth, and very bright and clean and shining, lying beyond. They came to a pause regarding this . . .

'I 'ave all dose lives to consider,' said Gerilleau suddenly.

Holroyd turned and stared at the captain, realising slowly that he referred to the unappetising mixture of races that constituted his crew.

'To send a landing party – it is impossible – impossible. Dey will be poisoned, dey will swell, dey will swell up and abuse me and die. It is totally impossible . . . If we land, I must land alone, alone, in thick boots and with my life in my hand. Perhaps I should live. Or again – I might not land. I do not know. I do not know.'

Holroyd thought he did, but he said nothing.

'De whole thing,' said Gerilleau suddenly, ' 'as been got up to make me ridiculous. De whole thing!'

They paddled about and regarded the clean white skeleton from various points of view, and then they returned to the gunboat. Then Gerilleau's indecision became terrible. Steam was got up, and in the afternoon the monitor went on up the river with an air of going to ask somebody something, and by sunset came back again and anchored. A thunderstorm gathered and broke furiously, and then the night became beautifully cool and quiet and everyone slept on deck. Except Gerilleau, who tossed about and muttered. In the dawn he awakened Holroyd.

'Lord!' said Holroyd, 'what now?'

'I have decided,' said the captain.

'What – to land?' said Holroyd, sitting up brightly.

'No!' said the captain, and was for a time very reserved. 'I have decided,' he repeated, and Holroyd manifested symptoms of impatience.

'Well – yes,' said the captain, '*I shall fire de big gun!*'

And he did! Heaven knows what the ants thought of it, but he did. He fired it twice with great sternness and ceremony. All the crew had wadding in their ears, and there was an effect of going into action about the whole affair, and first they hit and wrecked the old sugar-mill, and then they smashed the abandoned store behind the jetty.

And then Gerilleau experienced the inevitable reaction. 'It is no good,' he said to Holroyd; 'no good at all. No sort of bally good. We must go back – for instructions. Dere will be de devil of a row about dis ammunition – oh! de *devil* of a row! You don't know, 'Olroyd . . . '

He stood regarding the world in infinite perplexity for a space.

'But what else was there to *do*?' he cried.

In the afternoon the monitor started downstream again, and in the evening a landing party took the body of the lieutenant and buried it on the bank upon which the new ants had so far not appeared . . .

4

I heard this story in a fragmentary state from Holroyd not three weeks ago.

These new ants have got into his brain, and he has come back to England with the idea, as he says, of 'exciting people' about them 'before it is too late'. He says they threaten British Guiana,[97] which cannot be much over a trifle of a thousand miles from their present sphere of activity, and that the Colonial Office ought to get to work upon them at once. He declaims with great passion: 'These are intelligent ants. Just think what that means!'

There can be no doubt they are a serious pest, and that the Brazilian Government is well advised in offering a prize of five hundred pounds for some effectual method of extirpation. It is certain too that since they first appeared in the hills beyond Badama, about three years ago, they have achieved extraordinary conquests. The whole of the south bank of the Batemo River, for nearly sixty miles, they have in their effectual occupation; they have driven men out completely, occupied plantations and settlements, and boarded and captured at least one ship. It is even said they have in some inexplicable way bridged the very considerable Capuarana[98] arm and pushed many miles towards the Amazon itself. There can be little doubt that they are far more reasonable and with a far better social organisation than any previously known ant species; instead of being in dispersed societies they are organised into what is in effect a single nation; but their peculiar and immediate formidableness lies not so much in this as in the intelligent use they make of poison against their larger enemies. It would seem this poison of theirs is closely akin to snake poison, and it is highly probable they actually manufacture it, and that the larger individuals among them carry the needle-like crystals of it in their attacks upon men.

Of course it is extremely difficult to get any detailed information about these new competitors for the sovereignty of the globe. No eye-witnesses of their activity, except for such glimpses as Holroyd's, have survived the encounter. The most extraordinary legends of their prowess and capacity are in circulation in the region of the Upper Amazon, and grow daily as the steady advance of the invader stimulates men's imaginations through their fears. These strange little creatures are credited not only with the use of implements and a knowledge of fire and metals and with organised feats of engineering that stagger our northern minds – unused as we are to such feats as that of the *Saüba* of Rio de Janeiro, who in 1841 drove a tunnel under the Parahyba[99] where it is as wide as the Thames at London Bridge – but with an organised and detailed method of record and communication analogous to our books. So far their action has been a steady progressive settlement, involving the flight or slaughter of every human being in the new areas they invade. They are increasing rapidly in numbers, and Holroyd at least is firmly convinced that they will finally dispossess man over the whole of tropical South America.

And why should they stop at tropical South America?

Well, there they are, anyhow. By 1911 or thereabouts, if they go on as they are going, they ought to strike the Capuarana Extension Railway,[100] and force themselves upon the attention of the European capitalist.

By 1920 they will be halfway down the Amazon. I fix 1950 or '60 at the latest for the discovery of Europe.

NOTES TO *THE ISLAND OF DOCTOR MOREAU*

1 (p. 5) *Callao*   a Peruvian port

2 (p. 5) *Noble's Isle*   fictitious island

3 (p. 5) HMS *Scorpion*   fictitious ship

4 (p. 5) *copra*   dried coconut kernels

5 (p. 5) *Bayna*   either a fictitious location or a misspelling

6a (p. 7) *Medusa case*   a French frigate wrecked in 1816 which became notorious for the ordeal and cannibalism of its survivors, immortalised in the painting *The Raft of the Medusa* (1818–19) by Théodore Géricault.

6b (p. 7) *Daily News*   a real paper, but a fictitious article

7 (p. 7) *breaker*   water-cask

8 (p. 8) *gunwale*   edge around the sides of a ship or boat

9 (p. 8) *thwarts*   lateral beams that strengthen a boat's structure

10 (p. 8) *schooner-rigged*   The boat has two masts with sails fore and aft.

11 (p. 9) *bulwarks*   side of the ship above deck level

12 (p. 10) *Arica*   a Chilean port

13 (p. 11) *University College*   one of the colleges belonging to the University of London

14 (p. 11) *Tottenham Court Road and Gower Street*   London streets in the university district

15 (p. 11) *scuttle*   hatchway in the side of the ship

16 (p. 12) *duck things*   garments made of duck, a robust cotton or linen material

17 (p. 13) *companion*   ladder or staircase linking cabin and deck

18 (p. 13) *combing*   raised lip of the hatchway

19 (p. 13) *forward*   front of the ship below deck

20 (p. 14) *flush deck*   a deck all on one level

21 (p. 14) *spankers*   sails set aft of the mizzen mast

22 (p. 15) *forecastle*   raised deck at the front of the ship

23 (p. 15) *shrouds*   part of the rigging

24 (p. 15) *sawbones*   slang for a surgeon or doctor

25 (p. 17) *binnacle*   housing for the ship's compass

26 (p. 20) *mizzen spanker-boom*   The mizzen is the stern-most mast; the boom is the spar securing the base of the sail. See also Note 21.

27 (p. 21) *two standing lugs*   The launch is rigged for four-cornered sails called lugsails.

28 (p. 23) *painter*   light rope used for tying up a boat

29 (p. 23) *piggin*   small wooden pail-like receptacle

30 (p. 24) *struck the lugs*   lowered the sails

31 (p. 25) *Royal College of Science . . . Huxley*   Biologist and Darwinist Thomas Henry Huxley (1825–95), whom Wells admired and was taught by at the Normal School of Science, which later became the Royal College

32 (p. 32) *a crib of Horace*   Horace was a Roman poet; a crib was a version with both the Latin and the English translations.

33 (p. 34) *epiphyte*   a plant that grows on another plant, but not parasitically

34 (p. 44) *Comus rout*   This is a reference to John Milton's masque *Comus* (1634), in which Comus is the son of Circe, a sorceress in Greek mythology who turns people into animals; it also alludes to Edwin Landseer's painting *The Defeat of Comus* (1843), which depicts Comus's drunken revels with animal-headed women.

35 (p. 45) *canebrake*   patch of ground overgrown with cane-grass or similar

36 (p. 45) *bar of deal*   a piece of plank or other sawn timber

37 (p. 47) *scoriae*   rough volcanic rocky masses

38 (p. 53) *the ha-ha of an English park*   a ditch walled on one side to serve as a concealed fence

39 (p. 56) *Hi non sunt homines; sunt animalia qui nos habemus*   translates as 'These are not men; they are animals which we have . . . ' (Latin)

40 (p. 59) *Hunter's cock-spu*   experiment by anatomist John Hunter (1728–93) in which a cockerel's spur was successfully transplanted on to its head

41 (p. 59) *Algerian zouaves*   Algerian French light-infantry corps

42 (p. 59) *Victor Hugo . . . 'L'Homme qui Rit'*   'The Man who Laughs', an 1869 novel by French author Victor Hugo

43 (p. 61) *Mahomet's houri*   a beautiful young woman in the Muslim paradise

44 (p. 62) *six Kanakas*   south-sea islanders

45 (p. 67) *fumaroles*   volcanic vent emitting hot vapour

46 (p. 71) *Ollendorfian beggar!*   Heinrich Ollendorf (1803–65) was a German grammarian; 'Ollendorfian' describes stilted speech like that of a phrase book.

47 (p. 104) *before the days of Slöjd*   Slöjd (or Anglicised as Sloyd) was a Scandinavian craft-based education system

48 (p. 106) *Apia*   Samoan port

49 (p. 107) *gid*   ovine brain disease

50 (p. 108) *Note*   This refers to Wells's essay 'The Limits of Individual Plasticity' (see Introduction, footnote 8).

NOTES TO 'AEPYORNIS ISLAND'

51 (p. 111) *Cypripediums*   genus of orchids that includes lady's slipper

52 (p. 111) *atoll*   coral reef around a lagoon

53 (p. 111) *Aepyornis*   the elephant bird; a large extinct flightless bird

54 (p. 111) *Sindbad's roc*   The voyages of Sindbad the sailor appear in the *Arabian Nights*; during his second voyage, Sindbad rides on the leg of a roc, a mythical giant bird, to escape an uninhabited island.

55 (p. 112) *Antananarivo*   capital of Madagascar

56 (p. 113) *spirit-lamp*   lamp burning spirits rather than oil

57 (p. 113) *duck shot*   the right size of gunshot for hunting ducks

58 (p. 113) *whang*   noise of a resounding blow

59 (p. 113) *Dawson's and Jamrach's*   animal dealers. Charles Jamrach (1815–91) was a well-known London-based dealer and owner of Jamrach's Animal Emporium; Dawson is Wells's invention.

60 (p. 114) *phosphorescence*   a glow in the water caused by bio-luminescent plankton

61 (p. 114) *Cape Argus*   newspaper published in Cape Town

62 (p. 116) *parrot-fish*   brightly-coloured tropical fish with a hard beak

63 (p. 116) *Robinson Crusoe*   the eponymous protagonist of Daniel Defoe's 1719 novel, in which he is shipwrecked on an island

64 (p. 117) *wattle*   lobe of skin, often coloured, hanging from a bird's neck

65 (p. 118) *cassowary*   large flightless bird, relative of the emu

66 (p. 118) *sea-cucumber*   leathery-skinned marine animal, often somewhat cucumber-shaped

67 (p. 118) *shindy*   a quarrelsome noise

NOTES TO 'THE SEA RAIDERS'

68 (p. 123) *Haploteuthis ferox*   invented Latin name, similar to that for giant squid, *Architeuthis*

69 (p. 123) *cephalopods*   literally 'head feet'; a type of mollusc with tentacles surrounding a large head, such as octopus and cuttlefish

70 (p. 123) *the Prince of Monaco's discovery*   Prince Albert I of Monaco (1848–1922) was a keen oceanographer who made several expeditions in the 1880s, 1890s and 1900s to examine marine flora and fauna, thus discovering cephalopod pieces in cetacean stomachs.

71 (p. 123) *cachalot*   a sperm whale

72 (p. 124) *Sidmouth and Ladram Bay*   Sidmouth is a coastal town in Devon, halfway between Seaton and Budleigh Salterton (see Note 77, below); Ladram Bay is a small rocky bay south-west of Sidmouth.

73 (p. 124) *skerry*   small low-lying rocky island, covered by the high tide

74 (p. 126) *laminaria*   a kind of kelp, a seaweed with long flat fronds

75 (p. 128) *rowlock*   fork or pins in the gunwale to hold the oars while rowing

76 (p. 130) *Hemsley*   a fictitious biologist

77 (p. 130) *Seaton and Budleigh Salterton*   Devon towns on the coast of Lyme Bay

78 (p. 130) *Preventive Service*   the Coastguard, which was formed of an amalgamation of the Preventive Water Guard, the Riding Officers and the Revenue Cruisers in 1822

79 (p. 131) *Sark*   one of the Channel Islands

80 (p. 131) *Newlyn*   coastal town on south-west tip of Cornwall, near Penzance

NOTES TO 'THE EMPIRE OF THE ANTS'

81 (p. 135) *the Benjamin Constant*   The ship is named after the Brazilian mathematician, soldier, teacher, Positivist and Republican Benjamin

Constant Botelho de Magalhães (1836–91); the name also belonged to Swiss writer and political activist Henri-Benjamin Constant de Rebecque (1767–30) and French painter Jean-Joseph Benjamin-Constant (1845–1902).

82 (p. 135) *Badama on the Batemo arm of the Guaramadema* These are fictitious place-names; Badama is evidently a town on the river Batemo, a branch of the Guaramadema River.

83 (p. 135) *the Diario and O Futuro* Portuguese-language newspapers

84 (p. 135) *Creole* The captain is a descendent of Portuguese settlers.

85 (p. 135) *jiggers* a kind of tropical flea

86 (p. 136) *Alemquer* probably Alenquer, a Brazilian town on the Amazon's north bank some 400 miles from the mouths of the Amazon

87 (p. 136) *Southport* English town, in Merseyside

88 (p. 137) *Rio Negro* tributary of the Amazon, in north-west Brazil

89 (p. 138) *Caracas* capital of Venezuela

90 (p. 138) *Tamandu* invented place-name, possibly a version of the Portuguese word *tamanduá* (anteater)

91 (p. 138) *Pará* a state in east Brazil

92 (p. 139) *casa* house

93 (p. 140) *Mojû* relocated place-name, belonging to a town near Belem on the Mojû river 500 miles east of Alenquer

94 (p. 140) *cuberta* large covered canoe, characteristic of Amazon travel, with masts for sails

95 (p. 141) *Caramba!* an exclamation, like 'damn it'

96 (p. 145) *Saüba* name of a species of leaf-cutting ant (*Atta cephalotes*), sometimes considered a troublesome pest

97 (p. 147) *British Guiana* British colony between 1831–1966; now the country Guyana

98 (p. 147) *Capuarana* another fictitious river

99 (p. 148) *Parahyba* the Paraíba do Sul River in east Brazil, north of Rio de Janeiro. The industrious Saüba reportedly did tunnel underneath it, according to an 1875 account.

100 (p. 148) *Capuarana Extension Railway* fictitious railway